# ELIOT'S
# BANANA

## HEATHER SWAIN

downtown press

New York  London  Toronto  Sydney  Singapore

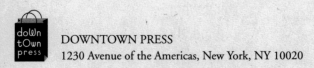

DOWNTOWN PRESS
1230 Avenue of the Americas, New York, NY 10020

ISBN: 0-7434-6487-7

First Downtown Press trade paperback edition September 2003

10  9  8  7  6  5  4  3  2  1

Designed by Jaime Putorti

Manufactured in the United States of America

For information regarding special discounts for bulk purchases,
please contact Simon & Schuster Special Sales at 1-800-456-6798
or business@simonandschuster.com.

# CAST OF CHARACTERS

(IN ORDER OF APPEARANCE)
without whom
I would merely be
a furious scribbler

| | |
|---|---|
| Mother. | Barbara Swain |
| Father. | Richard Swain |
| Brothers. | Christopher Swain |
| | Jason Swain |
| Husband | Daniel Vonnegut |
| Co-Conspirator. | Marybeth Raymond |
| Master Mind | Douglas Glover |
| Readers | Shawne Steiger |
| | Lisa J. Cornelio |
| | Ron Fletcher |
| Accomplice. | Laura Kriska |
| Agents | Megan Buckley |
| | Sheree Bykofsky |
| Editor. | Amy Pierpont |

FOR DCV

# CHAPTER
# ONE

When Eliot offers Junie a banana, she pauses in the entryway to his kitchen. He squeezes past her through the doorway, lightly touching her shoulder as he goes. He is only a few inches taller than she is, but he is sturdy. Broad chest, thick arms, strong legs. Junie wants to wrap her fingers around his biceps, which she imagines are solid but just a little soft.

The downward-sloping linoleum floor now separates her from where he stands by the cabinets. Coated in a slick patina of splattered grease over chipped and faded turquoise paint, the cabinets nearly gleam in the diluted evening sun. The countertops are slightly buckled. The color and texture of sand. A gently rolling dune. The walls have slipped from an optimistic yellow to a jaundiced beige. Junie imagines the former tenant in these rent-controlled Brooklyn digs. An eager newlywed bride, perhaps, twenty-five years ago painting her happy beach-inspired kitchen that is now so tired and spent it makes Junie yawn.

She covers her mouth to hide the yawn then adjusts her blue vintage cat-eye glasses. Her hands are restless for something to touch. She smooths her bright-red Louise Brooks haircut as Alfie, Eliot's tabby cat, tiptoes across the sloping floor. He stops to rub the side of his mouth against Junie's black-and-white saddle shoe.

Eliot grabs two conjoined bananas from the top of the refrigerator. She can picture him in twenty years, nearly seventy, when the few gray strands that meander through his hair have taken over and he shuffles around this same apartment, his burly muscle gone to fat. She'll be forty-five then. Leon close to fifty. She wonders if she and Leon will still be together.

"I'm not going to eat them," Eliot says. His brown eyes scan the bananas from behind wire-rimmed glasses. He cradles the fruit, then pulls it close to his face. The bananas are holding hands. Young and perfectly yellow from the tip to the top. Then green on the stem with no brown spots. He turns them over carefully as if they were delicate and rare and should be explored for hidden meaning. This is the look he gives Junie each time he sees her. The one that makes her want to peel off her clothes and stand before him shivering.

Alfie butters up to Junie's pant leg and mewls softly. She bends down to massage his tiny kitty shoulder blades and scratch under his chin. The cat watches her intently, blinking periwinkle eyes. (Jacob's favorite crayon color. All his skies were periwinkle.) Junie and Eliot met because of Alfie. Nearly three weeks ago, a few days before she moved in with Leon, she waited in the vet's office with her roommate Katie, who had gotten a kitten to keep herself company once Junie moved out. While Katie was in with the doctor, Junie noticed Alfie's piercing stare from across the room. The cat's handsome, disheveled owner gazed out the window.

Junie walked over to get a better look at both of them. "What a pretty kitty," she said and reached to pet the cat.

Alfie tilted his head toward her hand and sniffed, then licked her fingers. His tongue was smooth, not like the emery-board texture of most cat tongues. The feeling, as if a baby had licked her, lingered on her fingertips.

Eliot studied her. He didn't look away when it would have been polite. She pulled nervously at a string hanging off her sleeve and wondered what to do with her face. Smile? Wink? Furrow her brow? Run her tongue over her teeth like the Pearl Drops girl?

"He must like you," Eliot said, his voice a little ragged beneath mellifluous tones. A radio announcer who smoked too many cigarettes. "He's usually very surly."

"What's his name?" Junie asked and patted the cat's head again.

"Alfie."

"Like the song? 'What's it all about, Alfie?'" she sang.

Eliot frowned. "Absolutely not." Junie pulled at the string, until she had a tiny ball of red thread in her fingers. "Alfie was the computer on Barbarella's spaceship." Eliot stroked Alfie's back and continued to stare at Junie. "You do know who Barbarella is?"

"Sure," Junie said when really she had only a vague notion of

Jane Fonda straddling a missile, then thought that was something else entirely.

After the vet's, Junie ran into Eliot everywhere in the neighborhood. At the bakery on Seventh Avenue where pierced and tattooed teenagers sell seven kinds of sourdough bread. Getting coffee at Ozzie's on a chilly morning. Buying the Sunday *Times* at the Korean deli with the beautiful flowers. During each of those chance encounters she asked about Alfie.

"Why don't you come over to see him," Eliot proposed on a day when Leon was playing a gig in Philly. Junie, flustered and flattered by his attention, agreed.

She looks up at Eliot now. Uses glimpses of him to memorize tiny parts, like constructing a drawing one quadrant at a time. His hair is wild. Full of unruly curls. Dark-brown spirals that grow up and out, never down. Laugh lines like rays of sun reach out from the corners of his eyes.

"The bananas will turn black, you know." He says this like he is mourning the loss of the bananas' innocence. "You can't refrigerate bananas."

"Just like you can't teach an old dog or lead a horse or make a silk purse?" Junie asks.

A perfect comma sprouts in his left cheek as he grins at her stupid joke. "Come here," he says and waves her over with the fruit. "I'll show you what to do for Alfie."

Junie has agreed to take care of the cat while Eliot goes out of town to interview some actress for an article he is writing. They stand side by side in front of the open refrigerator. It is empty except for a jar of sweet pickles, two Chinese take-out cartons, three beers, and several boxes of insulin. Her mother kept Jacob's medicine in the fridge. All of the concoctions meant to save his life became mundane next to the milk and orange juice. "How's it taste?" Junie used to ask him after their mother spooned some liquid into his mouth. "Purple," he would say.

Eliot inserts the tiny syringe into a vial. Junie watches him closely. "The key," he says, "is to get Alfie eating so he doesn't really notice you." He reaches into an overhead cabinet. "The secret weapon." He holds up a tin of Fancy Feast salmon dinner.

"Perfect, darling. He'll have Salmon Chanted evening," Junie quips. Eliot grins the comma again. Their shoulders nearly touch.

"And don't use the electric can opener," he tells her. "It makes him nuts." He dumps the soft food into Alfie's ceramic dish. "Kitty, kitty," he calls.

Alfie darts across the room and winds between Junie's legs before settling in front of the food. Eliot squats down beside him. "I usually pet him a little so he knows I'm here. Then you just pinch the scruff of his neck like this." He holds a fold of Alfie's skin between his left forefinger and thumb. "You try," he says. Junie grasps Alfie's neck gently. "That's right. Hold it while I put the needle in. You have to get it just under the skin. He'll let you know if you go too deep." He slides the needle in expertly. "Hold it so you can feel the right way." Junie takes the syringe in her right hand. "Now push the plunger quickly." She does. Alfie doesn't twitch. "And pull it out." Eliot watches. She likes his eyes on her. Wants to take his glasses off and gently kiss his eyelids. "Perfect," he says.

They stand and she trades him the syringe for his keys. While he throws away the trash, Junie drifts into the living room jumbled with old typewriters and dusty books. The first time she came over she stood in front of the shelves filled with science fiction novels. Eliot told her he had written a successful book in the seventies called *Liberty Voyage* about an impotent astronaut stranded on an all-female planet. She confessed she'd never read any sci-fi. He lent her *Fahrenheit 451* and *The Left Hand of Darkness,* just to get her started.

She rented *Barbarella* and found a used copy of *Liberty Voyage* at the Strand. The back cover hailed Eliot as the Aldous Huxley of the New Wave for his combination of wry social commentary and titillating plot. While Leon played in smoky bars, Junie devoured Eliot's novel, turning down brittle corners to mark the most erotic parts. What fun to know the author! She and Eliot were on the planet. He was inventing sexual devices for her pleasure. She laid the book across her belly and snuggled down into the warm and twisted sheets with his words pressed against her tingling skin. She dozed with libidinous thoughts of Eliot and herself. Then woke suddenly, afraid Leon would return to find salacious passages tattooed across her midriff.

Now, she can't wait to stop by while Eliot is gone, dope up the cat, and explore his apartment. She wants to pick up the framed photographs to see who is important to him. Rummage through closed desk drawers to find secrets among broken pencils and old receipts. Smell his towels. Curl up on his bed. Maybe even try on his shoes.

She looks back at Eliot, who waits in the kitchen doorway with the bananas. A tiny stitch of guilt crosses her brow. Such scheming can't be right, she thinks, then tries to seem engaged in the conversation about fruit.

"Won't you eat them later?" she asks. "Before you get on the plane? You could take them with you."

"Bananas don't travel," Eliot tells her. He holds each one in his fingertips, gently pulls them apart and breaks the stem with a swift crack. "Anyway, I can't eat both of them. Here, you take one."

He lays the fat part onto Junie's outstretched palm. She wraps her fingers around it and considers the ingenious curve, then wonders if accepting phallic fruit from a man other than Leon would be considered cheating.

"They're still a little green. I don't think you can eat it yet," Eliot says.

"That's too bad. I'm hungry."

He opens the nearest cabinet. Saltines peek out. Packets of ramen noodles. Instant oatmeal. Kraft Macaroni and Cheese. Jim, Jack and Johnny stand at odd angles among the other half-empty bottles of hard liquor.

"You don't have to feed me," Junie says and turns to leave because if she really came over just to get the key and not to let her imagination flounder through illicit touches and pilfered kisses, she would be going now.

Eliot follows her to the door. "You sure you want to leave?"

He asks her this each time she goes. "You could stay. Let me show you my stamp collection." He wiggles his eyebrows and grins.

Junie smiles over her shoulder. "You don't have any stamps."

"Philately," he says.

"Is that some kind of proposition?" she asks, playing the innocent to his randy older man.

He rubs his hands together and nods. He has been tossing out these puerile hints since the first time she came over. She knows they are half-facetious. Designed to make her stammer and squirm. The first time he did it she audibly gasped, then blurted, "But, I have a boyfriend." He belly-laughed and Junie felt caught. The dumb rabbit that went for the carrot underneath the deadfall trap. She thought she'd cry and berated herself for not being a stronger woman. One who could dish it back or at least be offended and stomp out the door. And then what? Never return. No, thank you. Flirting with him was fun.

"So how about it, toots. Is today going to be the day?"

Junie knows if she says okay, the fun will quickly end. "You are forgetting about my boyfriend," she says demurely.

Eliot rolls his eyes. "I wish you would." He reaches for the doorknob.

Junie leans into him so that his fingers graze her arm, sparking tiny brushfires against her skin. She wonders if there is combustion of atoms when they touch. Her protons smashing against his neutrons, creating radioactive isotopes that glow in the dark for hours after they part. Or if all this flirting is really just for kicks.

Eliot pulls the door open and holds it for her. As she steps by, she can smell him—soap and shaving cream. She leans against the jamb, facing him and he smiles, showing his teeth and the rays of sun around his eyes. The anticipation of an embrace tremors in Junie's joints. Ball and socket. She imagines wrapping her arms around him. Dovetail. At least a friendly hug goodbye. Tongue-in-groove. But she knows her fingers. They are persistent. They would wind themselves into his hair. They would find the back of his neck. They would creep over his shoulders and pull him too close.

She thinks of Leon. Tall and lanky. Cleanly shaven head and a red-gold goatee. A little silver hoop dangling off the top ridge of his left ear. She fell in love with him a year ago when she saw him play the drums at a Mr. Whipple gig. She imagines him at home now, whisking up salad dressing with fresh herbs, marinating portobello mushrooms, waiting for her.

"Junie," Eliot says.

She stands on the threshold. Toes in the apartment, heels in the hall. It would be so easy to turn forty-five degrees, step into Eliot's arms, and send her life on a different trajectory. "What?"

He stops and looks away. Runs his fingers through all that hair.

She holds Eliot's banana against her sternum with both hands. "What?" she asks, a little smile playing at the corners of her mouth.

"Well," he says. "I'll miss you." He shrugs as if it were no big deal.

Junie's mouth blooms into a smile but she is uncertain. Is he serious? Should she step forward and pull him into a kiss, or run away before she gets herself into trouble, or stay cool and not react? Nothing seems appropriate but she has to do something so she tugs on the stem of the banana. The seams rip open to expose pale-yellow flesh. The smell is soft but momentarily overpowers the musty odor of the dank hall.

"Did you know that bananas break into three pieces if you squeeze them right?" she asks. It's a trick she and Jacob discovered. She pulls off the top third of the banana and rolls it gently between her thumb and forefinger. It loosens vertically into three long, thin triangular sections. That's how she and Jacob always ate their bananas. She hands one piece to Eliot. He puts it in his mouth. She does the same. It is dry and acrid on her tongue.

"Eww, gross," she says and steps backward out of the door. "You were right."

Alfie sits beside Eliot's foot. A long purr, or maybe a low growl, rumbles in the cat's throat. Eliot spits the chewed-up banana pulp into his palm. "See you in a few days," he says and slowly shuts the door.

Junie stands on the other side with the rusty bicycles and the granny shopping carts leaning crookedly against the slanting banister. She considers knocking again but hesitates. Obviously, she can't go back in. Eliot probably has the same flirtation going with lots of women. She is nothing special. In fact, she keeps waiting for this little game to wear thin. To see him not as an attractive accomplished artist who finds some spark in her. But as a sad-sack has-been, flirting shamelessly with someone half his age. She wonders when the whole thing will seem trite and terribly embarrassing. That day has yet to come.

For now, though, she decides to go. Leon is waiting. And there will be more of Eliot's attention later. She descends the creaking stairs with the half-peeled banana in one fist and the uneaten third mushy in the other. On the sidewalk, Junie looks for a place to toss the incriminating fruit. There is none but she doesn't want to throw it on the ground. Visions of silent movie banana-peel gags float through her mind. Old ladies with small dogs. Fat men. Women in high heels. They endlessly slip and fall with their feet above their heads. She doesn't want her indiscretion to cause such hazard. So, she carefully nestles the uneaten part into the open banana, then wraps the peel across its fleshy top. She pockets it in her cucumber-colored coat and walks toward home, banana on her breath.

# CHAPTER
# TWO

Junie detours through Prospect Park because she is not ready to go home yet. She needs this time to decompress. Empty her mind of Eliot like a deep-sea diver who must reemerge slowly to avoid nitrogen bubbles in her blood. She is relieved to be alone under the perfectly blue sky holding the last rays of sun before dusk. Before she goes home. Home? The word is deceiving. It's Leon's place with her stuff scattered around.

She cuts through the meadow. In front of her, forsythia bushes toss up majestic spires of yellow blossoms while every tree carries tiny buds like delicate gifts on the ends of long branches. She passes Rastafarian kite fliers in their Jiffy Pop hats. She counts the kites by twos, then threes. There are twelve. Dipping, diving. Tails wiggle-waggling. Buzzing from wind resistance like mighty, angry wasps.

She passes dogs and people romping happily across the green-grass hills. Past waify tiptoeing Chihuahua walkers. Barrel-chested pug paraders. Leon hates pugs. "They give me the willies," he always says with a shiver. Claims their eyes can pop out if they play too rough with the big dogs. Wants to invent pug goggles. "That way," he says, "you could just pick up the dog and shake it until the eyeball goes back into the socket."

With her hands deep in her coat pockets, Junie fingers soft and dissolving tissues left over from some past cold. She finds little football-shaped chocolate eggs wrapped in pink shiny foil and a pack of Starburst among the tissue shreds and half-eaten banana. She decides on an egg, pulls off the crumbling wrapper, and pops the candy into her mouth. It melts on her tongue and has a slight paraffin taste.

The path divides and she goes left. This takes her down the slope, away from home, through a copse of trees and by the duck pond where a blue heron stands like a hunchbacked old man watching the world. She thinks of Florida, of elderly men in plaid pants and wonders if other birds find the heron grouchy or his color tacky. She can imagine him complaining to the mallards in their golf shirts.

"What a world this has become," the heron would say. "The air's bad and I can't get a decent fish anywhere."

"And the people these days," the mallard might comment. "Look at that one there. What color is her hair? That red is not a real color. Used to be only harlots dyed their hair."

Junie laughs to herself. Where would a duck learn the word harlot? She sucks on a strawberry-flavored Starburst and imagines the birds' conversation if they knew she wanted to cheat on her boyfriend with an older man.

"An affair! How scandalous," the ducks might whisper to the

crows in the trees. But the crows are mischievous. They love sinfulness. They would cackle with delight.

Junie stands in front of the pond and silently implores the birds, Why now? Why couldn't she have met Eliot a year ago? Or a month ago before Leon asked her to move in with him, which had seemed like such a good idea at the time. She'd lived with Katie since their senior year at Ohio State and they had moved to New York together. She loved Katie but she was ready for a change. So when Leon asked, she was thrilled. Mundane tasks seemed imbued with romance then. Coming home to find him drinking a beer in his underwear and socks was wildly sexy. Buying peanut butter and milk at the deli might as well have been picking up a pound of oysters and a bottle of cold Chablis. Doing laundry together was practically orgasmic.

Now, she has the sneaking suspicion that something else had thrilled her. The promise of getting it right. Finally proving that she is not a flaky, goofy, bumbling mess who couldn't get into a good college or hold a real job or keep a boyfriend more than a few weeks. But someone who, at twenty-five, could conduct a relationship. A committed coupling. With hints of a future. The implication was that someday, maybe, if they chose, she and Leon might even find themselves married. With children and pets. There was the possibility of settling in nicely. Comfortably into a smooth groove. Junie might even get fat. And Leon, well, Leon was already bald.

She wonders now how she could have been so rash. The decision to move in with him was huge. The consequences immense. She should have meditated on it for weeks. Checked in with astrologers and soothsayers. Flipped a damn *I Ching*. At least paused before she nodded so eagerly and said yes. The vastness of being together indefinitely spreads out like an expanse of water. She can't see the other side. It is still and serene. What lurks down below? How could she have committed to something so vague and potentially rife with terrible outcomes? They may hate each other in six weeks. They may be bored in three months. Leon may have all sorts of horrible hidden habits. Worse, he might discover her most annoying traits. He just may figure out that her quirky front is a thin veneer covering a person who is unloved and unlovable.

The whole thing is especially awful because Leon is the first person she has really been in love with. There have been obligatory boyfriends in the past. Her first love in high school—a guy named Ronny who dressed like Robert Smith from the Cure. And she had sex with three guys in college. Even claimed to love one, a Japanese ceramics professor named Hiroshi. Looking back, though, it's clear that relationship was fueled by the excitement of screwing the *sensei* in his pottery studio while he grunted and groaned in his clipped and violent language. When he went back to Japan, she wasn't heartbroken. Just lonely and horny.

She fell in love with Leon, though. Toppled really. Caught off-balance and capsized into the relationship by the relentless itch to press her fingers against his skin, the greedy need to vacuum every thought out of his mind, and the luxurious comfort of his arms wrapped around her at night. Those feelings had gotten deeper and stronger over the past year and lulled Junie into thinking that maybe, after a quarter of a century on this earth, after seventeen years as the only daughter (however misdirected and disappointing), after eight years of making mistakes on her own, she could do something right for once. That this time, her parents might think, Wow, Junie has really gotten her life together! Instead of looking at her as if she were the consolation prize for having lost their son.

She's even thrown around the phrase *soul mate*. As if on some cosmic level, she and Leon belong together, and aren't merely two people who bumped into each other at a thrift store one day. But aren't soul mates supposed to endlessly bask in one another's presence? Finish each other's sentences? Know from just looks what the other wants and needs? Forgive each other of any indiscretion? Never tire of their love? And mourn for eternity if one is lost? That sounds more like what she had with Jacob when he was seven and she was eight.

And now, suddenly, when she stands toe to toe with Eliot, she begins to lean forward, tilt her head to the right and close her eyes. She imagines a first kiss. How his lips, loose as liver but oddly alluring, would press against her mouth. So what she has with Leon couldn't be a soul mate bond, could it? Otherwise, how could she have such thoughts of Eliot?

Besides, she is not even sure she believes in the soul. At least, not some immutable entity that exists forever. There is no milky outline of Jacob the Friendly Ghost floating around watching over her. She gave up a long time ago on notions of a benevolent God in heaven holding Jacob on his knee. For Junie, there is life and there is death. And Jacob is dead.

But she does hold out hope that maybe, inside of her, there is a pristine place, below all those layers of skin and bones and muscles and connective tissues. Behind the organs. Deep within the mind and heart. A little shimmering space that she could call her soul. A whisper of a thing that is impervious to the daily drudge of life. And maybe, there is another person out there who shares the same unguarded light deep within himself so that when they meet, their souls will cut through all the crazy shit in their lives and everything will melt away. That will be true love and bliss. And, it won't be something she has to work at.

So maybe she doesn't have a soul mate bond with Leon. Maybe she never will find such a thing. But at least he is kind and compassionate. He tolerates with good humor her idiosyncrasies. He loves her. Undeniably, this relationship has been good.

Why now? she asks the birds.

They are silent.

She looks up into the sky. The blue has faded to gray and purple as the sun retreats behind low clouds. The kites are floating downward. Some invisible hand reeling in their fun. Junie feels lost and dizzy underneath that sky, like the time Jacob blindfolded her and spun her around until she felt as if she were standing in a tipping canoe. Then he led her through the house, in and out of rooms, doubling back, and made her guess where she was. He wouldn't take the blindfold off until she guessed correctly.

Leon or Eliot? She compares them in her mind. Leon in the

kitchen, waiting for her to come home and eat the food he's made. Eliot with his head against the doorjamb, smiling at her. How long would he stay there grinning? Not as long as Leon would wait for her to come home. What if she never came back? She could go to Dubuque. By bus. Change her name to Loretta or Bobbie or Flo. Be a waitress in a truck stop and live above a bar. Fall asleep to a flashing Budweiser sign. Would anyone really miss her? That's an answer she doesn't want to know.

The sun sinks quickly. Under the thin fabric of her coat, goose bumps flash across her arms. The mallards turn their heads around backward and hide their beaks in silky feathers. She's hungry. She's cold. She wishes she could tell time by the angle of the sun. She's probably late and Leon is probably worried. And, there are no buses from Brooklyn to Dubuque. She hugs herself to get warm, then pushes her hands deep into her pockets so that her fingers touch the banana. She puts another chocolate egg in her mouth and works the candy over her tongue. Not now, she tells the birds. Not when I'm finally getting it together.

# CHAPTER
# THREE

Eliot bangs his head lightly against the door. He has sworn he won't do this again. Won't get involved with someone who is already involved. Certainly not with someone this much younger. Relationships, especially illicit ones, take too much energy and his search for inspiration in a woman eventually sabotages his writing.

Junie is so damn sexy, though. Like a character he would create. Lithe in her movements. A sweetheart-shaped ass and perky breasts. That crazy haircut and goofy glasses. The silly clothes she wears. He loves a woman with a sense of humor about herself. She flirts with him, too. Wriggles her hips and lets her hands flutter like dragonflies when she tells a story. Touches him with playful punches and pokes when he teases her. And, she keeps coming back.

She even bought a copy of *Liberty Voyage* and told him that she loved it. Oh, Junie, he thought. You could be my Erato if you would leave your big, bald-headed boyfriend.

Eliot loves to make Junie mention the boyfriend and then watch her sputter and blush like a baby that slips beneath the lip of its bathwater. He finds this a charming testament to her age and inexperience. He saw her with the boyfriend on Seventh Avenue one day. Stood on the corner and watched this guy, his head so shiny that he must wax it, casually sling his arm over Junie's shoulder. Eliot chuckled to himself at Baldy's confidence. As if nothing could wreck his bliss. Nothing but me, Eliot thought.

There is something else about Junie, though. It's not just the fact that she's cute or obviously smitten with him and can't figure out what she wants to do. Beneath that goofy getup there is someone he wants to talk to or sit beside quietly and do nothing with. Someone he suspects he could be comfortable with because she listens and seems interested in what he has to say. Christ, he thinks. I must be getting old if that's what I'm looking for.

He keeps his ear near the door until her footsteps trail away down the groaning stairs. The outside doors squeak and bang. She is gone again. He considers doing some work in the few hours before his flight, but he doesn't want to. Instead, he drops to the couch beside Alfie, who carefully grooms an extended leg on the middle of the cushion. Eliot strokes the cat, the only permanent thing through all the fucked-up girlfriends and abandoned novels. When the cat became diabetic Eliot couldn't let him go, even though the vet bills are enormous. Alfie claws at the couch, making tiny loops on the threadbare, lumpy lamé monstrosity. It came with the place. (The same way Eliot has gotten most of his furnishings.) It won't go through the door. How the former tenants got it in remains a mystery. But, it's functional, so it's good enough.

The phone rings. Eliot doesn't want to talk to anyone. Unless it's Junie from the corner pay phone. In saddle shoes and an oddball green coat. Calling to ask if she can return. Fat chance. She's gone home to Baldy. The machine picks up.

"Eliot, this is Margaret." Her grating voice, that Midwestern nasal twang, makes Eliot squirm and sweat a little under his arms. "I wanted to touch base with you and make sure we are on the same page about the Twyla Smart article." Touch base. Same page. Eliot despises her corporate catchphrase lingo. On the desk rests the unopened envelope with Twyla Smart's PR kit. He'll read it on the plane or in the hotel. Whenever he gets around to it. "I know I said this before," Margaret goes on, "but this article is important." She whines. She moans. He hates her self-righteous babble. "I have to have it by Wednesday." She pauses. Eliot waits. Hopes she'll hang up, then trip over the phone cord on her way to harass some poor editor-intern. "Look Eliot," she keens, "I was hoping to talk to you, not your machine, but you're never home. So I hope you get this message and I hope you understand that this article is really due on Wednesday. And I hope . . ."

The machine cuts her off. And I hope you get hit by a bus, Eliot thinks. He has tried to get along with Margaret, because even he has to admit that she is good at what she does. Not that that is enough. She is one cold fish. Never cracks a smile. A firm handshake hello and goodbye whenever he sees her. She'll be one of those women who, in five years when she hits forty, will be suddenly gripped by the knowledge that her ovaries have dried up and she has a better chance of getting eaten by a shark than finding a husband. Or, she's probably a lesbian. Worse, a celibate lesbian. Just as well. Screwing his editor never helped in the past. He'll get the article done, but he's not in the mood to start working yet.

A copy of *Liberty Voyage* lies on the cushion beside the cat. Eliot had barely looked at it in ten years until Junie started talking about it. Then he got curious again. Began to wonder what had made the book so successful and how he had lost that touch. Dug through old boxes in the basement until he came across a remainder crate. He picks up the book and rereads the scene when Doyle Hane, the American astronaut, lands on the planet Liberty.

Hane became aware of a deep pounding behind his closed eyes. The details of the crash resurfaced in his mind. The ship had been bullied by asteroids and sent into a tailspin. The blank vastness of infinite space spun for hours on his screen as the craft fell toward a luminous purple planet. When he awoke, he was lying beside the ship's demolished hull surrounded by lovely women with golden skin and gently curling hair. He pulled himself up to sit and a searing blade of pain sliced through his ribs, down into his groin. A stunning woman, tall and bronzed, leaned over him and said, "I am Ro El 3. Are you peaceful?"

Writing *Liberty Voyage* had been the happiest time of Eliot's life. He loved creating Rose Ellen Troy, the feisty American scientist who took her lesbian lover to space with a stash of human ova to start Liberty. At first, the critics loved it. A planet of self-sufficient women run as a peaceful free-love commune where they procreated by fusing ova in a lab. There were also Hane's Machines, the sexual appliances he invented since he couldn't perform.

Those machines had been Eliot's glory and his demise. Not only for the notoriety they brought him in literary circles, but also for the reactions from women who read the book. Some women assumed Eliot was impotent and wanted to cure him. Some assumed Eliot was a pervert and either wanted to castrate him or have sex with him because of it. And some assumed the machines were a metaphor for his own desire to please women in bed. Invariably, after every book signing, he had several offers.

He went from muse to muse, writing to impress his lovers, but every time those relationships ended the same way. She would want more of the pages that she had inspired and the sex would be good. Then the grind of two people together would wear away his motivation. He'd blame her for inhibiting his writing with niggling requests for attention. She would feel guilty and pissed. He'd lose interest. She'd leave and he'd be depressed and unable to write anymore. Until he met another muse.

Then the eighties came. The hoopla died down and feminist critiques relegated *Liberty Voyage* to just another piece of useless sexist fodder. He swore he would never let the critics get to him, and truthfully, they weren't what did him in. He was scared shitless to write another book and he knew it. He let the anguish of bad relationships with volatile women replace the thrill of writing a good sentence.

Now, he ekes out a living off the dwindling royalties of *Liberty Voyage* and by writing about movies. He interviews vapid up-and-coming stars and pretentious young directors that people in New York are supposed to like. Twyla Smart is the most recent dilettante who has captured the imagination of the imaginationless. Another gorgeous young actress finally given her big break. He already knows the story of her life. She will make a few semi-interesting indie films, then sell out for a boob part in a multi-million-dollar movie. He could write the article without the trouble of meeting her. But he'll go to Montreal and ask her questions and watch her preen, then turn the article in on time so he doesn't get canned from this job.

Then he will focus on Junie.

He drops the book and picks up the Play Station controls to play another round of the latest *Grand Theft Auto,* his most recent vice. An old man with a new toy. On some level he suspects it's pathetic but he doesn't care. His game has been paused since Junie came by. He starts again but is killed immediately. Too much on his mind. Margaret, deadlines, Junie, Twyla. He puts the controls down and rubs his eyes. They hurt from staring at the computer, at the Play Station screen, at books. He needs to rest. Take a nap. Eliot closes his eyes, tired of thinking, tired of grousing. He drifts toward sleep, telling himself just a half-an-hour snooze before his flight.

Soon, Junie comes to him, smiling with her arms outstretched, carrying the banana. She slides her fingers inside his jacket, across his hip to the small of his back. She steps up close and presses herself against him. Eliot murmurs happily in his half-sleep.

Alfie watches Eliot slumped beside him on the couch and thinks, I would devour you if you were smaller. Women have come and gone through their life together, but this time Alfie is pissed. In the past, Eliot has entertained overnight visitors and weekend lovers. Some stuck around for weeks or months. A few overlapped and one even made it close to a year. Their presence usually meant more attention for Alfie. Caresses and cuddles. Special kitty treats and balls with bells inside. Except for the few who didn't like cats or were allergic, but they never lasted long anyway. Junie, though, is different.

The first few times she came over, Alfie wound between her legs and pulled in her scent. Something so familiar about her. Even the first time he saw her at the vet's, he recognized the lilt in her voice and the way she moved as she reached out to touch him. He licked her hand to make sure. Yes, the same sweet taste he knew from before. Alfie is certain that he loved her once. Knew her intimately and then lost her. The feeling of recognition is vague. The memories deeply buried. As if he is staring into murky water, searching for a lost object. But she's there. Unmistakably part of his past. Only, which one?

His soul has seen ten lives and deaths. Incarnations as a weaver in Blackpool, a Russian serf, a sea cucumber, a violin prodigy in Prague. Killed by the plague, hit by a bus, and once a slug squished on a fat man's shoe. He ruled a small nation, shined shoes in Chicago, and danced topless for Japanese businessmen. Now in the body of a cat named Alfie, he lives with this scamp Eliot, who sits there obliviously snoozing while Alfie seethes.

The cat bats the Play Station control from Eliot's knee. It tumbles to the floor. This man suckles at the teat of technology like a greedy baby! His dependence on machines makes Alfie sick. Throw off your shackles man, the cat wants to yell. If only he had words. And if he had words, he would warn Eliot to halt this dalliance with Junie, for she is a delicate flower, a sweet sad egg who deserves much better.

The cat climbs carefully onto Eliot's stout chest and watches through the spectacles as the man's eyes move back and forth rapidly under the lids. Alfie has the urge to swat at them because he is certain that Eliot is dreaming of Junie.

The cat slinks across the cushions away from Eliot. Oh, the injustice of the universe! To reunite with his long lost love after all this time. But how can he, in this feline form, make darling Junie understand that Eliot is a depraved technocrat who does not deserve even her daintiest fingernail clippings? The only thing he can hope for is that she, too, feels the tug of remembrance and that together they can unravel this mystery entangling them. He rubs his ears and cheeks against the worn arm of the couch. He must be patient. She will return and again he will beg her to recollect. For now though, he hunkers down in a warm depression of a cushion to ponder the iniquity of his life.

Eliot wakes with Junie's touch lingering in the sensory synapses of his brain like an itch on a phantom limb. He tries to force himself back asleep with her in the center of his mind, but she slips away and Eliot is left with visions of tight-lipped Margaret demanding his article. He reaches to stroke Alfie meditating on the end of the couch. The cat's hair bristles and he hisses. Eliot withdraws his hand. "You old grouch," he says to Alfie. "What do you have to be so pissy about? Lounging and pampered all day."

Eliot hauls himself off the couch. His neck aches from sleeping slumped against the cushions. "You cats have it good," he grumbles. "Food when you want it. A warm place to live." He slowly circles his head, trying to work out the kinks as he walks toward the bedroom, muttering, "Unconditional love. No job to worry about. No sex-obsessed ego always getting you in trouble."

Alfie digs his claws into the fabric of the couch, creating a new patch of tiny snags. "Be warned," he snarls to Eliot's retreating figure. "I am watching you."

# CHAPTER
# FOUR

Leon stirs the spicy Moroccan stew he's made for Junie, who's late as usual. He glances at the clock above the stove. She said she'd be home by six and it is nearly six thirty. But she doesn't organize her life around a clock and Leon accepts her lateness as part of her charm. Besides, he loves to cook for her, especially now that they officially live together.

He asked her over goat cheese and sun-dried tomato omelets one Saturday morning when he had no gigs or rehearsals so that if she said yes, they could immediately move her stuff, then lounge around in bed all day until they were hungry again. Or if she said no, he could spend the day in a football coma in front of the TV.

He's known for a while that she was the person he'd never get tired of. Her feelings have been harder to read, but she is a thousand times better than any of his past girlfriends. Diva singers, frustrated actresses, even a perky realtor and a dour financial analyst. They were all just dates, though. A series of drinks, dinners, movies, and sex. Nothing like the connection and attraction he has with Junie.

He replaces the lid to the stew and goes to the sink to get a few dishes out of the way. He taps a fork against a glass. He digs the sound, the ringing tink tink. He tries the glass half full of water. The tone deepens. Against a salad bowl, the sound is hollow and forlorn. A chapel bell. He scraps the tine across the cheese grater. A rachety, metallic *guiro.* Junie says the world is his instrument. He can paradiddle anything resistant, flam anything with a little give, and play a wicked ride-cymbal pattern on every object with tone. His life, she says, could be transcribed in sixteenth notes across a five-bar staff. And she's right. He's always heard rhythm around him. In the dripping faucet, in the knocking pipes, in the radials bumping down the highway, and in the arguments his parents had. Doors slamming, cymbals crashing, it was all the same to Leon.

When he was ten, his mother gave him his first silver set of Pearl drums with *Rock Star* written in shiny blue letters across the bass. She even hired a local guy named Stan, who had played in New York for years before kicking his smack habit and moving out to Jersey where he gave lessons in his low-ceiling basement studio.

After the first lesson, Stan told Leon's mother that Leon was a natural. "Did you know he's already figured out the intro to 'Fifty Ways to Leave Your Lover'?"

"It doesn't surprise me," she said and flicked ash from her cigarette into the standing ceramic ashtray. "My family is musical."

Leon turned away. He never met a member of her family who played anything besides Yahtzee.

"Do you play an instrument?" Stan asked.

She took another drag off her cigarette. "A little piano. And I sing."

Sweat prickled under Leon's arms. They didn't even own a piano. Only a little organ his grandmother had given them when she moved to Arizona. Each Christmas his mother cajoled everyone to sing carols. After a few scotch and sodas, Leon's father picked a fight about the right key or the wrong lyrics.

"I've always harbored this little dream of singing in night-clubs," his mother said. "But then I got pregnant, and well . . ." She shrugged and smashed out her cigarette.

"I know a lot of people at local clubs," Stan said. Then he winked. She grinned. Leon felt his throat go dry and his skin prickle.

"My husband doesn't believe in me." She smiled sadly at Stan, who shook his wispy brown hair out of his eyes.

"I'm going outside," Leon said.

He sat on the curb throwing rocks into Stan's scrubby yard. Who cared about that guy, anyway? Mr. Long Hair. Mr. Never Played with KISS. And his mom was so stupid. She couldn't sing at all. Leon turned on the hose in Stan's side yard. He drank the iron-tasting water, then wet his head and arms to cool his fiery, scratchy skin. A puddle formed in the grass and a mangy dog trotted over from the neighbor's to drink. Leon threw a rock that splashed beside the dog. It scurried away and glanced over its shoulder as if it were hurt and disappointed that such a nice boy could be so mean. Leon cocked his arm, ready to lob another rock but the dog ran away and Leon dropped the rock on his foot. It hurt.

When his mother finally came out, a halo of smoke hovered around her head. "Stan thinks you're really talented," she said as she unlocked the door to her baby-blue Firebird. "I'm increasing your lessons to twice a week."

At home, Leon discovered the benefits of his rhythmic talent during dinner. "Evelyn, pass the spinach, would you?" his father grumbled. His mother absently flipped pages of *People* magazine while smoking a cigarette. Dinner for her was a kind of revenge. She'd cook. But only crap. Her meat loaf was a mix of dehydrated onion soup mix, ketchup, and bloody hamburger meat molded into a bread pan. Potatoes came from a box. Spinach from a can. She picked around the edges of her meals, nibbling on bread or sipping a spiked Diet Coke. His father ate everything but always complained. Leon sat between them and laid down a backbeat to keep everything together.

"Pass the spinach," his father said again. When she didn't move, his father's tone changed, something darker, deeper, more growling. "Pass the goddamned spinach!"

"Pass the goddamned spinach! Pass the goddamned spinach!" Leon chanted and banged out the rhythm with his palms on his thighs under the table. His mother and father stopped in midmotion to stare. His mother's cigarette dwindled halfway to her mouth. A thin line of spit like a spider web hung between his father's partly opened lips. A spoonful of dripping creamed spinach paused over the serving bowl held between them.

"What the hell are you doing?" his father snapped as his mother dropped the green blob.

"Four over three," Leon said loudly never missing a beat on his legs that stung and felt good all at the same time.

"Is this something Stan taught you, honey?" His mother gave a sidelong glance to his father. His father shook his head and shoveled a bite of meat loaf into his mouth. "Baseball is a hell of a lot cheaper," he said. "And quieter."

The cost of the drum lessons and the noise were always points of contention between Leon's parents. (What wasn't?) For years, he thought the drums had driven his father to leave. As an adult, he realized that his parents' problems were seeded long before he started banging on the cans. Regardless of whether the drumming pushed his father over the edge or not, Leon remains grateful to his mother for getting him started. Without the drums, he's sure he would be a prematurely bald burnout working in a record store in Weehawken. And he certainly would have never gotten someone like Junie.

Junie who loves his music, loves his food, adores even his balding skull. She keeps mementos from their dates—cocktail napkins, ticket stubs, snapshots of them together with their arms around one another. She used to stash little notes and candies in his drum cases when he went on the road. Leon has never felt more loved in his life.

He glances at the clock again. Six forty-five. Maybe her train got stuck. Or maybe her job went late. She usually comes home with funny stories about her daily temp assignments. She has had more strange jobs in the three years she's lived in the City than anyone else he knows. She's made sandwiches in a deli, delivered flowers from a beat-up van, given tours of South Street Seaport to school groups, and bussed tables at a Greek restaurant in Queens. She's pamphleteered. Sold little laser lights outside of Madison Square Garden. Been the personal assistant to a crazy brilliant sculptor and checked facts for two alternative press magazines. She claims she wants to drive a cab. Sometimes she talks about going to law school or getting certified as a massage therapist.

Leon finds her ever-changing jobs amusing but has always assumed she'd eventually find something that she loves to do. In fact, he has a secret fantasy about the two of them opening a business together. They will move upstate. To a small college town where they will scrape together enough money to buy a house on a country lane with a yard and a dog. Then they will open a restaurant. Nothing fancy. Just a small place on the main drag of town. Leon will cook good solid food with a few specials every night. Junie will bring the people in, beguile them with her quirky charm. They will showcase local artwork. Weekends they'll bring in great bands. Push the tables to the side so people can groove. Leon will even play sometimes with a few guys from around town. Nothing too serious. Never any touring. His commitment would be to the restaurant. And to Junie. Who will be pregnant and glowing with the anticipation of their first child.

He stirs the stew again and turns the burner down to low. The fantasy is pointless. For many reasons. He knows nothing about running a restaurant. And where would they get the money to buy a house, let alone open a business? Plus, he has no idea if Junie would be happy outside of the City. They've never talked about it. Nor have they talked about a family. Just alluded to children in a vague way as if in another life the two of them could be parents to some mischievous three-year-old. Hell, they haven't even talked about marriage.

No wonder. Both of them come from such screwy families. He used to think Junie had an enviable childhood when she talked about piano lessons and dance recitals. The fact that her parents are still together seemed to indicate a level of mental health and stability that his family could never claim. But, the more he's gotten to know Junie, the better he understands that things in her house were not what they appeared. He'd like to ask about her brother sometimes, but she doesn't have much to say on the topic. Leon supposes that's because she was so young when Jacob died. What little she's said about it has given Leon the impression that Jacob's death was like an earthquake along a fault line that left a huge rift between Junie and her parents.

So, maybe he and Junie have been ruined for marriage and parenting by the fucked-up circumstances of their families. Or maybe their mutual dissatisfaction with their childhoods makes them perfect candidates for monogamy and procreation because they will work hard to get it right.

That is, if Junie ever comes home.

Leon lays out bowls and spoons at each end of the little Formica table they picked out together from the Manhattan Salvation Army. Junie wants to cover it with a tablecloth, but Leon loves the table's shiny metal legs with brown freckles of rust and the wide metal band that skirts the marbled Formica table-top. There are even matching chairs with red vinyl seats. He digs old beat-up furniture with character. No Pottery Barn crap made to look old. He has a real wrought-iron bed frame and crazy quilts from his great aunt's Pennsylvania farmhouse. He enjoys browsing antique shops on Atlantic Avenue and has collected some of his best bookshelves and rugs from stoop sales and Dumpster dives. Nicked-up finds from street corners, buys from second-hand stores, and rescued family heirlooms that no one else wanted. He's taken all those orphaned accessories and made an electric, cozy place. Maybe it was so many formative years without his father. Maybe his feminine side is overdeveloped.

The guys in Mr. Whipple used to call Leon a pussy for all the decorating and cooking. Asked him if he was secretly gay. They all about shit their pants when Junie moved in. Especially Steve, who couldn't believe that a girl as great as Junie could be in love with Leon. Steve thinks every woman is in love with him, or should be. One good thing about him, though, he packs girls into the Mr. Whipple shows.

Junie promised to come to the gig tonight. She hasn't come for weeks. It must get old to see them play the same thing every show. But Leon's leaving tomorrow for the whole weekend. He wants to see her in the middle of the crowd watching him, swaying to the music and finding the beat with her hips. He knows everything is okay when she smiles at him and blows kisses from the floor. She swears someday she'll toss her leopard print bra to him during a drum solo. Junie told Leon once that she's always had a thing for drummers.

She never said anything about chefs.

Leon checks the bread in the oven. Warm, bordering on hot. Pretty soon it will be dry. It's nearly seven o'clock. An hour late is bad, even for Junie. He closes the oven door and sighs. She'll get here when she gets here. No use getting mad over it. Hopefully she'll be in a good mood.

He goes into the living room, flops to the couch, and flips through TV channels. He settles on an *I Love Lucy* rerun. Red-haired, kooky Lucy takes apart the television and gets inside so Ricky will know she could be a star. Ricky teases Lucy and Lucy gets pissed. Their fighting was oddly sexy, even if they slept in separate beds. Not at all like Leon's parents, who screamed at each other with hatred in their eyes. He could never get mad and yell at Junie that way. Funny, kooky, sexy Junie. He's so glad they never really fight. If she gets pissed, he can always joke her back to happy.

He should do something special for her. Something to show her how much he loves and appreciates her. And that he can be patient while she settles in. Moving in together has been harder on her than it has been on him. They should have found a neutral place instead of fitting Junie into Leon's space. But it's so expensive and such a pain in the ass to find an apartment in New York. He could make her a tape. A special moving-in-together tape. Or a two-week anniversary tape.

From the shelves he pulls out CDs. "Bring It on Down to My House" by Bob Wills and "Our House in the Middle of the Street" by Madness. The music should also narrate their relationship. "We Belong Together" by Rickie Lee Jones. Distill his feelings into something entertaining. "Silly Love Songs" by Wings, a wink and nod to show he knows the tape is goofy. He pulls out Aretha, *Live at the Filmore West*, "Love the One You're With" and "Let's Stay Together" by Al Green. His finger cruises past the plastic spines of jewel cases. "I Need Your Love So Bad," Irma Thomas. He wants this tape to tell Junie exactly what he's thinking. "Stand by Your Man," Tammy Wynette.

Leon flips through the stack of music cradled in his arms. He doesn't like the mix at all. It's whiny and will piss Junie off. She hates it when he's needy. He should think it over more. Decide exactly what he wants to say. He'll make it when he comes back from the road. Talk to the guys in the band about it and get some suggestions. He slides the CDs onto the shelf one by one, except for the Rickie Lee Jones. One of her favorites. Some music with dinner would be nice. Help her relax and cheer up if she's grouchy. Remind her how happy he is that she is here with him.

# CHAPTER
## FIVE

Junie trudges up the stairs. Heavy black marks line the walls where Leon's drum cases have banged on the way up and down. Since she moved in she has feared the landlord will stage a surprise inspection and evict them because of the damage. They could never afford another place in Park Slope. Where would they go? Redhook? Sounds like a slaughterhouse. Gowanus? Any neighborhood with "anus" in its name speaks for itself.

Now Junie thinks it wouldn't be such a bad thing to lose their lease. She could even make an anonymous call to the landlord. Tip him off in a fake accent. Her Irish brogue isn't entirely unbelievable. She does a pretty good Southern belle impersonation. If they were kicked out, she could tell Leon she'd made a big mistake. Move back in with Katie. Pursue Eliot without the guilt. It wouldn't exactly be like leaving Leon.

She stops on the first landing and sighs over her predicament and her complete inability to deal with the situation.

What's she supposed to do? Forget she's ever seen Eliot Bloom? That would be nice but it isn't going to happen. Especially when he has infused her thoughts like tea in hot water. And now, she has to go upstairs and try to carry on some semblance of her relationship with Leon while Eliot lurks in the shadowy corners of her mind. It would be easier to plunk herself down on the stairs and become part of the banister. A newel post with a finial for a head. Too bad transmogrification isn't in her repertoire.

So, onward!

She gathers breath for the next flight and catches a whiff of something tomatoey with lots of spices. No doubt Leon's latest creation. The rich odor pulls her up the stairs like a finger in her nostrils. This is how he wooed her when they first met. Taking her out on eating adventures in different boroughs. Queens for Indian and Korean. Brooklyn for Italian. Chinatown for dim sum. He courted her with homemade multilayered casseroles, rolled and stuffed and fried things, soups and sauces so thick that spoons could stand up in them. Until then, food had been merely sustenance for Junie. Something practical she had to have when her stomach rumbled and her arms felt weak. The only food she made overtures toward were desserts and candies, filling her cupboards and pockets with small treats.

As she nears the door the scent becomes stronger and Junie realizes this is a new recipe. Something he has created, perhaps just for her. She'll eat it with a side of shame. How could she share a dry and bitter banana with Eliot while Leon was home coaxing herbs to release their essence in hot oil? She wants to slip inside the door without Leon hearing and slink to the bathroom where she can brush her teeth or at least gargle with something minty before she tastes his concoction. But the kitchen is the first thing in the door. She makes a mental note to start carrying breath mints.

The smell of his food envelops her as she enters. Leon is not there. The clock above the stove reads seven-o-eight. What time did she say she would be home? Surely before now. She closes the door quietly and tiptoes to the stove, curious to see what he has made. Lifting the lid of the large soup pot releases tendrils of steam from the spicy stew. Her glasses fog up as she inhales and Rickie Lee Jones softly croons, "Spring can really get you down," from the living room. Then Leon is behind her, wrapping his long arms around her shoulders and drawing her into the familiar contours of his body. She stiffens.

"Hey," he whispers. "I was getting worried about you." He kisses her ear.

"Sorry." She wriggles free from his grip and pecks him lightly on the cheek. Rough with bristly stubble. Fragrant with good clean soap and cooking smells. Her hand rests against his arm. Solid and warm beneath his tee shirt. Those muscles toned from pounding on the drums. When all her prepubescent friends were licking lead-singer photos from *Tiger Beat,* Junie was looking in the background for the guy behind the drum kit. Quiet, unassuming, but essential. Arms and legs flailing. She cried real tears when the drummer from Def Leppard lost his left arm in a drunken car accident.

She rubs the foggy lenses of her glasses with the corner of a dish towel. "I had to run some errands after work." She stays beside the refrigerator and picks at the corner of a dancing lobster magnet Leon brought her from Boston. He brings her tacky magnets when he's on the road with Mr. Whipple. They have a whole collection on the fridge. Billy Ray Cyrus. Union 76. Baltimore Orioles. I'd Rather Be Bowling. Trinket tributes to their love.

"Where did you work today?" he asks as he stirs the stew.

"I handed out samples of cheesecake to tourists in Grand Central Station."

Leon smiles over his shoulder. "Did anything funny happen?"

Junie knows he is waiting for a story. He loves it when she regales him with impersonations of the weirdos she meets during her day as a temp. His favorite is when she walks dogs on the Upper West Side and mimics the old women in Chanel who kiss their Yorkies on the lips. Junie shrugs. "Today was pretty boring," she says.

He turns back to the pot, his smile gone. "Your mom called."

"Was she civil?" Junie asks.

"She's always very polite to me."

"That's right. It's only me she has a problem with."

"You're so hard on her," Leon says. He tastes the soup then grinds fresh pepper into it.

"Right," she says and rolls her eyes. Leon is so damn forgiving, a trait Junie normally adores except when he applies it to her mother. "What did she want?"

"She's doing a Leukemia Walk-a-Thon and wants you to sponsor her."

"Good Christ," Junie grumbles. "Another one?"

Leon reaches for her and pulls her to the stove by the elbow. He waves the spoon under her nose.

"Smells great," she says.

Leon dishes out two bowls of the steaming stew, lays a leaf of fresh parsley across each one, and sets them on the table. Junie thinks of the leftover Chinese take-out cartons in Eliot's fridge.

"Hope you're hungry," Leon says.

"What?" says Junie, snapping out of a fantasy of feeding Eliot noodles from the tapered ends of chopsticks.

"I said, I hope you're hungry."

"Oh, yeah." She unbuttons her coat. "Starving. All I've eaten today is cheesecake." Junie remembers the banana in her pocket and realizes she's told her first lie. She carefully lays her coat over a chair.

They sit. She digs her spoon into her bowl and takes a big bite. The tastes are complex. Paprika and fruit, sweet potatoes and garbanzo beans. "This is delicious," she says.

"I'm glad you like it." Leon smiles.

They eat. Chew and swallow words and food. She hates this strained hush that falls between them because within it thoughts of Eliot bubble into her mind. She sees herself across a table from Eliot. They are sharing a bottle of Merlot. He reaches for her hand and she weaves her fingers into his. She crawls through the plates of heavy, garlicky food to get to him.

"So," says Leon. A few bread crumbs have gathered in the

reddish scruff on the bottom of his square chin. He smiles at her again. His soft hazel eyes are wide beneath the sketch of his eyebrows, waiting for her response. He is such a beautiful and gentle man and Junie feels remorse just then for thinking of Eliot at the dinner table. She wishes she could go to Leon, sit on his lap, and brush the crumbs away. Hold his head against her breast. Tell him she is sorry that she is late. That she is such a bad person, a terrible friend, a horrible girlfriend. And that she will try harder from now on.

Before she can will her limbs to move, Leon says, "Have you ever thought about leaving New York?"

"For a vacation?" She tears off a hunk of warm bread and dismisses her plan for a spontaneous apology.

"No, for good. Moving somewhere else."

"Not really."

"Do you ever think about going back to school?"

"Huh?" Junie says through a mouthful of bread.

"Grad school. Or something. You mentioned law school once."

She swallows, chokes a little. "You want me to be a lawyer?" Is this some kind of trap? Is he commenting on her lack of moral fiber? Her inclination toward duplicity?

"You talk about it sometimes." He leans forward thoughtfully and folds his hands over his bowl of stew. "What do you want to be?"

Junie is momentarily stymied. Normally this line of questioning is reserved for her mother, who relentlessly reminds Junie that she is twenty-five and careerless and directionless with the attention span of a gnat. A classic underachiever by today's standards. Junie likes to think that fifty years ago her lack of career ambition would have been the default setting for marriage and motherhood. By now she would have three kids and a collection of Jell-O salad recipe cards. Not that she would have been happy or fulfilled, but she wouldn't have been deemed a slacker. One who hasn't found herself yet. Sometimes Junie worries that she actually has found herself and that this self truly has no aspirations. She never thought Leon would mind.

"What do you feel passionate about?" he asks.

"Passion?" she asks. As in ardor and desire? Her mouth hangs open. Is this a trick? Does he know about Eliot? Surely not. Leon couldn't know. Even if he did, he's not this conniving.

"Yeah. What makes you really excited?"

"I . . . I . . . ," Junie stammers. She can think of nothing professional that could thrill her. Filing? Data entry? Rescuing stray dogs? Teaching blind children to knit? None of it is orgasmic. Maybe she's one of those people who doesn't have a passion. It's not as if she moved to New York with a dream and a song. Brooklyn was far from Indiana and Katie had an apartment lined up. Seemed like a good reason three years ago. "Since when do you care so much about my job?" Junie snaps.

Leon shrugs. "I don't care what you do as long as you're happy." He leans forward more, so he hovers over his soup bowl and he stares at her intently. "Are you happy?"

Junie grabs the edge of the table with her free hand, holds her spoon like a spear in the other. "Do I not seem happy? Because, I'm fine. You're the one who seems suddenly unhappy with my career choice." She points her spoon menacingly at Leon.

"Hey, hey." Leon reaches across the table and strokes her white-knuckled hand. "Don't get upset. I was just talking. Blah, blah, blah. Dinner conversation. You know. It was nothing. Let's forget it. New subject!" he says brightly. "You know what I was thinking about today?"

Junie relaxes her grip on the table, on her spoon. She shrugs out the kink that has formed in her shoulders and tries to forget the past two minutes. Just like Leon has. Bring up something important. See that it causes tension. Then drop it. He's good at that.

"I was flipping through TV channels," Leon says. "And I saw a rerun of *Charlie's Angels*. The one where Sabrina goes undercover as a trapezist who's afraid of heights. And I was wondering what happened to your tee shirt?"

That shirt is how they met. At Domsey's, a huge thrift store converted from a factory in the industrial part of Williamsburg. It sits across from the Domino sugar factory. Mothballs, must, and burnt sugar are the smells of their first encounter. Junie was examining the tiny tee with the *Charlie's Angels* silhouette. Leon stood behind a rack of deliveryman shirts with names like Bud and Cecil embroidered over the heart. She saw him eyeing her as she held the shirt up against her body. "What do you think?" she asked, simply for the fun of flirting.

"I like a girl who's not afraid to be seen with Farrah Fawcett across her chest," he said, then stepped closer. "But I'd have to see it on."

"You'd like that wouldn't you?" she answered and was all set to ignore him but then he adjusted his hat. A silly hat. A black leather apple cap with a bill that he wore slightly askew. It hugged his head and puffed out on the sides then came back together on top under a black button. With the shadow gone from his face, Junie noticed his eyes (brown with flecks of green and gold), his nose (triangular with delicately flared nostrils), and his smile (a little lopsided so that he looked slightly chagrined).

"I'm playing with a band tonight," he said, pulling a weedy little ponytail across his shoulder. "If you wear that shirt, I'll get you in for free."

"Where are you playing?"

"Far Bar in the East Village. You know it?"

"Yeah." She slung the tee over her shoulder and smirked. "And I also know that there's never a cover. So you can't get me in for free."

Leon readjusted the hat, casting a shadow over his eyes again. "You're right," he said. "But if you come, I'll buy you a beer."

"Maybe." She scooted a few hangers across the rack indifferently. "Depends on what you play."

"What'd you mean? Like jazz, rock, pop?"

"No, I mean what instrument."

"Why? You only like guitarists?" Leon asked.

She gazed straight at him. "No," she said slowly. "I like the drums."

Leon repeated the rhythm of her sentence with his palms

against his thigh, I-like-the-drums, ba-da-da-da. "Then you should definitely come," he said. "And you should definitely wear that shirt."

Leon taps his spoon in quarter notes against his bowl. "You haven't worn the shirt to bed since you moved in," he says.

"It's only been two weeks."

"I know, but you used to wear it a lot when you spent the night."

"It was the only shirt I had here."

"It's kind of special," Leon says. "Like our song, only it's a shirt."

"Not everything can stay the same."

"But things don't have to change just because you moved in with me."

Junie drops her spoon into her half-eaten bowl of stew. "Maybe this was a big mistake," she blurts. "Maybe we weren't ready to move in together." She pushes her chair back. It makes obscene noises across the linoleum. She stands, unsure what to do. Dump her soup on the floor, then stomp out of the room in a fury of protest? Over what?

"Junie?" Leon says. "What's going on?"

She stares into the soup bowl at the floating bloated chick-peas and little currant blimps. "I don't know," she mumbles, then feels tears pressing at the corners of her eyes. It would feel so good to confess it all. That there's this man, Eliot. And she can't stop thinking about him. And she doesn't know why and she's so sorry. So terribly, terribly sorry.

"Junie." Leon extends his hand for her. She stays outside his reach. "This isn't a mistake. It's a big change but we just have to relax and take our time." He stands and walks behind her. Massages her shoulders. Kisses the back of her neck and nuzzles her ear. "I'm glad you're here."

It's impossible to argue with Leon. He's just too nice and understanding and reasonable. She and Eliot could have some good knock-down-drag-out fights. If Eliot told her to get a real job, she would tell him to kiss her ass. If she said moving in with him was a mistake, he'd tell her to go ahead and get the fuck out. But not Leon. He will nice her to death. She turns to him and buries her face in his shirt. She has no idea why he loves her when she can be such a bitch. She wants to impale herself on the bread knife, choke herself on a garbanzo bean, run screaming through the apartment, and jump out the front window because Leon is so good and kind and fair and she is such a schmuck with banana breath.

"Hey, let's not have a big stupid fight, okay? I have to leave pretty soon," Leon says into her hair.

"Where are you going?"

"Mercury Lounge," he says slowly. "Remember? You said you'd come. Steve claims an A&R guy from Epic is showing up."

Junie looks up. "That's tonight?"

"And I'm leaving tomorrow for the weekend."

"The whole weekend?" she asks a bit too eagerly.

"What's wrong with you? Are you tired?"

She shrugs. Shakes her head. "I just forgot."

"You want some ice cream? There's butter pecan in the freezer."

This is always Leon's answer. Ply her with food if she's tired, grouchy, sick, unhappy. He's kept the freezer stocked with her favorite flavor since she walked through the door with her clothes and her grandmother's juice glasses. "No. Thanks," she mumbles.

"I have to go get set up. You want to come with me now or meet me later?"

"I'll meet you later."

Leon kisses her forehead. She lifts her face to find his lips but she feels confused. Part of her wants to latch on to him fiercely and not let him go. Part wants to push him out the door so she can be alone.

"Promise?" he says.

She leans into him again and rests her cheek against his sternum. Familiar space. Comforting place. She listens to his heartbeat. Listens to him breathe. It would be so easy if this were all there were to being happy.

"Promise," she says and holds him lightly around the small of the back, waiting for him to let go first.

# CHAPTER

# SIX

In the middle of the bedroom floor, Junie discards her clothes to change for the gig. She kicks the remnants of her day into the corner where laundry encroaches toward the worn Navajo rug that Leon scored from an estate sale in Woodstock. Junie has never cared much about the décor of her living spaces. A few posters. The same faded purple polka-dotted comforter dragged from place to place. Katie covered their shared apartment with bright tapestries and handmade throw pillows. Now Leon's medley of furniture surrounds Junie.

Sometimes she thinks it would be fun to have her own place. She would paint the walls different colors. One orange, one blue, one yellow. Have no furniture. Only pillows on the floor. Her own private harem. Who is she kidding? She doesn't have enough money for rent. Maybe Leon would give her a corner to decorate. A shrine to her own skewed taste. But everything in the apartment is so perfect and he's worked so hard to get it that way. She could never ask him to change it.

She kicks her clothes again and catches her reflection in the mirror next to the closet. Stands with her hands on her hips in a bra and white cotton panties. In college she went through a phase of wearing boys' tighty whitey Y-front underwear and never shaving. Her uniform became Mary Janes and baby doll dresses with furry armpits and boys' briefs underneath. She claimed to be making a statement about the objectification of women. She could rage on quite unpoetic about the impracticality of intimate apparel. Boys' briefs don't push and pinch and reconfigure! Totally utilitarian with their clever escape hatch. And shaving. You didn't want to get her started.

But darling dresses and little-girl shoes didn't fit with her rebellion against sexism. Slowly she recognized the more subtle statement of her half-girl/half-boy look. For the first time on her own, there were no reminders of Jacob. At least at home she had the familiar pattern of the wallpaper that they pretended was *Willy Wonka* lickable. Or the yard full of interred paraphernalia from their childhood. All she needed was a shovel to find him. At college, Jacob was buried in her mind and she felt so lonely, then. She had always been afraid of losing him too much. If she completely let him go, what would be left? Just herself. Not enough. Clearly, since it wasn't enough for her parents. Everyone wanted Jacob back. Most of all, Junie.

The dresses, the shoes, the briefs, the soft wispy hair on her legs and underarms were all comforting in her new surroundings. A way to be him and her, together. Again. When it dawned on her what she was doing, she quickly shaved and bought some respectable panties. She didn't want to be one of those crazies who carried the dead around like a stinking alba-tross. Especially not at college where she could re-create herself into anyone she wanted to be. Not the girl with the dead brother. But someone else. Someone completely herself.

She studies her reflection in the mirror. Now she is tired of these practical white cotton panties. No more of this nun under-wear she's currently sporting. She wants something a bit more feminine. Matching bra-and-panty sets with lace and flowers. Perhaps a thong. Or slutty lingerie with straps and buckles. Leon would be just as happy if she wore the *Charlie's Angels* tee shirt to bed again. When did she wear it last? Was it a Wednesday or a Friday, an ordinary night? Did she and Leon have sex? At some point, she took off that shirt and shoved it in his dresser. She rummages through the top drawer. Not it. Not it. Not it. She digs harder and finds the Angels wadded up in the back.

The tee shirt was old when she bought it and now the white has become dull, almost gray, and the logo has lost its sparkle, a little rip has intruded beneath the collar. She works her finger into the hole. The fabric separates easily at the seam. Subtle, she thinks and laughs. She buries her nose into the fabric and inhales deeply. Musty pressed particle board. Sour sweat. Faint traces of bitter cigarette smoke.

The first time she wore the shirt was at the Far Bar. She cou-pled it with a blue-suede miniskirt and red cowgirl boots. The fringe at the bottom of the skirt shimmied across her thighs when she walked into the bar with Katie by her side. An old Sly and the Family Stone album played over the p.a. and cigarette smoke hung thick from the ceiling. As her eyes adjusted to the

dim light, she recognized Leon leaning against the bar. The little ponytail and silly apple cap were dead giveaways. Plus two
drumsticks stuck up from the baggy back pockets of his jeans.
She elbowed Katie and pointed.

"Definitely cute from behind," Katie whispered.

Leon turned around. In the few seconds before he recognized her, Junie caught her breath. Was it his eyes, his forehead,
the notch between his bottom lip and chin? Could she take
measurements and scientifically prove the attraction? Was it the
ratio of arm length to torso? The space between his ears? The
way he slouched, his curving back? Was it all merely reminis-
cent of someone else, comforting in its familiarity? Or was it the
newness of this person? The possibility of discovery. How were
his toes shaped? Where was he ticklish? Whatever it was,
describable or not, Junie was smitten just then, as pliable as
warm taffy, ready to yield.

When Leon saw her, he smiled anxiously. "Hey, Junie." He
held out his hand.

Junie curtsied. He remembered her name. Just like that, first
thing, he smiled his little crooked smile, then said her name and
reached for her. She took his hand. His fingers were callused
from the drumsticks but his palm was warm and soft. Perfect to
lay her cheek against on a cold day.

"Nice shirt," he said. He didn't let go of her hand just yet.

"Thank you," she said. "I got it at a very exclusive boutique
on Park Avenue."

He laughed loudly and his shoulders danced. A belly-
laugher. Junie liked that. They drew their fingers apart.

"This is my friend Katie," Junie said. "Leon, Katie. Katie, Leon."

As Leon and Katie shook hands, Junie leaned back against the bar to steady herself. She tried to appear cool and collected rather than this giddy, jumpy spaz she had become. An eleven-year-old at the junior high school dance who just brushed shoulders with her secret crush.

"So, I owe you a beer," Leon turned to her and said.

"Can it be a whiskey and soda instead?"

"Sure. And you?" he asked Katie.

"Whatever's on tap," said Katie.

While Leon ordered the drinks, Junie caught Katie's eye, then pretended to pinch Leon's butt. Katie snickered.

Leon glanced over his shoulder. "Everything okay?"

"Just fine," Junie said as he handed her the whiskey.

"Wish I could hang out but I have to go warm up." He pulled the drumsticks out of his back pocket. "Will I see you after the show?"

"Yeah, sure." Junie took the first sweet sip of whiskey and soda, which calmed her a bit.

Leon looked at her for a moment and grinned again. "I'm glad you came."

Blood bolted to Junie's cheeks. "Thanks," she said but it came out a squeak as Leon left for backstage.

Katie slid up next to Junie. "He was waiting on you."

"You think?" Junie asked and fanned herself with a cocktail napkin.

"Absolutely." Katie hopped onto a bar stool and took a drink of beer. "Waits to see if you come. Grins all goofy like that, then buys you a drink. Whew doggy!"

"He's cute, right?"

"And totally sweet," said Katie.

"He remembered my name," Junie said.

"God," Katie said. "You're blushing like a virgin."

"Shut up," Junie said. "He's adorable."

"But he's gotta lose that hat," said Katie.

"I'll drink to that," Junie said and raised her glass again.

When the band came out, Leon settled in behind the drums. Junie perched on a bar stool to get a better view as he counted off the rhythm to the first song. Then the band exploded into a chaotic ska tune about Little Debbie Snackin' Cakes. The lead singer flailed around the stage, lunging at the mic and stomping over cords. He jumped and shouted and beat his head with the microphone while the rest of the band grinded on their instruments. The singer was undeniably sexy in those wild antics but Junie barely paid attention to him. She sat at the bar, nursing whiskeys and sodas, feeling every cymbal crash in her shoulders, tom-tom throb beneath her belly button, and bass drum beat between her hipbones. When Leon smiled out at her, her nipples stood erect like tiny soldiers.

After the gig, Leon said he needed some fresh New York air. Junie followed him outside. Katie conveniently stayed behind. The two of them stood under a streetlight on the corner of Stanton and Allen streets breathing in the exhaust fumes from city buses. "Did you like the music?" he asked.

"Had a good beat. I could dance to it."

"Ten?"

"Eleven!" she said. "How about my shirt?" She plucked at the fabric just below her breasts and stretched the tee toward Leon.

"I like it even better on."

"You want to borrow it?"

He stepped a bit closer. "Only while you're wearing it."

"I think that could be arranged," Junie said as she stood on tiptoe and titled her head. Leon closed his eyes. They kissed, small and tentatively at first, then with more urgency. She didn't know what to do with her hands, so they fluttered by her sides.

When they separated, Leon said, "Can I have your phone number, Junie?"

Her stomach flopped like a slippery seal and she smiled big. "Do you have a pen?"

He patted his pockets. "No, but I'll remember. Just tell me."

"How will you remember?" Junie frowned. Did he not like the kiss?

"Just tell me."

"962-8145," she said rather petulantly.

"9-6-2-8-1-4-5," Leon repeated. He put a rhythm to the numbers as he said them. "9-6-2-8-1-4-5." Added a backbeat with his palm against his thigh, repeated each digit like hits on a drumkit, added crash cymbals in the middle by sucking air against his teeth. When he was done and stood grinning at her, she kissed him again, pushed her tongue inside his mouth, eager to find out how his lips and teeth created music just for her.

Then they were spending every day together. An instacouple. Just add water and watch them grow! Sea monkeys. Every date with Leon was so exciting at first. Picking out clothes to wear to his gigs where her name was always on the guest list. Standing in the crowd watching him watch her as he played. Hauling drums out the back exits of bars. Waking late the next morning, still smelling of beer and cigarettes, tangled in his arms and legs. She never imagined that lifestyle could be anything but exhilarating.

So what changed? Not Leon. Maybe that's the problem. Or maybe she stopped trying as hard. She hasn't been to one of his gigs for several weeks. The last time she went, she only stopped by for the last few songs. Even then, she was in a bad mood after stuffing envelopes for some German conglomerate all day. Maybe if she made more of an effort things with Leon would improve. She hasn't flirted with him in a while. Dressed for him. Instigated sex.

She looks at herself in the mirror again. She still looks good. Smooth tummy. Firm breasts. Tapered calves. But, she also looks older. Not in a bad way. No deep lines or wrinkles, yet. What's changed in her is subtle. Something around her eyes and mouth. The way she holds her head and shoulders up and back. As if she's become more of an adult. When she was a kid, she thought that kind of change would happen all at once—the second she got her period or turned eighteen or lost her virginity. Now she knows that growing up comes in fits and starts. Giant leaps, then long lingering periods of nothing. Evolution of the soul. Moving in with Leon was one of those big steps. Perhaps now they are at a plateau, getting used to the mutation in their relationship. And if she wants to keep moving forward, she's got to put some effort into it.

She scoots hangers across the closet rod. What would Leon like? Something equal parts sexy and funky. Black bell-bottom tuxedo pants with a purple spangly one-shoulder top. Too disco. She trades the pants for a beat-up denim skirt. Appalachian chic? She slips the top over her head and pulls on a red bra under a filmy red polka-dotted sleeveless blouse. Not bad. Which shoes? Boots? Heels? Loafers? It's not warm enough for sandals. She hasn't worn her red ballerina slippers for a while. But they don't go well with the skirt. She pushes hangers left and right to uncover her favorite pair of navy-blue linen Capri pants with a big white stripe down the side. Perfect with the top. Righteous with the shoes. And she has the perfect coat. A little red poncho she found at a stoop sale. She retrieves it from the front closet, then looks at herself one last time in the mirror. Very Audrey Hepburn on a budget. Leon will love it!

# CHAPTER
# SEVEN

The front bar of the Mercury Lounge is long and narrow and always packed on a weekend night with people trying hard to appear not to be trying too hard. Hipsters lean against the bar in their casual city chic, smoking lazily and sipping drinks. Jostling through this crowd while carrying a single beer is enough to inspire muttered curses, but schlepping drum gear into the bar sparks looks of death and hatred. Everyone loves a band, but only when they are on stage.

Leon holds his bass drum in front of his belly and his cymbal bag over his shoulder and shouts, "Excuse me! Coming through," as he plows into the crowd. At the end of the bar, he spies Steve and Randy bumming cigarettes from two girls who look younger than Junie. Leon "accidentally" bumps Steve's ass with his drum, then says, "How about helping me out, man?"

"I already got my gear," Steve says and opens his vintage suede jacket to reveal himself in patchwork leather pants with a giant silver zipper running up the middle of his crotch and a tight red tee shirt that says Porn Star in gold. "This is all I need, baby." Steve holds up his hand for Randy to slap. The girl with spiky blue-striped hair rolls her eyes and the other one laughs.

"You paying if I get a ticket for double-parking?" Leon asks.

Steve lets his jacket fall closed. "Dude, drink a fucking beer and relax." He glances around the bar. "Good crowd." One of the girls taps him on the shoulder and hands him a beer.

"I got it, man." Randy grabs Leon's keys and muscles through the crowd to the front door.

Leon threads his way backstage to set up his kit while the first band finishes their set. Tim is already there replacing a string on his bass and squinting against the smoke of the cigarette hanging loosely from the corner of his mouth. He and Leon go way back. Both came to the City right after high school and started slogging away at the clubs. They met Randy and Steve five years ago at an audition. They all shared the ambition to be rock gods by the time they hit thirty. Now, as they each zero in on the big 3-0, they're getting antsy.

"Need help?" Tim asks.

"Nah," says Leon. "Randy's on it. I just got one more load, then I'll park."

"You see Steve?" Tim flicks the cigarette to the ground and grinds it with the heel of his worn cowboy boot.

Leon nods.

"He tell you he's scrapping my tune from the set list?"

"Why?" asks Leon as he opens the bass drum case.

"Wants to do some fucking Deep Purple song instead.

60

Dude, I'm telling you, I'm tired of being treated like some lame sideman."

"What'd Randy say?" Leon attaches the legs to his bass drum.

Tim sneers. "Nothing. As usual. Thinks every idea Steve has is money. Fucking Berklee pricks. Just because they went to music school they think they are God's gift to music. But I'm telling you, I'm going to shove a metronome up their asses. Both their time sucks."

Whenever Tim gets on one of his tirades, Leon swears to himself that he's going to quit the band. He hates all the tension and fighting, but then he remembers the other option. Playing endless fifty-buck showcase gigs with this year's parade of new singer-songwriters who've descended upon the city with something meaningful to say. At least Mr. Whipple has a small label that's putting some cash behind them and distributing their CD. At least one of their songs charted on AAA-format college stations. Last summer they did a song for an indie film soundtrack that got them some attention. And now, Steve claims Epic is interested in the next CD.

"You think this A&R guy will really show?" Leon asks.

Tim shrugs and tightens the string with one hand while plucking it with the other. The sound climbs up a wobbly scale. "How many times a month does Steve claim someone from a label is showing up?" He cocks his head and listens carefully as he strums all the strings on his bass.

"Sharp," Leon says.

Tim nods and twists the keys until the notes all blend when

he plays. "I'll believe an A&R guy showed up when I see a big wad of cash in my pocket."

Randy opens the door and slides in the Army duffel full of Leon's hardware. The girl with the blue-striped hair from the bar peeks in and grins. She carries the tom and snare. "I found a roadie," Randy says and smirks.

Leon takes the drums from her. "Thanks," he says. "You didn't have to . . ."

"I'm used to it," she says. "I play, too." She hands Leon a card from her back pocket that says "Pussy Willow" in big bold letters with Austin Healy underneath and two phone numbers.

Tim looks over Leon's shoulder. "Which one is your name?" he asks.

She rolls her eyes. "Austin," she says. "My parents have a sense of humor."

"They could be James Bond fans," Tim says.

Leon sticks his hand out to her, hoping to shut Tim up. "I'm Leon . . ."

"I know who you are." She shakes his hand and grins. "You ever need a sub, give me a call."

"Cool," Leon says as she waves and leaves the room.

"I'll take that." Randy holds out his hand for the card.

"You planning on replacing me?" Leon jokes.

"She has nicer legs."

Leon holds the card out of Randy's reach. "I might need a sub someday."

"For drums or for Junie?" Randy asks.

Tim laughs.

"Now you're definitely not getting it." Leon tucks it into his wallet. "I have to park the car."

The back of the bar is crowded with Mr. Whipple fans and hangers-on from the last band that played. Beer bottles line most tables and the ashtrays are full. Leon tightens the snare-drum head as he pumps the bass drum pedal to warm up his foot. A tall gorgeous blonde leans on the edge of the stage and laughs at everything Steve says as he unwinds a long mic cord. She doesn't look like one of Steve's normal groupies. She's at least thirty and she is put together. Even Leon notices that her white shirt is very crisp.

He leans down close to hear the snare over the din of drunken conversations and the Radio Head album the sound guy blasts over the p.a. Sometimes all this work and worry over the exact right pitch of each drum head seems futile. Once the band starts playing everything gets lost and muddy through the crappy sound system beneath Tim's grinding bass, Steve's screeching vocals, and Randy's wailing guitar. Leon might as well be banging on trashcan lids.

He scans the crowd for Junie. She's easy to spot with that red hair and those goofy blue glasses. The first time he saw her in Domsey's, he wrote her off as just another image hound, trying to create a distinctive look to make up for being uninteresting. On second glance, he saw what was under the hair and glasses and absurd plaid pants. Big green eyes and pouting lips. Great body, too. Not heavy, not thin. Perfectly in between with soft, curving hips and a perfect little butt. At first Leon wished she would get rid of the weird getups and just go natural. He loves it when she comes out of the shower with no glasses and her hair slicked back off her face. Now he understands her better.

Junie likes to hide herself beneath a layer of absurdity. It's a way to hold others at bay. If people think she's ridiculous then they won't expect too much. It's taken Leon a year to get beyond her protective cocoon. Now he knows her as a smart, kind, and loving person who can make him laugh harder than anyone else. She can also be serious. She listens to him and offers good advice. The past year has been bliss but lately their relationship has felt as if it could disintegrate at the smallest provocation. Maybe he pushed too hard for them to move in together. She can be so skittish sometimes.

The woman from the edge of the stage has disappeared into the crowd. Steve grabs his microphone with both hands, stands on his tiptoes, puffs out his chest, and puts his lips against the bulb of the mic, as if he is going to tongue it. "One, two, one, two," he croons with his eyes closed. On the other end of the stage, Randy noodles on his electric Fender, distorting his warm-up with the wah-wah pedal. The guy loves effects. Peter Frampton is his God. Why can't either one of them tune up and check mics without acting as if they are lost members of the Rolling Stones?

Tim hops onto stage and hands Leon a seltzer water with lime. "That was her," he says as he settles onto the monitor next to Leon's right knee.

Leon squeezes the lime and takes a long sip of the cold bubbles while continuing to pulse his foot against the bass drum pedal. "Who?"

"The A&R guy, only he's a she."

"Which one?" Leon looks out at the crowd again.

"The one who was talking to Steve just a minute ago."

"The blonde?" Leon asks.

"Randy told me." Tim takes a drink of his Guinness. A thin mustache of foam gathers beneath his nose.

Leon shakes his head. Watches Steve accept a squat glass of amber liquor from a smiling waitress in a tube top and pony-tails. "Figures," Leon says.

"You guys ready?" the sound guy asks through the monitors. Leon checks his watch. Ten-thirty exactly. Since when did Mercury run on time? He scans the crowd again. Still no Junie.

Tim puts his beer on top of the monitor and slings his bass down low across his hips. Randy flicks the butt of his cigarette off stage. Steve strips off his Porn Star shirt to reveal a blue dragon tattoo on his shoulder. The tail wraps around his arm and disappears across his chest beneath a white ribbed tank top. Some girls whistle and Steve flashes them a grin.

The sound guy says, "Let's hear it for Mr. Whipple."

Decent applause erupts. A few people yell as Leon counts off the first four beats and then smacks the ride cymbal as hard as he can. Steve takes a giant step backward, then leaps for the mic to begin the set.

Leon watches the door, waiting for Junie and worrying that she won't come. She's never on time, he reminds himself, but she'll come because she said she would. His divided attention makes no difference as he plays through the first two songs. The music is so ingrained in him that he barely has to pay attention.

Except when Steve pulls some pseudo–Jim Morrison stunt and starts writhing on the floor, expecting the band to cater to his every gyration. He doesn't usually start that until late in the set when he thinks he's whipped his groupies into a Steve frenzy.

Sometimes Leon is embarrassed to be playing the same shit in the same clubs as the first time he met Junie. She says she likes Mr. Whipple and thinks they have potential. She's right, of course. Of all the bands Leon has played with in New York, this one is more poised for success than any other. But how long should he hold out? There is always some big promise of a record deal, an opening slot on tour with a bigger band, a producer who's interested. Eventually any accomplishment starts feeling monumental, because most of the time prospects for any band are completely hopeless.

They all thought things would really change six months ago when Crop Duster distributed their second CD. They got a better manager because of it. But all Howie does is book the same kinds of bar gigs and festivals, just further away, all in the name of building a fan base. Now here's this supposed A&R woman, who looks more interested in screwing Steve than signing the band. Sometimes Leon wonders if it's all still worth it.

Junie comes in halfway through the third song, when Steve is screaming lyrics into Randy's ear. It's their schtick. Randy stands stoic, feet planted, face rigid, hands working over the strings of his guitar while Steve bumps him, screeches at him, and sometimes pounds him with the microphone. They work it up in rehearsals. The crowd loves it. Leon thinks it's gotten old. He sees Junie as soon as she steps in the door. He nods hello.

She blows him a little kiss, then parks herself in the back near the sound booth where she can see the stage. Leon perks up and plays harder. He loves when Junie watches.

After the last encore, after Steve has fallen to his knees, shrieking lyrics to a row of moshing girls, after the applause and whistles have finally been replaced by the Radio Head CD blasted through the p.a., Leon quickly dismantles the drums. Another band is already waiting at the foot of the stage. Junie stands off to the side.

Steve saunters over and slings his arm around Junie's shoulders. "Hey gorgeous!" He leans down to kiss her on the cheek. Leon hates the way Steve shamelessly flirts with Junie. "Haven't seen you for a while. Did you miss me?" Steve asks.

Junie slips away from his arm. "You're sweating like a pig," she says with a smile.

"It's hard work up there." Steve lifts the bottom of his tank top to wipe his face. He keeps the shirt folded up to show off his perfectly sculpted abs.

Leon leans over the edge of the stage and Junie stands on tiptoe to kiss him lightly on the lips.

"Sounded great," she says.

"Thanks," Leon says. "I'm almost packed up."

"Want me to get the car?"

"If you don't mind."

"Shouldn't treat your lady like a roadie," Steve says. "You want a beer, Junie?"

She shakes her head and holds her hand out to Leon for the keys.

"It's on Allen. Right in front of The Hat." Leon holds on to her hand for a moment and squeezes. "Glad you came," he says.

She squeezes back. "Meet you out front."

Leon hops down from the stage and pulls off his drums. Steve makes no move to help as Tim struggles to drag his amp off stage.

"You know about this radio interview Sunday morning, right?" Steve asks.

"No," Leon and Tim say together.

"College station. No big deal. Just a quick in-studio thing. We'll answer some questions and play a song before we drive home."

"I hate that shit," Tim says.

"Of course you do," Steve says. "Anything that might generate some interest, you're against it."

"Fuck you, man," Tim says. "That's not it at all."

"What's up." Randy joins them. He hands Steve a beer and then takes a long draw off his own bottle of Dos Equis.

"Usual shit," Steve says.

"I hate it because you do all the talking while the three of us sit back like a bunch of mute assholes."

"Then say something!" Steve yells. "Who's stopping you?"

The blonde woman in the blinding white blouse steps into their half-circle. "Hope I'm not interrupting," she says.

"Hey!" Steve opens his arms and leans forward to kiss her on the cheek.

"Sounded great," she says directly to Steve. "Really fantastic. Loved the encore."

"Guys, this is Angeline Hopkins," Steve says. "She's with Epic Records."

Leon holds out his hand. "Nice to meet you," he says.

Angeline distractedly grips Leon's hand, then quickly shakes hands with Tim and Randy. "So Steve," she says and jerks her head toward the door. "I have an early day tomorrow and I'd love to talk a bit before I call it a night."

"Sure, sure," Steve says. He drains his beer and puts his arm around her shoulders. "We're all set here. See you guys bright and early tomorrow," he calls over his shoulder as he leads Angeline out the door.

"Fuck," Tim says.

"What's your problem?" Randy asks.

"Get your head out of your ass," says Tim. "She blew us off."

"She's just talking business with Steve," Randy says.

"It'll be alright, man," Leon says.

"It better be," says Tim. "It sure as hell better be."

Junie leans against Leon's beat-up Honda double-parked in front of the bar. A crowd has gathered on the sidewalk, making it difficult for Leon to haul his drums out of the club. Randy stands on the corner talking to Austin Healy and her friend. Austin waves as Leon struggles to lift the cases over people's heads. "Better you than me!" she shouts and laughs.

Junie grabs each drum and shoves them into the open hatch-back. When everything is locked and loaded, Leon slides in behind the wheel and sighs.

"You okay?" Junie asks. She strokes his thigh.

Leon leans over and kisses her on the mouth. "I am now."

"Did the A&R guy show up?"

Leon snorts. "Yeah."

"That's great, Leon!" Junie says. "Did he like it? What did he say? That's so exciting!"

Leon starts the car and pulls into traffic. "Well first off, the A&R guy is a woman who, like every woman, seems to have the hots for Steve."

"Don't be cynical," Junie says. "So he's a huge flirt. It might work to your advantage for once."

Leon circles the block and heads toward the Manhattan Bridge. "When we first started going out, I was always afraid you would dump me for Steve."

Junie laughs. "I told you I like drummers."

Leon weaves his fingers into hers. "So if Steve played the drums . . ."

She nudges him with her elbow. "Shut up," she says playfully. Then she settles herself against the seat and closes her eyes.

"Tired?" he asks.

"Mm-hmm," she murmurs.

"But do you think he's good looking?"

"Who?"

"Steve."

"He's an idiot."

Leon squeezes her hand as they inch across the congested bridge back to Brooklyn. "I'm glad you think so."

• • •

Leon kills the engine next to the fire hydrant in front of their apartment building. It's chilly outside and he is tired. Junie naps in the passenger seat. In bed, she sleeps on her stomach, her hands held in fists beneath her hips. Long eyelashes and pouting lips. He imagines this is how she looked as a child. In the pictures he's seen she is always making goofy faces or frowning but never quite smiling. Always looking somewhere else. His favorite picture is of a dance performance. Junie dressed as a shaggy dog with floppy brown ears and furry oven mitts, lurching while the girl next to her struck a pose and beamed confidently at the camera.

He gently massages her knee. "Hey, darling. We're home," he whispers.

Her eyes pop open and she yawns. "Sorry. I dozed."

She climbs out of the car and helps Leon pull drums out of the hatchback one by one. On these cold nights he fantasizes about deflatable drums or collapsible ones shaped like camping cups. His past girlfriends wouldn't deign to carry drums, but Junie slings the cymbal bag over her shoulder, grabs the snare with her right hand and the small tom-tom with her left. As they haul the equipment up three flights, Leon wishes he played an instrument that could fit inside his pocket. He could learn the harmonica. Would Junie find that as sexy?

Upstairs, Leon tucks his gear away inside the drum closet. He can hear Junie brushing her teeth in the bathroom. She takes a long time to get ready for bed. Brushes her teeth carefully. Always flosses. Washes and moisturizes her skin. He could easily leave the car parked illegally and risk the fifty-dollar ticket for a chance to watch her nightly ritual, then crawl into bed while she is still awake. So many nights when he comes home, she is already sleeping soundly. When she first moved in, he imagined she would wake up when he came home and they would immediately fall into frisky midnight sex. Of course, that's not the way it works. She has a job. She is tired late at night.

"Junie," he calls into the dark of the apartment.

"Mm-hmm," she answers sleepily from the bathroom.

"Will you be awake when I get back?"

He hears her tap her toothbrush against the sink. "I'm so sleepy," she says.

"I'll hurry. Try to stay awake." He rushes out the door.

# CHAPTER
# EIGHT

Junie drops to the bed and curls around rejected outfits from earlier in the night. One by one, she tosses pants and skirts and tops toward the closet until she uncovers the *Charlie's Angels* tee shirt tangled in the wrinkled bedcovers. The shirt fits perfectly in her plan to try harder for Leon. He is such a sentimental guy. She could reduce him to a simpering, syrupy mess if she wore the tee to bed tonight. She wriggles out of her clothes, flinging them into the mounting pile half-in her jumbled closet. Her bra sails across the room and catches a dresser knob. It hangs deflated. She puts on the tee shirt, then sits up to look at herself in the mirror across the room. The shirt pulls tight across her breasts and her nipples peek through, advertising coming attractions. Leon will be pleased when he comes home. It is the least she can do for him. Or maybe it is the most.

The front door locks tumble. Junie quickly turns out her lamp and burrows down into the warm covers as Leon walks through the apartment, flicking off lights on his way back to the bedroom. She peaks at him in the dim light cast through the window by a three-quarter moon. He undresses, neatly tucking his clothes into their proper spaces. When he slides into the bed beside her, Junie rolls onto her back with one arm slung over head and a smile on her face.

"Hey," Leon says happily. "You're awake." Then with a gentle finger, he traces the Angels three-pronged pose. "You found it," he says nearly reverently. He tucks his head beneath her raised arm, laying his cheek against her breast, then turns to kiss her nipple. His head travels up and down with her breath. He lets out a satisfied sigh.

Junie brushes her lips lightly across the top of his smooth skull. She talked him into shaving it. On their third date before they ever slept together. Told him to lose the silly hat and the little ponytail and embrace his baldness.

"It'll be sexy," she assured him.

While Leon lathered his scalp with shaving cream, Junie perched herself on the side of his bathtub. She watched him make careful strokes across the curve of his skull. He worked slowly, rinsing the razor between each run. When he was done, he bent over the sink, splashed water over his head, then came up and toweled himself dry. He looked in the mirror with wide eyes.

Junie went moist at the sight of him bald. She stepped into the doorway of his bathroom and began to strip off her clothes, leaving a trail of tee shirt, jeans, and bra for him to follow. In the doorway of his bedroom she hooked her thumbs into the sides of her panties and swung her hips from side to side as she lowered her underwear to the floor and stepped out. She turned to look for Leon. He stood in the hall, watching her. "You coming?" she asked.

Junie enjoys sex with Leon. Always has. He is a considerate lover, concerned about her orgasm. She rolls to her side and grinds her hips into his lap. He pulls her tighter against his body. She fits perfectly in his fierce hug. This is her chance to make up for her earlier transgression. Be a good girlfriend. A better lover. Make things right with him before he leaves. But as he moves his hands across her body as if he were reading Braille, possibilities of sex with Eliot float through her mind.

Eliot would be aggressive. Perhaps he has a stash of sex toys in his apartment. Would he handcuff her to the bed? Fuck her on the floor? Leon would never fuck her. He makes love to her. Isn't that what she's supposed to want? Not this Eliot of her fantasy. The one who would come to bed, wake her up with his thick fingers groping in her panties, then bulldoze her into fervid sex. Twice. She tries to concentrate on Leon kissing a circle around her belly button. She tries not to think about Eliot while Leon's tongue brushes delicately across her inner thigh.

If she were a stronger woman, with a better sense of herself, and a good dose of confidence, then she would want what she has with Leon. Right? Isn't that how the rhetoric goes? That there must be something wrong with her. A deep flaw in her character to fantasize about something so base and defiling as rough-and-dirty adulterous sex with a man nearly twice her age. The thought makes her hot and she grabs for Leon. She wants him inside her now. Surely her actions aren't so bad. *Cosmo* approves. She's read articles like "Use Your Desire for Other Men to Enhance Your Sex Life with Your Partner!" So it must not be cheating to imagine it is Eliot above her, rocking her back and forth and chanting her name, "Junie, Junie, Junie. Oh, Junie!"

When they are through and both lay twisted in the covers, Leon drapes an arm around Junie's shoulders and strokes her hair. "This is what I love about having you here," he says.

"Basically I'm here for sex," says Junie as she fishes among the covers for her underwear and tee shirt. She didn't really orgasm. She faked it. Lost her concentration halfway through because she felt bad about pretending Leon was Eliot. So she moaned into his ear and said his name. She has never done that before with Leon, but tonight the battle in her brain between fantasies of Eliot and the reality of Leon made it impossible to focus.

"That's not what I meant."

She slips on her panties. "What did you mean?"

"I don't want to fight with you before I leave," Leon says. "Let's just lie down and be happy." He slides onto his pillow and smiles up at her.

"Sometimes couples fight, Leon."

"What do you want, Junie? For me to be really mean to you?"

"No," she says.

He rests his head against her bare arm. "Then what's the problem?"

76

She tugs the shirt over her head. The tag tickles her face. She has it on backwards. She struggles to turn it around and punches her arms through the holes. "The problem is ever since I moved in, you keep asking me what the problem is."

"I just want things to be okay with us."

"Well, I get tired of you asking me if I'm okay over every little thing. Sometimes it's too much."

"I can't win here. Everything I do pisses you off." In the dusky moonlight, Leon looks like he might cry.

"I'm not mad at you," Junie says. "I'm just . . ." She pauses. Tries to find the most accurate words to describe what she is. Confused? Riddled with doubt? Guilty? "Tired," she says, then lies down beside him.

He wraps her in a hug. Kisses the nape of her neck. She tries to relax in his embrace. Tries to remember what it is about this position that should be comforting.

"I know this move hasn't been easy for you," he says. Junie fidgets. He strokes her arms. Her skin feels chaffed by his touch. "But everything will be okay. I know it will." He squeezes her tighter. "I love you, Junie," he says into her hair.

"I love you, too" is her automatic response. They are quiet and her words fade from the room, replaced by the night noises of Brooklyn. Doors open and shut. Muted voices float up from the sidewalks into the dark. Car alarms trill their awful songs. Junie wonders if her declaration to Leon is true. If she is even capable of what Leon defines as love. Some mix of voracious emotion and constant forgiveness. Sometimes she thinks that kind of love is impossible for her. Maybe that is the draw of

Eliot. She can't imagine ever really loving him. Having sex with him. Being amused by him. Getting dumped by him. But not loving him.

Leon breathes smooth and easy already. His arms are heavy around her. She wiggles away from his limp grip, then sits up and hugs her pillow against her chest. Junie resents how easily he sleeps. How he can blindly accept that everything will be okay. For her problems weigh heavily, making it impossible to close her eyes and rest. Lately, she wants to slip out of bed and escape the apartment in the dead of night. Go into the streets, searching for a quiet place where no one will find her.

When she and Jacob were overwhelmed, they took a flashlight from their father's toolbox and hid in the coat closet. Tossed out boots and shoes, then crawled around the vacuum cleaner into the depths beneath the overcoats and fall leaves smell.

"Let's turn on the flashlight," Junie begged because she hated the dark. But Jacob wouldn't do it. They lay side by side with their fingers woven together. She had trouble distinguishing whose fingers were whose in the dark.

"Maybe it won't be dark when you die," she said. "Maybe it will be like summer when the sky stays kind of light. You know, when you can see all the lightning bugs and the sky's kind of blue?"

"Shhh," Jacob whispered. "Just don't think, Junie. It's nice in the dark when you don't think."

"How can you not think?" Junie asked. "If you don't think, you'd be dead."

Jacob didn't answer and they lay in silence until their mother came looking for them. For a long time their hiding place was secret, until their mom noticed all the misplaced shoes in front of the closet door. A slice of light slid across the floor. "You guys in there?" she asked.

Junie and Jacob stayed quiet as their mother got down on all fours and crawled toward them, groping for their legs. She found Jacob's calf and shook it gently. "Why didn't you answer me?" she demanded. "What are you doing in here? You alright, Jacob?"

"I'm fine," Jacob whispered.

Her mom let go of Jacob's leg and Junie waited for her mother's cool fingers against her skin. Instead, her mom held her head in her hands for a few silent seconds, then lifted herself on all fours again. "Junie, be sure you clean up when you're done." She crawled backward out of the closet, then she shut the door.

Junie let go of Jacob's hand and sat up. "I don't want to play this anymore," she said. "Give me the flashlight." She held out her hand, which felt disconnected from the rest of her body. She wondered if death were like that. Would Jacob have his body but just not know where it was?

"Here," he said.

"Where?"

Jacob's fingers brushed hers then moved across her hand again and grabbed it. "Here," he said and laid the flashlight in her palm. "But don't turn it on."

Junie hugged it to her chest. She sat quietly, considered

turning it on and shining it in Jacob's eyes. She wanted him to squint against the bright light. To make him mad. She wanted him to hit her so she could hit him back but he never hit anymore. She placed her hand over the light and flicked it on. Jacob simply closed his eyes and turned his face away.

"You don't know that it will be dark," Junie said. She shined the light toward the front of the closet. "You can't know that."

Junie crawled out of the closet and slammed the door. She pressed her back against it, then kicked the shoes scattered on the carpet. They looked as if people had run by and tripped, then disappeared, leaving their shoes as the only reminder they had been alive. She threw the flashlight against the wall. It bounced to the floor and left a heavy black mark on the pale-yellow wallpaper with tiny red flowers. She knew her mother would get mad but she wouldn't yell. She hadn't yelled as long as Jacob hadn't hit. Junie was the only one who yelled and hit anymore.

She turned around and opened the closet door again. "Come on, Jacob. Let's do something else," she said. "This is boring." Jacob didn't answer so Junie crawled back in the closet and shut the door. She felt carefully along the floor until she found his body, perfectly still. "I left the flashlight out there," she said quietly.

"Good," Jacob answered. "It's better in the dark."

Junie lay down beside him and groped for his hand again. His fingers were still cool.

"It *will* be dark, Junie," he whispered.

She squeezed his hand. "I believe you," she said.

# CHAPTER
# NINE

In the morning, Junie wakes to the sound of drums banging and rattling as Leon loads his gear out the front door. Usually she sleeps through his comings and goings, but this morning she is annoyed by the racket and wishes he would leave already. The door closes and she is miffed that he has left without saying good-bye. Of course, he didn't know she was awake, but he used to kiss her on the cheek and whisper his good-bye on early mornings. She's not the only one who has changed. She rolls over and squishes her face into the pillow, hoping that sleep will come back to her. Then, the front door opens again. Leon rushes through the apartment and kneels beside the bed with a Styrofoam cup of coffee. Of course he's back. What was she thinking?

"Sorry, sweetie," he says as he strokes her hair. "Got to go quickly. The guys are downstairs, waiting." He plants a tender kiss on her forehead. "Love you," he says.

She feels bad for being mad at him first thing in the morning. She reaches up and pulls him down to her again. "Love you, too," she mumbles and puckers her lips. He quickly brushes his mouth over hers before he scurries out the door.

Junie tries to go back to sleep after Leon leaves, but she's already awake. She might as well get up even if it is early. The day is spread in front of her with almost no obligations. She used to hate it when Leon went away, but she has been looking forward to this time alone. She can do anything she wants today. Go to a museum. Take a run. Find a yoga class. Bake a cake. Read a book. Or she could do nothing at all. Lie around on her fat ass and wallow in seclusion from the world. She kicks off the covers and smiles. Stretches her arms and legs, taking up as much space on the bed as she wants.

She rolls across the bed. Lies sideways. Then scooches herself backward until her head and arms hang over the edge. What if this were her bed and she lived alone? What if she were independent, successful (at something), and slightly lonely. She would wear a fabulous cashmere car coat and boots, smoke cigarettes, take cabs. She would even have a shrink downtown. In this daydream world, she would meet Eliot at a cocktail party. Introduced by a mutual friend. An editor who still believes in Eliot's work. When he returns tomorrow the fantasy Junie would call him up and in an alluring voice, gruff from cigarette smoke, she would bluntly state her desires. Then take a cab to his apartment. Stand on his doorstep in slutty buckle-and-strap lingerie beneath the cashmere coat.

Eliot said that he would miss her. She sits up. Did he really mean it? What if he was lying? Why would he lie? Men lie.

Leon doesn't lie. Junie does. She slumps down to her back again, too close to the edge, and slides off the bed backward. Her legs flip over her head and she lands crumpled on all fours, twisted in the blankets and sheets. An inauspicious way to start the day. She needs to talk to someone. Hash everything out. Get a second opinion on the situation. She pops up and squints at the clock. It's just past eight. Katie gets up early.

Katie answers on the third ring but sounds sleepy.

"Aunt Myrtle," Junie whines. "Aunt Myrtle is that you?"

Katie giggles softly. "Aunt Myrtle is dead," she barks. "She died. Now stop calling here!"

Katie cracks Junie up. Has since they lived on the same dorm floor at college. Junie can see her, lounging on her beat-up futon, twisted in the flannel sheets with her long black hair tucked behind her ears. Her paint-splattered faded corduroys and old sweaters tossed carelessly to the floor. She is vegetarian and doesn't own leather. Her passion is painting small canvases of decaying fruits and vegetables but she refuses to send slides to galleries or sell her paintings on the street, so she works on the forty-third floor of a midtown high-rise as a secretary for accountants.

"Hey," Junie says.

"June Bug, my sweet. So long it's been since we've talked. How the hell are you?"

"I'm good. I'm okay. I don't know. How are you?"

"Me. Can't complain. My husband left me last week for his assistant, my kids are juvenile delinquents, and I've got cervical cancer. But other than that, I'm pretty good."

"You aren't married, you don't have children, and if your cervix is cancerous, I'll donate mine to you."

"You are so sweet. What's up?"

"Want to get coffee or something?"

"Oh, mon petite peach pit. I'm sorry. I really can't. I have company just now."

"A male-type fellow?" Junie asks in her best British accent.

"Oui."

"Good for you," Junie says, hiding her disappointment. "Everything okay?"

"Yes. No. Not really but nothing that can't wait."

"You sure?"

Junie knows Katie would come over right now if she asked her to. But she can't ask her to leave a boy in her bed to dish about Junie's perverse fantasies of older men. "I'm fine," she says.

"Leon gone?"

"Yep."

"I'll call you later," Katie offers.

"I'll be around." Junie hangs up. She picks herself up off the floor and shambles around the bedroom, kicking clothes into new piles. Leon is very tolerant of her messes. She should really straighten up. But that's no way to start her Day of Junie. She could do something for herself this morning. Go out to breakfast. Buy a paper and a coffee. She stops kicking at the clothes. Who is she kidding? All she wants to do is go to Eliot's. Now.

She pulls on dark jeans and a purple cowgirl shirt. Quickly brushes her teeth and runs a comb through her messy hair. On her way to the door, she grabs her cucumber-colored coat from the kitchen chair. The pleasant aroma of a ripening banana shrouds Junie as she swings the coat over her shoulders. Makes sense that tropical fruit is the scent of lust. She reaches into the pocket and pulls out Eliot's banana. Brown now and decaying, it looks like one of Katie's paintings. Junie opens the garbage and tosses it in. Good-bye, for now, she tells the slippery fruit. Until we meet again.

As she is gathering her wallet and keys, the phone rings. She pauses by the door and waits for the answering machine to pick up.

"Junie, it's your mother." Junie's shoulders tense and she grips the doorknob tighter. "I called last night. Didn't Leon tell you?"

"Yes, mother. He told me," Junie says to the room.

"I hope I can count on you for a pledge. I know this is important to you, too. Even though you're only temping, surely you can afford a little something. Call me as soon as possible, please." The machine clicks and whirls.

"You have no idea what's important to me," Junie mutters as she walks out the door.

# CHAPTER
# TEN

There are four hundred seventy-eight steps from Junie's apartment to Eliot's door. Junie knows this because she has counted them. Four hundred seventy-eight steps, two hundred thirty-nine sidewalk squares, and ten and a half blocks with twenty-eight trees. On the way, she will pass three bodegas, two video rental shops, a fishmonger, three coffeehouses, and a hardware store. There are also several restaurants, two bookstores, a school, and a game shop. It takes her fifteen minutes to walk there, seven minutes to run. She wonders how long it would take her if she skipped. She wonders how long it would take her to crawl back to Leon on her hands and knees.

She gets to Eliot's building. Stands on his stoop and her pulse revs. What if he didn't really go to Montreal and he's there, waiting? Sitting on the couch, wild hair run amuck on his scalp. Would she be able to leave? Would she want to?

Inside Eliot's apartment, the sun streams through the living room windows, exposing corridors of floating dust over the dying ficus tree and wilting peace lily in the corner. Dust seems natural in his unruly living space. Precarious stacks of books and magazines compete for floor space with mismatched chairs and battered end tables. Cup stains, cigarette burns, and criss-crossed scratches cover every wood surface.

"Eliot?" Junie says quietly. The rooms are silent.

She passes by the bookshelves, the Star Trek library she calls it. The books are shoved in at odd, uncomfortable angles and the boards beneath them sag from the burden of the weight. Eliot also collects old typewriters. Anything precomputer he considers worthwhile. He has manual and electric on the shelves, on his desk, on the floor. QWERTY models and a rare alphabetical-style monster. He can speak at length about each machine, hold it up and examine its underbelly as if it were a priceless relic.

So many words trapped in that nearly airless space. Junie fears that at any moment, if she steps too heavily, all the books would come tumbling down and the typewriter keys would click ferociously. Angry words would fly dangerously around the room and bounce off furniture, leaving bumps and bruises in the shape of words like *cheater* and *liar* across her back that she would have to hide from Leon. She tiptoes.

On Eliot's desk she sees a writing pad with an uncapped ballpoint pen. Her name is written in his small, even script at the top of the paper. The discovery thrills her and she greedily grabs the notepad. He was writing instructions for feeding Alfie but he's drawn a big squiggly line through the message.

That's okay, though. He was thinking of her. He could have

written the instructions without putting her name at the top. Just a list. Impersonal. But he didn't. He wrote her name. And when someone writes your name, that person thinks about you. That person sees you in his mind. But how did he see her? Attractive? Appealing? Annoying? She looks carefully at his handwriting. Junie wants to filch the note off to a handwriting analyst. See here? The analyst would say. The way he's written the "J" with a wide cross on the top? That shows he was feeling amorous. Junie wants to take the note, roll it up in a tiny tube, and store it in her sock. Walk around on it all day so every time her foot hits the ground and she feels it, she will think, Eliot.

She puts the note down on the desk and pulls her hand away. Her fingers leave a thin streak across the dusty wood. She can't resist the temptation to write something. In curly cursive she traces "Junie" across the desktop just below the mouse of his computer. She studies her work from various vantage points and realizes the word is only noticeable from certain angles where the sun skims the top of the wood.

She imagines Eliot finding her scribbles one morning. He'll walk out of his bedroom as the sun streams through the windows at this exact same angle. He'll be carrying a coffee cup, wearing baggy pajama bottoms and a white tee shirt. His hair will be out of control, a not-so-scary fright wig. He'll come to his desk to turn on the computer and there he'll see streaks across the wood. He'll start to swipe his hand across it but will notice curvy lines forming letters, making a word. He'll squint, move his head around until the name becomes clear in the sunlight and he'll wonder if he wrote it himself and when.

She shouldn't waste this opportunity on merely writing her name. She draws a heart, ❤, then writes "Eliot." This makes her laugh. It's so goofy. Where else could she write the secret missive? Scratch it in the soap scum in the bathtub? Arrange the magnetic poetry into an acrostic poem so the first letter of each line spells out her message? Or in red lipstick across the bedroom mirror? Subtlety has never been her strong suit. She stands back and admires her handiwork: "Junie ❤ Eliot." She laughs out loud, delighted by her audacity.

Alfie crawls out from under the bed and listens carefully to the noise coming from the living room. Something quick and chattery. Like an excited squirrel. Perhaps pesky rodents have invaded his home. He slinks from the bedroom through the hallway, prowling like a lion through tall grass, blades parting and brushing the fur on his belly. Each step silent. Ears back. He is invisible. That squirrel chatters away at the base of a tree, preoccupied in its small-minded way with where it hid the nuts.

Alfie stops dead when the chatter lulls. One paw lifted. Body perfectly still and quiet. He is taking his time getting there in order not to startle the intruder. He rounds the corner slowly and sees Junie. Oh exquisite, beautiful Junie who laughs like a squirrel! She has come to him at last and he is elated. Alfie stops and rolls, rubbing his backbone on the floor, swinging his legs in the air with paws dangling from limp kitty wrists. He stands and twitches his itchy ears. What he wouldn't give for a long index finger to poke inside of there.

Junie turns to him and grins. She luxuriates in her body. Her gestures are grand. She throws open her arms and cries, "Alfa Romeo!"

Alfie hunkers down and leaps to the desk. She scratches under his chin and behind his ears as he walks back and forth in front of her. Alfie meows, then purrs from deep inside his belly and ducks his head into her caress.

"Lonely, sweet kitty." She rubs his back. "Hungry?" He slinks under her arm, rubbing his flexi-spine against her wrist. "Do you want to eat?"

He answers with a long meow. Just as he is preparing to hop down and dart into the kitchen for his tender victuals, he sees something scrawled across the desktop in the dust. He is no dumb kitty and reads the message clearly. "Junie ♥ Eliot" it says.

That cad! Eliot has infiltrated sweet Junie's mind and filled it will such garbage that she is now playing his infantile game. To find such a note and at the base of that evil automatic writing machine is too much of an insult to bear. Alfie cannot take it! He runs across the desk and skids to a stop, knocking the mouse to the ground. He bats at the words, scratches the surface of the table, anything to erase this disconcerting message.

"Alfie!" Junie says. "You nut." She grabs him and drops him on the floor. "Be careful," she scolds as she returns the mouse to the desktop, then walks into the kitchen. Alfie pounces up on the desk again and walks across the message, leaving paw prints in the dust. Satisfied that he has thwarted Junie's plan, Alfie hops down and trots into the kitchen after her.

●　　●　　●

Crusty dishes and empty beer bottles clutter the countertops smattered with crumbs. Junie sees another note next to the cat food and the manual can opener. She skips across the kitchen and snatches it.

*Junie,*
*Thanks again for your help. Alfie will be glad to see you.*
*I'll be back tomorrow afternoon. Dinner or something?*
*Eliot*

Junie reads the note twice, both times savoring the last line. Is Eliot moving their association beyond the walls of his apartment and chance encounters on the streets? The note seems to be an invitation for a date, cleverly cloaked in an offhanded question, Dinner or something? What clues does the rest of the note hold? He trusted her to know what to do rather than leave a list of instructions. Alfie will be glad to see her, ha! That's projecting emotions if she's ever seen it. And telling her specifically when he will be back. Maybe he really does miss her. Maybe he wants more than audacious flirting. But he only signed his name. No "Sincerely" or "Take Care" or "Best." Certainly no "Love." She reads the note one more time. As with everything Eliot says to her, this message is ambiguous. She folds the slip of paper carefully and puts it in her pocket before slinging her coat over a chair.

"So now," she says to Alfie, who rubs the side of his face against her shin. "How about some breakfast?" She reaches into the cabinet for a can of salmon-flavored Fancy Feast. Alfie twists and turns between her legs as she sets the bowl of cat food on the floor. Next, she opens the fridge and extracts the vial of insulin, then loads a fresh syringe. She imagines putting the needle into her own arm. Just like when she was a kid. Fantasizing about Jacob's medicine.

They had known for so long that he would die from the disease infinitely dividing in his bone marrow. Jacob knew its real name, chronic myelogenous leukemia. He tried to teach Junie to say it. She could never remember the order of syllables. Her parents called it CML to the doctors, nurses, pharmacists, and people who put their hands on Jacob's bald head and asked why. She chanted the abbreviation CML, CML, CML until it became *See ya', Mel* and Jacob laughed. Every time he left the waiting room to get pricked and poked by the doctor, Junie whispered, "See ya', Mel," in his ear and watched a silly grin spread across his face.

Then she waited outside the room where doctors huddled over Jacob. Junie imagined his medicine was thick and green, the color of snot when you have a bad cold. In her mind, his medicine came in a little plastic cup like how their mom gave them cough syrup. And it tasted terrible. Lima beans and Swiss steak put together. She wished she could slip inside the room and gulp the medicine while no one was looking. She wouldn't even make the face she normally made when she took yucky medicine. Wouldn't they all be surprised when her hair fell out and she threw up all her food? She never did it, though. Too much of a chicken.

Now in the kitchen, with Alfie at her feet, she is tense with the needle in her hand. She doesn't want to hurt the cat. She squats beside Alfie and pets the top of his head. He continues to eat. Junie knows she has to give him the injection quickly before he finishes the food. She holds her breath, grabs the scruff of his neck and pinches it in her fingers. Alfie's ears twitch but he continues eating. She slowly brings the syringe toward his neck and with a deep exhale slips the needle beneath his skin, then plunges in the insulin and extracts the needle. Alfie looks up and to the left at her, then turns back to his bowl. Junie pats his head. "Good kitty," she says.

After tossing the syringe into the garbage, she notices a lone banana on the counter. She picks it up and examines it in the sunlight. The matching glass slipper. The long-lost twin. It has turned a bit more yellow, but still doesn't look good enough to eat. Eliot held this banana. Offered it to her. She carries it with her as she goes off to explore the rest of the apartment.

Flipping on the bathroom light, she sees the toilet seat up. Ah-ha! she thinks, then wonders what that proves. The bathroom is mucky, ripe with mildew in the grout. Dark blue towels hang crooked on the rack. She lays the banana on the counter and opens the medicine cabinet. A half-used tube of Tom's of Maine Cinnamint toothpaste rolled carefully from the bottom. Yes, his breath smells like cinnamon. Old Spice deodorant. She opens it and inhales the spicy scent that Eliot exudes sometimes. She replaces it and extracts his shaving cream, then squirts a seashell-shaped blob onto her index finger. It smells creamy, fresh, just like his cheeks when she's close to him. She rinses her fingers and wonders if she'll ever do more than quickly hug him and smell his personal hygiene products.

She picks up the banana and tiptoes to the bedroom where she stands in the doorway. His boudoir is not what she imagined. She and Eliot have stayed in the demilitarized zone of the living room or kitchen when she's been over and her fantasies of him take place in a nondescript room where the sheets are tangled as they roll together across some enormous bed. Sometimes in this imaginary room it is the next morning with sun streaming through an open window as they read the *New York Times* strewn across the sheets.

Eliot's room is stark. His bed is queen-sized, the dark-green covers twisted with dull white sheets. Jane Fonda as Barbarella with her minimissile launcher looks down over the bed. On the nightstand are two framed photographs, a clock radio, three wadded-up tissues, and three books, *The Female Man* by Joanna Russ, the most recent *Best Science Fiction Stories of the Year,* and one of Eliot's own dog-eared copies of *Liberty Voyage.*

First she sets down the banana and picks up a photograph. It is old, black and white, a couple in wedding garb, squinting into the sun. The woman holds calla lilies. The man wears small round glasses and has curly hair like Eliot. His parents? Grandparents? How precious that he would keep their wedding photo near him. The other photo shows two boys in jeans standing beside an old car with exaggerated fins. The smaller boy has wild curly hair and a perfect comma in his chubby cheek. Eliot as a chunky little boy with his older brother, perhaps. She's seen pictures like this of her mother and father when they were kids. She wonders what her parents would think if she brought Eliot home. Would they be scandalized by their daughter: coveter of bananas, writer of secrets in the dust, seductress of older men?

They like Leon. Or seem to anyway. Which surprised Junie at first. After all, he is a poor musician with no college degree. But it's hard to dislike Leon and they've only met him twice. Once when they deigned to visit New York for a long weekend. Leon claimed her parents were delightful on that trip, but by Monday morning, her father's passivity and her mother's terribly polite but indifferent smile had nearly driven Junie to drink bleach. Then last Thanksgiving Leon offered to come home with Junie. Her mother, full of Martha Stewart grace, made place cards by writing each person's name with a gold glitter paint pen on a tiny pumpkin. Her father pressed a roll of crisp twenties into Junie's palm, saying he didn't know how she could make it in New York on the money she made.

Junie puts down the photo, then opens the closet door. Eliot's smell wafts out. She runs her hand over the row of shirts and pants. They swing lightly, releasing more of his redolence into the warm air. She wonders what Eliot would taste like.

Alfie jogs into the bedroom and hops onto the bed. He rubs his shoulders against her butt and twists his tail around her thighs. Junie runs her hand over his back. The room is warm and Junie feels sleepy. Like a little kid who got up too early on a big day. She lies down on the bed. Alfie settles in the crook of her arm. He licks her cheek and she smells the salmon on his oddly smooth darting tongue.

From the nightstand she picks up *Liberty Voyage* and flips to her favorite part.

Hane strolled through the ovular pink tunnel with his hands in his pockets. He loved to come to his Sexual Amusement Park and browse through the History of Sexual Appliances exhibit, which showed the chronology of his inventions. The women usually laughed as they picked up the first crude vibrator he made with salvaged parts from his ruined spacecraft. They still seemed intrigued with his Pumping Hump, a phallus on bellows that hooked over both knees and worked by rapidly opening and closing the legs. There were also The Swing and The Undulator in the museum, but Hane's favorite device was a rotating wheel covered with soft tongue-like feathers built into the center of a chair that he had dubbed The Lap of Luxury.

Junie's eyes grow heavy and she drifts, half in and half out of sleep. The book falls across her chest. In her mind, Eliot comes home. Unexpectedly. His trip was canceled. He opens the front door and walks straight back to the bedroom, lugging a heavy shoulder bag. There he finds her on the bed, lying with his cat snuggled into her side and his book against her body. Junie's skin tingles. On her breasts, around her nipples, across the plane of her stomach, and between her legs. Eliot comes to the bedroom and drops his bag on the floor when he sees her. She looks up and smiles slowly. "I missed you. I came back here to smell you," she says.

Alfie has climbed onto her stomach, riding up and down with her breath. He presses his paws into her belly and kneads. A deep and urgent purr rumbles in his throat.

Eliot doesn't hesitate. He immediately climbs onto the bed and wraps his arms around her shoulders. His hands find their way under her shirt, across her breasts, in her pants. A slick of dew, anticipation, warm mizzle between her thighs. Junie wants to touch herself then. Feel with her fingers the moistness gathering between her legs. Knowing that it's slightly kinky to touch herself on Eliot's bed while fantasizing about him makes her want to do it more. To think that she could have an orgasm on Eliot's bed without him even knowing almost makes her come right then.

She slips her hand past the cat and into the waistband of her jeans, under white cotton underwear, beyond the tuft of hair. She feels the warm moisture collected between her legs and inserts her fingers, then circles her hand as she pictures Eliot kissing her neck and chest. Her body exhales the musky odor of sex. She slips another finger inside. She could fit the world in there sometimes. She moves her hand. Her hips. Alfie kneads and purrs.

She waggles her head from side to side as she rocks against her fingers. The book falls off her chest. She opens her eyes and sees the banana on the nightstand. I couldn't, she thinks. But she wants to. She removes her hand from inside her pants and lifts the banana to examine it. The perfect size, the perfect shape. That ingenious curve. She fondles the end and wonders if it would scratch her inner walls if she inserted it. She brushes at the tip with her thumb. Dried brown foliage flakes off leaving a smooth tip. Junie thinks again that she couldn't do it. But she wants to.

What if she did and died right here on the bed? Had a heart attack or punctured her cervical wall with it. Or what if Eliot suddenly returned? He would find her in his room with a banana in her cunt. How would she ever explain that one? But her body insists. Can't let it go. Greedy little devil. If she stops now she will be hot and bothered all day. Rubbing up against lampposts and panting at the sight of mounted police officers in the park. She inserts her fingers inside herself again but they won't do. She can't get excited enough. She wants the banana inside her body. She dumps Alfie off her stomach and whispers to him, "Don't tell."

She slides her jeans over her hips so she is naked from the waist down. Alfie puts his paws on her bare belly and gently, without claws, begins to massage again. She slips the banana between her legs and starts to move it in and out. She feels her body giving over to the rhythm of the movement. Imagines it is Eliot. Beneath her. Behind her. On top of her, galloping. She bites her lip and squeezes her eyes closed as everything comes together in the middle of her body. Her knees lock, her toes point, then the ebbing releases down around the banana gently swaying inside her. Alfie shudders with her and lets go a strange moan. Junie lingers in those few delicious moments while her body shudders and shakes with lonely little paroxysms of joy.

Junie removes the banana to examine it. It is moist but barely bruised. She pulls her pants on again and strokes Alfie's shoulders. "Our little secret," she whispers into his fur.

Junie tilts her head back to see Barbarella smiling down at her. The ebbing of her orgasm turns into queasiness. Barbarella would never secretly fuck a banana on someone else's bed. Barbarella is tough. She can crash-land her spaceship, have incredible sex with different men, and defeat the evil Duran Duran all while wearing see-through breastplates and fishnet hose. That is who Eliot would want. Not a little twit like Junie in thrift store clothes and goofy glasses who sneaks around his house sniffing his deodorant and putting his banana in her pants. She sees the photos on his nightstand. Everyone stares at her with disgust. She knows they would rat her out if they could speak from their two-dimensional mouths.

Junie walks quickly to the bathroom where she washes her hands and the banana. In the mirror she appears disheveled with messy hair and bleary eyes beneath her smudged lenses. She splashes water on her face, runs her fingers through her hair, cleans her glasses on the damp hand towel. She is unsure what to do with the banana, though. She can't very well put it in his trashcan. He would find it and wonder how it got there. He was probably saving it for tomorrow when he gets back. But she can't leave it for him to slice on top of cornflakes! She'll take it with her, she decides. Tell him she got hungry while she was here and ate it. He won't mind. He offered it to her in the first place. Then she shakes her head at her own stupidity. Looks down at the fruited dildo in her hand. As if he will even notice the banana is missing.

She returns to the bedroom to erase any evidence of her misdemeanor. Alfie refuses to get off the bed. Junie could swear he smirks at her as she tries to put the covers back the way she found them. The cat smirks, Barbarella's eyes follow her, the photos gossip back and forth. She marches to the living room and wipes her hand across the desk to erase the words she had left in the dust. No more playing this silly game. It's nonsense. Eliot is no more interested in her than Alfie is in the banana.

She goes to the kitchen to retrieve her coat. Shoves the banana into one pocket and puts her hand in the other to extract the keys. She feels Eliot's note. "Dinner or something," it says. What the hell does he want with her? She's tired of all the cryptic messages. She needs to talk to someone who will understand and help her sort everything out. She usually talks to Leon when she has done something stupid. He laughs and tells her she's adorable. But who would want to hear that you just fucked a banana with a cat on your stomach?

Katie, Junie thinks. Katie will listen.

Alfie lies on the bed remembering Junie's creamy skin, the tiny mole on the top of her left thigh, the slight depression of her knotted belly button. A hint of fragrant mackerel on her hands. Her chin tilted up and a slight smile stealing across her face as pleasure enveloped her quivering body. It is all familiar somehow.

He kneads the mattress where her smell lingers. He remembers water, spread out forever, and the sound of sails slapping against the wind. Men's voices and the aroma of fish. He feared the vast ocean but she was not afraid. The water was part of her life, as simple as the ground. That's not what stood between them. It was something more profound. Stolid and insistent that they would never be together. Has fate always kept them apart? Perhaps they were never really united. Maybe this burning passion he has carried over nearly two hundred years will forever be unrequited. But he knew that look of desire on her face today and is certain that he was once the cause.

Alfie paces across the disheveled bedcovers. Does she remember anything? Have even an inkling of their connection? Surely, she must. This thought stops Alfie cold. He sits and ponders the question. Why else would she come to this place so often? And today on the bed? Some part of her soul, locked away perhaps but present, must have known that once they were lovers, delighting in the discovery of one another. Why else would she pleasure herself in front of him?

Yes, of course! Some part of her must know. Alfie is elated. He jumps from the bed and scurries to the front of the apartment, ready to pounce into her arms again, lap up the nectar of her skin, and whisper into her ear, "It is I!" Rounding the corner, he sees the edge of her coat swirl through the threshold as the door swings shut and he hears the decisive clank of the lock. "Do not fret!" he calls after her in a series of meows. "You and I, fair Junie, will be reunited yet."

# CHAPTER

# ELEVEN

Leon wakes in the front passenger seat of the band van on the outskirts of Alexandria, Virginia. Urban sprawl quickly gives over to lush forests and steep rocky inclines where highways have been blasted through the foothills of the Blue Ridge Mountains. He glances at the green numbers of the digital dashboard clock. It's nearly noon. They've been on the road since seven thirty that morning and Randy is still driving with one knee propped up against the door and two fingers on the steering wheel. He cruises at eighty miles per hour as Nine Inch Nails wail softly from the CD player. Tim and Steve snore from the back of the van.

"Want me to drive?" Leon asks through a yawn.

"I have to piss like a racehorse," says Randy. "There's a rest area in ten miles. We'll make a pit stop then switch."

"Where the hell are we?" Steve calls from the back where he is sprawled across the seat.

"Virginia," Randy says.

"Yee-fucking-haw!" Steve yells and throws a pillow toward the front.

The pillow wallops Tim in the head and he snaps awake yelling, "Jesus Christ! You fucking asshole." Then hurls the pillow back at Steve, who catches it and stuffs it behind his head.

"Hellfire and damnation! I need me some grits and red-eye gravy over mama's home-cooked biscuits," Steve yells in a fake Southern accent. "And a pretty little Southern belle ready to suck my cock! I have the biggest goddamn hard-on." He rubs both hands against the bulging zipper of his jeans, then hollers, "Woo-wee!"

"Shut the fuck up," Tim says. He resettles himself across the two middle seats and closes his eyes again, resting his chin against his chest.

Randy turns off the CD and looks into the rearview mirror at Steve. "What went down with Angeline last night?" "You mean speaking of giant hard-ons?" Steve asks, then laughs. Randy laughs, too. Tim sits up and runs his fingers through his greasy hair.

"Actually, nothing much," Steve says. "We just talked."

"About what?" Tim grumbles.

"I don't know. Stupid shit."

"You talk about the CD?" Leon asks.

"A little. Not really. It was just a get-to-know-you meeting."

"She like us live?" Tim asks.

"Yeah," Steve says. "I guess so."

"What do you mean, you guess so? Either she did or she didn't," Tim says.

"We didn't really talk about the band, so much."

"When are you talking to her again?" Tim asks.

"God, I don't know. What are you? My mother?"

Tim turns in his seat to face Steve. "No, we're your fucking band, man."

"Shit," Steve says. He throws the pillow at Tim's head again. "Just relax!"

Tim ducks, then swoops the pillow off the floor. He lunges and smashes it against Steve's face. They struggle, arms and legs flailing across the backseat.

"Do I have to pull this van over?" Randy yells.

Steve pushes Tim off. "Fucking asshole."

"Prick," Tim answers.

"Now, now," Randy says.

Leon checks the clock again. Four minutes have passed, another four hours to go.

After the rest stop, they reconfigure in the van. Leon drives with Tim in the front passenger seat. Randy crawls into the back to sleep and Steve slouches in a middle seat with a copy of *Rolling Stone* and his CD player. The van already smells like ass. Body odor, fried food, and exhaust fumes. Some people love being on the road with a band. Leon knows musicians who go out for months and months at a time. They tell stories about drunken nights in cheap hotel rooms and wicked hangovers on the bus, as if they are reminiscing about summer camp.

Riding in a van with a bunch of sweaty guys has never been a high point for Leon. Even if Mr. Whipple made it big, it would be more of the same. They'd go on the road to bigger gigs in a bigger van, but Steve would continue to be an asshole, Randy would be his lackey, and Tim would want to beat the shit out of both of them. Leon could quit. Only play around town. Try to join the union and get Broadway gigs? Those shows will suck the life out of him faster than flipping burgers at McDonald's would. In fact, sometimes he thinks he might enjoy a shit job, like being a short-order cook. Get into the Zen of spatula against grill.

Of course, what he really wants is his own little establishment where he gets to make the menu, order the ingredients, and oversee the creation of his recipes. He would call the place Leon's. No, too boring. June Bug. Too cutesy? He likes it. Would Junie?

He watches the green highway signs pass. They are coming up on Richmond and the exit for Norfolk down on the coast. Why couldn't he and Junie be happy in a place like that? A quiet little town in a beautiful part of the country where everyone is a little bit nicer and he and Junie wouldn't have to work so hard just to pay rent on a crappy apartment. In Norfolk his restaurant could cater to both tourists and townies. He could buy from local farmers. Organic even. And go out to the boats in the morning to pick up fresh crabs, lobsters, and fish. Junie could be in charge of the garden.

"Hey." Tim taps Leon on the shoulder, bringing him out of his daydream. "Mind if I put in a CD?"

"None of that 80s glam Hanoi Rocks shit you were playing last time," Steve says.

Tim turns in his seat to glare at Steve. "Shut the fuck up. Listen to your headphones if you don't like it."

"Driver's choice," Leon says.

Tim grimaces but pulls the CD case out from under the passenger seat. "What do you want?"

Leon thinks. "Something old," he says. "Something with a groove. Is that Donny Hathaway CD in there?"

"Man, not that shit again," Steve says. "Leon, you need to join the twenty-first century."

"Are you driving?" Leon asks.

Tim flips through the CDs. "Can't find it. We've got Leroy Hudson, Marvin Gaye, and Al Green."

"Let me ask you something," Leon says. "If you were going to make a tape for your girlfriend, what would you put on it?"

"What are you? In high school?" Steve says.

"A tape? For real? Like a cassette tape?" Tim asks.

Leon glances at Tim, then in the rearview mirror at Steve. Both smirk.

"Dude, at least burn her a CD," Steve says.

"Okay, whatever. Tape, CD. What would you put on it?"

Tim puts one foot up on the dash. "What's the occasion?"

"Sort of a moving-in-together anniversary tape."

"Didn't she just move in with you?" Steve gets up and moves in between Tim and Leon. He drapes his arms over the backs of their seats.

"A few weeks ago," Leon says.

"How about 'Let's Pretend We're Married' by Prince," Steve says. He punches Tim lightly on the arm as he laughs. Tim smacks his hand away.

"That's funny," Leon says, completely deadpan.

"Okay, I know. You want something old and outdated." Steve

pretends to think, tapping his forefinger against his chin. He breaks into an air guitar riff, then sings in a deep moan, "Well, I just want to make love to you!" More guitar. "Remember that one? Foghat. That's about your speed, right, grandpa?"

"No, wait. I got it. 'Make Love Like a Man,' Def Leppard," says Tim.

"'Love Em and Leave Em,' Kiss," Steve says.

"'Do It All Night,' Prince," Tim adds.

"'Sex Bomb Boogie,' Sigue Sigue Sputnik." Steve holds up his hand for a high five but Tim ignores him.

"'Fuck Kitties,' The Frumpies," Tim says. Steve laughs.

"You guys done?" Leon asks.

Steve rubs Leon's head. "Not what you're looking for, precious? Or not what you're getting at home? How about 'Slave to Love,' Bryan Ferry."

"Quiet Riot did that, you nimrod," Tim says.

Steve snorts. "Quiet Riot? Who the fuck listens to Quiet Riot? It was Bryan Ferry?"

"It was both of them," Randy yells from the back.

"'Slave Lover,' George Jones," says Tim.

"Country?" Steve rolls his eyes.

"George Jones could kick Bryan Ferry's ass," Tim says.

Leon shakes his head. "You two are both idiots."

"Just trying to help." Steve drops back into his seat and picks up his *Rolling Stone* again.

They ride quietly for several minutes. Leon thinks maybe they are right. Maybe making a tape is too much like high school. He should do something better for Junie. Buy her something nice. Or take her somewhere. Maybe a play. Out to dinner first. Surprise her. Tell her to get dressed up and then not tell her where they are going until they get there.

"What's it like, anyway?" Tim asks.

"What's what like?"

"Living together."

Leon considers this. He smiles. "It's good." He nods. "It's real good." He shrugs. "But it's hard."

"Truth comes out," says Steve.

"It's not like anything's wrong," Leon says.

"What's hard about it then?" Steve asks.

"I don't know." Leon wishes he did know. "It's a big deal. A big change. She's just a little bit . . . I don't know. I think it's been harder on her because she moved into my place. That's all. It just takes time for everything to settle in right."

"Leon, man." Steve rolls his magazine into a tube and whacks Leon on the head.

"Goddamn it!" Leon slaps at the air above his head. "Don't be fucking with me when I'm trying to drive."

"You're probably smothering her," Steve says.

Leon catches Tim nodding. "You're like that," Tim says.

"What do you mean I'm like that?" Rumble strips grind beneath the tires.

"Watch the fucking road, man!" Tim yells.

Leon jerks the wheel to the left, then he eases the van back into the lane. "What did you mean?" Leon asks again.

Tim clutches the dashboard. "Maybe you should just concentrate on driving before you send us over a fucking cliff, man."

"Now, now." Steve leans up between them. "Leon has a right to know. Tim, care to wager on how many minutes it will take for Leon to sniff out a pay phone and call Junie when we get to Raleigh?"

"Minutes?" Tim says. "How about seconds? I'll give him thirty."

"So what if I call her?"

"Just checking in?" Steve asks. Leon nods. "It's like she's your fucking mom."

Again, Tim agrees.

"I like talking to her," says Leon.

"Sure. Fine. But you're so predictable. Pull into town, you're on the phone. Get to the hotel, you're on the phone again. Next morning, you call her when you get up."

"Hate to admit it," Tim says. "But the man has a point. Girls like you to be more mysterious."

"Have either of you ever had a girlfriend longer than a week?" Leon asks.

Steve shrugs. "All we're saying is, give her a little space. Keep her guessing."

"What do you want me to do? Not call her?"

"Sure. Why not?" Tim says.

"What's the big deal?" Steve adds. "Call her tomorrow. Or the next day. Whatever. Then she'll be really happy to hear from you."

Leon stares at the passing yellow lines. "You're both fucked up," he mutters, but he wonders if they might be right.

# CHAPTER
# TWELVE

Eliot sits in the Montreal hotel room and stares at his laptop screen, thinking about Junie, then getting mad at himself for thinking about her when he should be writing. He could send her an e-mail. Flirt with her electronically. Maybe they could have cyber sex. Bouncing desires off satellites or funneling them through fiberoptics could be oddly erotic. Even Doyle Hane didn't come up with that one.

He lies down on the bed and surveys the room. Standard hotel décor. Hanging lamp over the round table in the corner. A blue quilted polyester spread over the queen-sized firm mattress. A landscape watercolor. The only thing a hotel room like this is good for is a tryst with a mistress. That's when the mildewed grout in the bathroom would seem seedy and sexy and not just neglected by the maid service.

If Junie were here, they would have sex on this bed, clean up in that shower, and then she would drag him out to some wacky place like the Insectarium or the Just-for-Laughs Museum because Junie is fun. Not like the women in Eliot's past with their dark and twisted eccentricities. Such as Annabelle, that crazy manic painter who worked only in the nude. Or Sheila, who'd been raised by Hare Krishnas and named Shiva, but changed her name and left Eliot to marry a contractor from Connecticut. A few years ago she invited him to an Amway party. Then there was Astrid, the Wiccan who didn't believe in tampons and desperately wanted her cycle to coincide with the moon. And all the others. He told each one that she was the reason he could write. Each one inspired some mediocre attempt at a follow-up novel. Each one left.

A woman has inspired everything he's tried to write, no matter how good or bad, except *Liberty Voyage*. He wrote that when he was twenty-three, a pudgy, sci-fi dweeb and a virgin. After the reviews and interviews and book signings came the endless parade of women. Of course, they had always been there. Eliot was the one who had been invisible. The only thing that changed was his sense of self. He was burly instead of chubby. His hair was lion-like instead of Bozo-esque. He said the things that were on his mind, instead of conducting imaginary conversations in his head, and people crowded around to hear.

He's made various attempts at celibacy over the years for writing's sake, but then he produces nothing. Sits in front of the blank page and confronts his fears that he will always be a pudgy, sci-fi dweeb who only had one good book in him. Invariably he goes back on the prowl and ends up with a crazy woman in his life.

With Junie things would be different, though. She's not a nut. Just quirky. Light. Fun. And the sex would be great. She's young. She probably does yoga. Everybody her age does yoga. He tries to imagine what possibilities such flexibility could bring. Could she wrap her legs around her shoulders? Do acrobatics on the bed? Sex with Junie would be a circus with dancing elephants, bears riding bicycles, and a lion tamer cracking a long black whip. But then afterward, they could lie together quietly, dose off, get up and cook something light, eat on the couch, stay in and drink decent wine from water glasses.

Thinking about Junie makes Eliot want to read his own work and figure out what she liked, if he still has it in him, and if he could get it back again. He opens a copy of *Liberty Voyage* and finds the part where Hane falls in love with Ro El 3.

Hane sat in back of the large amphitheater where the Libertarians had gathered to debate the pros and cons of Hane's Machines. The opposition made impassioned speeches about how the society would soon forget ways to pleasure one another if sex became fully automated. Then Ro El 3 stood and surveyed the crowd. Everyone grew still as she paused before she spoke.

"I am Ro El 3," she said in a commanding voice. "I am a user of these devices and I believe my grandmother, our founder, would have approved." As he watched Ro El 3 dominate the gathering, Hane felt a physical sensation like the tide of the ocean, ebbing and flowing, deep inside his body—something he hadn't felt since he left the earth many years before. "Rose Ellen Troy believed in self-satisfaction," Ro El 3 continued.

"She came from a world where women were denied this basic right. The devices of Hane do not impinge upon the doctrine of Liberty. They enhance it."

Eliot skims the chapters where Hane creates a device he can wear to overcome his impotency. Ro El 3 agrees to the experiment and they become lovers, which outrages the society. Ro El 3 and Hane slip away to Rose Ellen Troy's original cabin high in the hills outside the main occupation center. Then Ro El 3 takes off Hane's device, drops to her knees, and cures him of his impotency.

Eliot rests the book against his belly and closes his eyes. It's Junie on her knees beneath him on the plush purple ground of Liberty. He slips his hand into his waistband and gently pulls at the pubic hairs, rubs around the tender edges of his balls. He hasn't had sex in months and months. Another experiment with celibacy that has produced nothing. He wonders what Junie thought of the part when Ro El 3 becomes pregnant and she and Hane are cast out to wander the barren plains of Liberty. That's the part the feminists hated the most. His hard-on fades. They couldn't stand that Ro El 3 would choose the conventional life with a man.

He opens his eyes. His erection is gone. He wants to know if Junie had a problem with that part. He could call her right now. She might be in his apartment, feeding Alfie. Lucky cat. She coos to him, makes up silly names, and cradles him against her breasts. He could call his phone. She would hear his voice on the answering machine and pick up. They could talk about the book, then make plans for tomorrow, when he returns.

He stares at the ceiling. He knows what will happen if he pursues her now. He'll become consumed with her. Screw around and not get the article done in time. Then he'll have to beg for an extension. Margaret might give it to him. Or fire his ass. He'll have to start over again. Calling in favors. Querying magazines.

He looks at his watch. He only has an hour before he has to meet Twyla Smart. He should start the article or at least read her bio. Learn something about her so he can ask intelligent questions. But he knows all the questions to ask and she'll know all the answers.

The challenge of Junie is much more stimulating than this idiotic article. She thinks she is in love with Baldy but is clearly enjoying the flirtation she and Eliot have started. She thinks she is not the kind of person who would ever cheat. But she wants to. Eliot can tell. Why else all the visits? She's looking for permission. Eliot knows just the things to say to woo her away. He has enjoyed insinuating himself into her thoughts, making her squirm, watching her slowly crack. It is only a matter of time. If he puts enough energy into it, he could be sleeping with her in a few days.

But screwing Junie won't pay the rent. Even if he could find between her legs the incentive to write. He pulls himself up off the bed and sits down in front of the laptop again. He thumbs through the press kit about Twyla Smart. He can't concentrate on the words. They mean nothing. He taps out *Junie* on his computer. Then, *Ju Ni 1—granddaughter of Ro El 3 and Doyle Hane.* Now that, Eliot thinks, is interesting.

# CHAPTER
# THIRTEEN

Junie sits by the coffee shop window and looks out on Seventh Avenue at the couples nearing forty who walk their golden retrievers and push baby strollers. She wonders if she will be one of these older mothers with a neurotic child someday. Oddly, the prospect feels soothing. As if there is hope that she will eventually get her life together enough to procreate. But, she's not sure she wants to be a mom. The possibility of watching another child die is enough to shrivel her ovaries. Not to mention what it would do to her parents to have a grandchild die, too. Neither of them have much emotion left as it is. Losing someone else would annihilate their souls, leaving them empty carapaces working in the garden and thawing out chickens. Junie doesn't want to be responsible for any more disappointment in their lives. Anyway, thinking about it is absurd since she can't even figure out if she wants to live with Leon or screw old men, let alone bear someone's baby.

She sips her milky coffee and debates which details of her

predicament to divulge to Katie. She pats her coat pocket and feels the banana bulge. Brazen hussy, she thinks and swallows a giggle. Katie walks in as if on cue, black hair flouncing across the shoulders of her Army surplus jacket. Junie stands and opens her arms. They hug.

Katie shrugs off her coat and pulls up a chair.

"Where you been?" Junie asks.

"Leavenworth. Three to five for arson."

"Finally burned down the accounting firm?"

"Yes. I set all the miserable schmucks free."

"Have you ever thought about flirting with the accountants to liven things up a little?"

"Honey," Katie says. "Those boys wouldn't know flirting if I laid across the copy machine with tassels on my tits."

Junie laughs. She loves this banter. Why did she ever leave Katie's apartment? "Quit. You should."

"Like I could ever make a positive change in my miserable-ass life."

"What about the boy who spent the night?" Junie asks.

Katie rolls her eyes and shrugs. "It's nothing. We had a few drinks, he came over. Neither of us had any condoms so we just messed around but then he fell asleep so I let him stay."

"You're such the hostess."

"Just call me Miss Vanderbilt."

"You going to see him again?"

"If the batteries in my vibrator die."

"Imagine Amy Vanderbilt with a vibrator."

"The Vanderbrator!" Katie says.

They both howl. Junie wipes laughter tears from her eyes.

"Let's not talk about me, dear," says Katie. "What's up with you? You sounded sad."

Junie cradles her chin in her hands. Her head feels heavy, full of milk sloshing between her ears. She can't think of how to begin.

"Okay," Katie says after Junie's silence. "How's about I get some coffee, then we talk?"

Junie nods. Katie bounces up to the counter and pulls wadded bills from her pants pocket, then hands them to the skate-rat kid working the espresso machine. She returns with a tiny steaming mug. "So, how's living in sin with that no-good, deadbeat boyfriend?"

Junie collapses back against her chair.

"Ah, just as I suspected," Katie says. "Shacking up ain't the bliss you imagined?"

Junie sits silently and inhales the steam from her coffee. She feels tired, then. Too tired to even lift her mug to her mouth, she imagines herself slumping to the floor and sleeping there for months. "I don't know. Maybe I made a mistake."

"You mention that to Leon yet?"

Junie dabs at the crumbs scattered across the table. "Sort of. But he just thinks I'm adjusting."

"That's not how you see it?"

"There's more to it than that," Junie says. Katie leans in closer. "You'll think I'm such an asshole if I tell you," Junie whispers, then her eyes fill with tears and she is mortified that she might cry in public.

Katie slings her arm around Junie's shoulders and pulls her close for a quick hug. "Crying? There's no crying in the Chocolate Factory. Besides, you can't say or do anything that will shock me. I know you too well."

Junie dabs the tears away with the cuff of her sleeve. "I kind of met someone else that I find . . ." She hesitates. "Interesting." She peers up at Katie half expecting her to scowl and shake her head in disapproval.

Katie sits back and twirls a long strand of hair, then grins. "Are you fucking someone?"

"No," Junie says quickly, then realizes her indignation is entirely false. This is Katie, the person she can tell anything. She thinks about her tryst with the banana. Well, almost anything. "But, shit," she adds and grins. "I want to." She feels lighter after saying it out loud, as if she has removed an iron chastity belt.

"But you haven't done anything?" Katie asks.

"Nothing but feed his cat."

"Is that a euphemism for a blow job?" Katie whispers. They both laugh loudly. "God, Junie, relax," Katie says. "So you have a little crush on somebody. Big deal. Women probably flirt with Leon at gigs and you think he's never been tempted?"

Junie pictures Leon at a club, in between sets, sipping soda water and talking to some woman leaning against the bar. "You don't think he's ever . . ."

Katie shakes her head. "He's too sweet and loyal."

"Yeah," Junie agrees.

"So what's the problem?"

"It's not that I expected never to meet anyone else I thought was attractive after Leon and I moved in together, but Christ, after two weeks? That's pathetic. And I certainly didn't think I'd have a crush on someone so much older."

"How much older?" Katie asks.

"I think he's close to fifty."

"Electra, you slut!" Katie says and slaps Junie's arm.

Junie is grateful that Katie can make a joke out of even desperate circumstances. "So far it's been just flirting and that's been fun. But what if I do something?"

"Then you have a problem," Katie admits. "And," she adds with a wicked grin, "I want to hear all the details."

Katie is a crow.

"Let's not talk about it anymore," Junie says. "All the words out loud make it seem more real and complicated. It's easier to ignore."

"That's my girl," Katie says. "Cleopatra, Queen of de Nile."

"God, I've missed you," says Junie. "What are you doing tonight? Want to go out? See a movie or have dinner? Play darts somewhere?"

"Can't," Katie says and grimaces apologetically. "Wish I could."

"Same boy?" Junie asks and feels a twinge of jealousy.

Katie nods.

Junie cups her chin in her hands. "When are you going to give me the dirt?"

Katie shrugs. "I'm not so sure he's worth it, yet. I have to go out with him again to know if he's worthy of serious conversation or merely fodder for endless hours of ridicule."

"I'll be waiting for the prognosis."

Katie reaches over and covers Junie's hand with hers. "Really, tell me, are you going to be okay?"

"I'll figure it out."

"I can cancel this date."

"No way," Junie says. "But thanks for talking. You're the best."

Katie slips into her coat. "The cat's meow."

"The bee's knees."

"Don't do anything I wouldn't," Katie says.

"Oh goody," Junie calls as Katie heads for the door. "Free rein!"

# CHAPTER
# FOURTEEN

Eliot slouches into the French restaurant, notepad under his arm, pen behind his ear, hands shoved deep into his baggy chino pockets. Twyla's agent told him to meet her at this place tucked between narrow streets in Vieux Montreal. He hates these dinners. Sitting across from a gorgeous, nubile woman, listening to her blather on about herself. It's supposed to be the other way around.

He spots Twyla perched in a circular booth, sipping red wine. He recognizes her from her PR photo. She is svelte, pale as paper, with cropped black hair and blood-red lips. Snow White. Does she travel with an entourage of dwarves? She wears some sort of shimmery silver dress that ties around the back of her neck and exposes her long arms with two thin bracelets on her right wrist. She smiles when he stands in front of the table.

"You must be Eliot." Her voice rattles in her throat as if it's caught between the bars of a cage. She extends her hand toward him. Her bracelets tinkle. "Glad you could make it."

"Didn't think I was late," he says as he slides into the booth. She smells of lilacs.

"I'm not timing you." She hands him a menu. "But I am starving so let's order quick."

Another fucking princess, Eliot thinks.

"This place is supposed to be good for steak," she says as she glances over the menu.

"Aren't you a vegetarian?"

"Nah." Twyla shakes her head. "I grew up in Oklahoma. My daddy raises cattle." She speaks with a bit of a drawl. "I can't remember a day when I didn't eat some poor defenseless animal." She snaps her menu shut and grins. "I'm having a T-bone. Rare." Her smile is gorgeous. Full of teeth. The kind that translates well on camera. "Will you join me in the carnage?" she asks, sounding slightly British.

Eliot closes the menu. "Sure," he says. He doesn't care what he eats. Hopes it's the most expensive thing on the menu since the magazine is paying.

Twyla motions to the waiter then speaks to him in French. She looks at Eliot. "Shall I order for you?"

Eliot shrugs. She could irritate him if he let her but her assertiveness is sort of sexy. The waiter leaves and she licks her index finger, then runs it around the edge of her wineglass, making the crystal moan.

"Wine?" she asks.

"Sure," he says.

She fills his glass with a dark Merlot, then refills her own. "Bottoms up," she says and grins.

Eliot hunches over the table and opens his notepad. He knows this is the worst way to start an interview. No small talk. No putting her at ease so she will trust him. No watching her interact naturally. But he doesn't care. He wants to get it over with quickly, go back to his hotel, and write more about Ju Ni 1 so he can show it to Junie tomorrow.

"What do you want people to know about you?" he asks.

Twyla sits back against the booth and pouts. "Nothing. I hate interviews and publicity shit."

Eliot tosses his pen down, annoyed. "Why did you agree to do this then?" He takes a long drink of the wine. It is dry and fruity on his tongue. He drinks some more.

"My agent assures me it's for the best. And I'm sick of hanging out with the people from the set. All they want to talk about is this movie or the movie they just did or what movie they'll do next. Like they are so much more important than I am. It's just such a bore." She rubs her hand across the top of her head. Her hair bristles like the fur of a terrier being rubbed the wrong way. That motion could be terribly unattractive, but on Twyla it is oddly seductive. "You're a nice diversion from all that," she says. "Cute, too." She winks.

Eliot's cheeks grow warm. He blames it on the wine. Or maybe it is the sweet fermented grapes on her breath.

"You write anything besides magazine articles?" she asks.

"Used to."

"Like what?"

"Sci-fi. I wrote *Liberty Voyage.*"

"Never heard of it," she says flatly.

Eliot realizes his days are numbered with this younger generation. "It got a lot of attention at the time."

"I'd love to read it," she coos.

Eliot knows he is an easy mark. A glutton for attention, just like Twyla. Opposites might attract, but such soul mates can make an impervious connection. "I'll send you a copy."

"Autographed," she demands. "To my darling Twyla . . ."

Eliot studies her carefully. Her eyes are gray, not blue as he had assumed. And she has a scar over her left eye. "So, how did you get into acting?" he asks, more interested now.

"Didn't you read my bio?"

"No."

"It's all lies anyway. It says I was discovered in a mall when I was sixteen, then became a model before I broke into film." She forms her hand into a little puppet and makes it say, "Blah, blah, blah." She turns the puppet to her face and kisses it on the fingertip lips.

"What's the truth?"

Twyla cups her cheek in her palm. "I was a child actor." She closes her eyes and shakes her head. "No," she says. She holds her chin in both palms now, framing her pretty face with long, thin fingers. "Actually, I ran away from home when I was twelve and started turning tricks in Hollywood. Just blow jobs, though."

She is definitely a lunatic and of course Eliot is intrigued. It's always the nutcases that do him in. He can't resist watching them wind themselves up and then spin out of control. "No really, Twyla," he says and leans near her. "Tell me the truth."

She scoots closer to him and says quietly. "Really, I'm the bastard daughter of a major rock star." She glances over her shoulder and under the tablecloth. "I can't tell you who. My mom signed an agreement never to reveal his identity. But I blackmailed him. Told him if he didn't get me some acting gigs, I would expose him."

"You're having fun, aren't you?" he asks. She nods. "But what do you want me to write?"

She leans way back and drapes her long arms over the booth. "Okay, I'll tell you the truth. You get the scoop, Sparky." She has adopted a slight Katherine Hepburn accent now. "It will be an absolute coup." She drops the Hepburn inflection and says in what seems to be her regular gravelly voice, "I worked as a dominatrix to put myself through graduate school in LA. One of my clients was a USC film student. He put me in a few shorts. They won some awards at festivals. I got other parts." She shrugs. "Same old story."

Eliot pictures her in black leather with a whip and wonders if she's still lying. She probably is, but like she said, this is a nice diversion. "What were you studying?" he asks. She looks at him blankly. "In grad school."

"Philosophy," she says quickly, then taps the side of her head. "I'm very, very smart."

"What happened to the film student?"

"I chained him to the air conditioner in a West Hollywood hotel and left him there." She grins, full of teeth.

Eliot leans in closer. He reaches for her bracelets. Spins one lightly on her wrist. "Do you still, you know?"

"Philosophize?" she asks.

"No, the other thing."

"Only if you ask me nicely," she purrs.

"More wine?" he asks and fills her glass.

The steaks arrive and Eliot cuts into the bloody meat. He's never cared for rare steak. Twyla devours everything on her plate, even the lettuce leaf for garnish. Eats crusty bread in big bites, then swipes her hand across her dress to dismiss the errant crumbs. And drinks lots of red wine. With her sharp little pinky nail, she picks a string of meat from between two teeth when she's done.

"So what now?" she asks. "I don't want to go back to my hotel with all those assholes." She clutches his forearm. "Please don't send me back. Anything but that!"

"Why don't you come with me," Eliot says. "We'll have a drink. Talk some more. I have a feeling there is a lot more to learn about you."

Twyla bows her head demurely and looks up at him through long, blinking eyelashes. She is no longer the philosophizing, carnivorous Jezebel she has been portraying for the last hour. "Okay," she says gently and turns to wave the waiter down. Eliot notices a small tattoo of an ankh on the back of her neck, just below the hairline. The vision gives him a small hard-on. He thinks of Junie and wonders if he should do this. But it's not like he and Junie have anything going. She's the one who always leaves. Maybe it will be good to fool around with Twyla. Then he won't be sex-obsessed when he gets back to New York and he can take things more slowly with Junie.

He reaches out and lightly touches the tattoo. Twyla leans her head back and murmurs, "Is your hotel far from here?"

"Just around the corner," Eliot says into her ear.

Twyla walks ahead of him in the hotel hall, swinging a little silver handbag. "Which number?" she asks over her shoulder.

Eliot digs the key out of his pocket. "Seven seventeen," he says. She trails her finger across the numbers of every room, making tiny tapping noises on the doors. Eliot finds this amusing. He imagines disheveled Canadian sleepers poking their heads out to see this long, tall woman with an ankh on her neck strutting through the hall. And he will be behind her. Following. Doing as he's told. His hard-on returns.

Inside his room, she heads straight for the minifridge and pulls out tiny bottles of liquor. "What'll you have?"

"Something pale."

She tosses him a baby vodka and opens a Bacardi for herself before settling on the desk chair with her legs stretched in front of her. "Have you started writing about me, yet?" she asks and tilts the bottle to her lips.

"It's all up here," Eliot says, tapping his head. He perches on the edge of the bed across from her.

Twyla extracts her foot from her strappy sandal and works her toes under Eliot's pant leg. "Tell me what you're saying up there."

"You'll have to wait and read it."

"But I want to know now," she whines, then pinches him on the leg with her toes and pulls a few strands of hair.

"Ouch!" he says and grabs her foot. "That hurt."

"I think you like it," she says with a smirk.

Eliot stands and walks behind Twyla's chair. He touches the tattoo on the back of her neck. A nice diversion. They'll have a little fun. He'll be inspired to write tomorrow. Margaret will get her article on time. He'll go back to Junie. Everybody wins.

"I've never been with a dominatrix before," he says.

"I'm not practicing anymore."

"What will it take to bring you out of retirement?" he asks as he kisses the ankh.

She pulls his head down beside her mouth and whispers, "Bark like a dog, monkey boy."

# CHAPTER
# FIFTEEN

When Junie returns home in the evening, the message machine light blinks. She tosses her coat aside and eagerly pushes the play button, expecting a call from Leon, hoping for a call from Eliot. The first message is from her mother earlier in the day. Junie rolls her eyes and holds down the fast-forward button. Her mother's scrambled voice chatters incoherently while Junie sits impatient, like any normal conversation between the two of them. The next message is for Leon about a wedding gig on Long Island with the Band of Gold. She saves it even though he hates those gigs. The Band of Gold pays well but Leon swears that playing instrumental versions of Kool and the Gang tunes and honoring requests for Bob Seger songs from drunken fratboys-cum-groomsmen sucks every ounce of joy out of being a musician. The last message is the high-pitched squeal of a lost fax machine searching for its kin. Then the tape cuts off and automatically rewinds.

Leon didn't call. He always calls her from the road. Usually from a rest stop in the late afternoon. Sometimes when he gets to the bar before the band has to sound-check. But always before the gig because he knows that by the time he's done playing, she'll either be asleep or out with Katie. Junie pushes the play button again. The same three messages tease her before the tape rewinds.

She counts up the hours Leon has been gone. They should have made it to North Carolina by now. They are likely setting up their gear, arguing about the set list, and trying to weasel the bar into letting them drink for free. Leon's had plenty of time to call. So, either he is mad at her for her vile behavior last night, which would be perfectly justified. (Although he's never been spiteful and she can't imagine that he wouldn't call even if he is irritated with her.) Or something horrible has happened.

He could be smashed against a bridge outside of Baltimore. Trapped on I-95 beneath the grinding wheels of that piece-of-shit van they drive. Or catapulted headfirst through the windshield into the Rappahannock River. The last person Leon would ever see is Steve, flying through the air with his arms spread open as if he were embracing the experience of death so he can write bad lyrics about it in the afterlife. Would Leon think of her in the moments before his body shattered the cloudy surface of those deadly river rapids? Would she be the center of his mind as he sank into the cold depths claiming his last breath? Would her name be trapped in the final air bubble to escape his bluing lips?

This has been the worst part of living with a musician. Every time he is gone on a gig, she makes herself crazy, glancing at the clock every ten minutes until she convinces herself that he is dead. Knifed outside a Bleeker Street bar. Bleeding to death behind a Dumpster full of restaurant garbage. Or he could choke on a slice of pizza. No one would find him until morning. Sitting upright behind the wheel of his Honda, blue in the face, grease congealed on his chin. How would she ever find out? There are seven million inhabitants on the island of Manhattan. Dead people ride subways. It could be days before someone would find Leon's body and even more time before the system would connect him to her.

Junie's fears are worse when he is out of town. She can reach frantic in a matter of minutes if she hasn't heard from him. Who would call her if there were a fiery crash somewhere near the Allegheny Mountains? She's not the next-of-kin. Her name appears on no insurance forms. She's merely the girlfriend shacking up with him. The authorities might track down his mother. And she would hold the information hostage, use it to her best advantage with all her acquaintances and relatives to procure pity and favors. She certainly wouldn't share it with Junie because she doesn't like Junie. Told Leon once that Junie needs to grow up and get over herself. Junie didn't ask for clarification on what part of herself appeared to be an obstacle, but ever since then any unintentional phone conversations between Junie and Leon's mom are notably terse. No, if Leon dies anytime anywhere, Junie is certain that she will be the last to know.

At least with Jacob, they had a chance to practice before he died. She found him once inside the old wooden storage bench where their mother kept extra blankets. Junie lifted the lid to look at Jacob inside, lying perfectly still with his eyes shut and arms folded loosely over the cold flashlight held against his sternum.

"What are you doing?" she whispered.

"Rehearsing," he said.

"Can I try?"

"I'm not done yet. Close it."

Junie lowered the lid and wrote her name in the pale yellow carpet with her index finger. They weren't supposed to play in the living room because of the nice furniture and the sweeper marks their mother wanted undisturbed. Junie drew a scowling face next to her name. She wished Jacob would come out so they could do something else. Something fun. She pressed her eye against the crack under the top of the bench and tried to see him in there. She pictured him with dark, curly hair and eyebrows like caterpillars over hazel eyes even though by then he was mostly bald from the chemo.

"Do we still look alike?" she asked when his hair began to fall out in downy fluffs. They had studied themselves in the bathroom mirror.

"It's our noses," Jacob said as they scrutinized their reflections. "They're the same. It's mom's nose. It's round on the end. Like a little tiny doorknob."

Junie pushed the cartilage at the end of her nose. She imagined Jacob opening her face door to expose her brain like a TV screen where he could see the pictures of what she was thinking. Would he see her thinking about him thinking about her? It would be like the time they held the hand mirror in front of the wall mirror to create never-ending hallways of reflections. She wondered if death would be like that for Jacob and if he would find his way.

"Jacob," she whispered into the crack. "What's it like? Let me try."

"In a minute," he said.

"Come on, Jake. This is boring," Junie whined.

Jacob lifted the lid and sat up. "Okay. Your turn. You won't be afraid will you?" He slung one brown-corduroy leg over the side. He was wearing his baseball cleats. Junie stood eager for her chance.

"I don't know," she said. "Is it scary?"

"No." Jacob slid over the edge of the bench onto the carpet and handed her the flashlight. "It's nice. I think I'll like being in my coffin."

Junie pressed her palm over the light and turned it on. She liked how it made her hand look pink. That must be her blood. She wondered if Jacob's hand would still be pink after he was dead for real.

"You can turn on the light if you get scared," Jacob said.

Junie climbed into the bench. She settled her shoulders against the warm, soft blankets where Jacob had lain. "It's comfy," she said.

Jacob leaned over the edge on crossed arms. "See. It's nice. You want me to close the lid?"

Junie nodded. Jacob lowered the bench top very slowly. The wedge of light got smaller across her body until it was dark inside and her heart sped up. "Jake, you still there?" she whispered hoarsely.

"Yes."

She promised herself when Jacob was in his real coffin she

would stay beside it forever in the same black dress with a white Peter Pan collar and her favorite Mary Janes. And she'd make sure Jacob had a flashlight. But he hadn't even turned on the light when he was in the bench. He was brave. Junie was the chicken. She pressed her palm against the top of the light and flicked it on. Her hand shone pink. She could make out the shadows of her body surrounded by the box of wood.

"You turned the light on," Jacob said through the crack.

"Nuh-uhn," Junie lied. She flicked it off again.

"Yes, you did." He lifted the lid.

Junie sat up. "So what?"

Jacob shrugged. "Doesn't matter," he said.

How clever of Jacob to practice for death, Junie thinks now. With cleats on. This makes her laugh. Worn Wrangler cords, a Cookie Monster tee shirt, tube socks, cleats, and sweat bands, Jacob's little-boy uniform. Once their mother would have wrestled him out of his favorite clothes to make certain they were washed, then rotated through a variety of outfits. But when death hovered over them, most household chores went to hell in a handbasket, as Junie's grandmother remarked each time she came over and soaked stacks of forgotten dishes or ran loads of mildewing laundry. In the midst of the domestic confusion, Junie and Jacob skipped right along, simplifying death into something rehearsable while the adults around them fretted and fell apart.

Why can't she now accept the inevitability and capriciousness of death as she did when she was a child? Junie knows her endless what-iffing about Leon is futile. He isn't dead. Because she's thought about it and things don't happen that way. In fact, Leon is probably just fine. Bastard. Going off for the weekend, leaving her alone and not even calling. Probably met some insipid Southern college girl named Tallulah in short shorts with a big sexy gap between her teeth. Just like Katie said.

Junie opens the cabinet over the stove where Leon keeps all of his fancy oils and she stashes her one bottle of Maker's Mark. She pours two fingers of amber liquor into her grandmother's juice glass and swirls the drink. Light refracts off the ice and dances a faint rainbow on the speckled countertop. She sips the bourbon. Loves the first burning gulp. She hardly ever drinks when Leon is home. His mother is a lush and his father a surly drunk. That combination is enough to steer Leon clear of alcohol for answers. Junie's parents, on the other hand, believe in a civilized four-thirty dry martini and wine with dinner. Junie likes to drink alone when her mood is right. And right now her mood is perfect for solo imbibing. Leon might not be dead, but he didn't call and that makes her irritable and frustrated.

She ambles into the living room and drops into an easy chair where she slings her legs over the armrest. She can't blame her bad mood entirely on Leon's lack of communication. Eliot didn't call either. Of course, he doesn't have an obligation to call but he knows Leon is gone for the weekend. Tonight would have been the perfect chance to up the ante. If he were serious about this flirt they have going, which clearly he is not, then he would have called. Bastards. She chokes back a big swig of liquor. Both of them.

# CHAPTER
# SIXTEEN

When Junie wakes early the next afternoon, her head feels full and sloshy. The bourbon glass sits dejected on her nightstand. Leon never called and she drank herself into a stupor. Pathetic. Drooling over a stupid answering machine, pining away for men like some poor Miss Lonelyheart with nothing better to do. She doesn't need any stinking men to fulfill her life. Today she will be productive. Read a book or at least rent a movie based on a classic novel. Or get crafty and make a lampshade out of dried flowers and a milk carton. Better yet, get industrious and clean the apartment. Or she could think about her career. Go to the library. Look at reference books. Surf the Web until she locates her WWW.PASSION. Wouldn't Leon be surprised if he came home to find the apartment spit shined and Junie studying for the GREs?

She curls around her pillow. Fat chance that will happen. None of those ideas seem remotely interesting and self-motivation has never been her style. Sloth and self-loathing are more her method. The truth is, the relief of being alone for the weekend wore off as soon as Leon closed the door and now Junie is bored. She has never been good at entertaining herself, which is odd since she's spent the majority of her life as an only child. She blames this trait on her stars. A palm reader, Mr. Lee, even told her that was the case.

He was a young, prim, Chinese guy in plaid pants who had a shop on Houston Street. Junie and Katie walked in on a whim one night after the bars closed. The room was clean and spare and smelled of sandalwood. They sat across from Mr. Lee on metal folding chairs with a wobbly card table between them. He delicately stroked Junie's palm with his well-manicured thumb, then pronounced that she would live long, had lost something important, and should surround herself with friends because being alone would always make her melancholy. She loved that he had used the word melancholy, as if she were a Victorian-era depressive prone to fainting spells and black moods.

She wonders if Mr. Lee is still in business. She could track him down and ask him, Leon or Eliot? What would she want the answer to be? If he said Leon, would she happily accept her life with him and never give Eliot's wicked grin another thought? If he said Eliot, could she abandon Leon's love for something so uncertain? She weighs them in her mind. Loads each image on a balance scale and watches it tip back and forth. Calm, predictable happiness versus fervent, impulsive shenanigans. It's not a choice she can make because she wants them both. And what's so bad about that? So she wants more than Leon's undying devotion. And she wants more than Eliot's wily attention. Isn't today's sexually aware modern young woman supposed to be voracious and uncompromising in her pursuit of satisfaction?

The phone rings. Junie sits up and kicks back the covers. It rings again and she is out of bed running toward the kitchen. It could be her mother. In which case, Junie should answer the phone breathless and distracted, as if she were terribly busy with no time to talk. But it could be Leon. In which case she has to make a snap decision. Should she sound frantic with worry to induce maximum guilt or seem aloof, as if she has barely even registered his absence? Before she can decide on her demeanor, the receiver is in her hand and she is nearly shouting, "Hello!" into the handset.

"Are you alone?" The rough edges of morning catch on the corners of Eliot's words and Junie slides down the wall to the floor, grinning into the phone.

"Where are you?" she asks.

"Sitting on my couch. Where are you?"

"You're back already?"

"Didn't want you to miss me too much." He laughs.

What would be the snappy repartee? Before Junie can formulate anything remotely clever, Eliot is on to something else. "Thanks for yesterday," he says.

Junie remembers Eliot's note. Dinner or something. She remembers the banana. The thought makes her blush and pulse.

"You free this afternoon?"

"Yes," she says too quickly and wishes just once she could hold back, play his game, make *him* squirm a little.

"You sure? Because I don't want to tear you away from anything important."

Junie forces herself to inhale, then exhale before she says, "Well, I have plenty I could do, but . . ."

"But what?"

"But if you had something in mind, I might be interested."

"I need to get my keys back."

"Oh." Junie feels herself shriveling down to the insignificance of the dust bunnies gathered in the corners.

"Plus," Eliot adds and Junie perks back up. "It would be nice to see you today."

Junie makes herself breathe again before she says, "Yeah. Okay. I'll stop by later."

"I'm around," Eliot says and hangs up.

Junie showers, shaves her legs, plucks her eyebrows, and stands in front of her closet. She debates about what to wear. All of her clothes seem tired. Nothing like Barbarella would wear. She pulls out a short plaid skirt and holds it in front of her body. She matches it with a little boy's argyle sweater. With kneesocks and her saddles she should look okay. A naughty schoolgirl. How trite. But Junie likes it anyway. It fits her mood. When she's ready, she pulls on her cucumber-colored coat to walk the four hundred and seventy-eight steps to Eliot's apartment.

The air is crisp like two cold hands pressed against her cheeks. She passes blossoming cherry trees. Tiny white petals flutter against the brownstone buildings. She shoves her hands deep into the pockets of her coat. There she finds the banana.

She pulls it out to study. The yellow has darkened and a few small brown spots freckle its surface. She hates to throw away a perfectly good banana so she shoves it back down, deep into the recesses of her pocket.

In the other pocket she finds crumpled paper. Cinnamon gum wrappers, a receipt from the deli on Eliot's corner where they bought cat food once, and his note from yesterday. She wonders how he crawled into her pockets in the first place. When she memorized his smile so that every time she closes her eyes, he grins at her from the back of her eyelids?

In the past few weeks, she has walked down Seventh Avenue and let her mind wander toward him, hoping she could trip some cosmic wire so he would be drawn to her for conversation that was slick and smooth and delicious, like some food she craved but could not name. She prayed to the love gods, "Let me run into him one more time." Those chance encounters were barely enough to sustain her. Now everything is different. He called and invited her over. She accepted. Her actions are premeditated and cannot be excused as fate dragging her through its wake. She knows what she is doing. When he opens the door she will step up to kiss him. When they go inside, she will tell him she wants him. She will say it with a sultry, sexy voice because he bothered to call her, invited her over, and she said yes.

Junie walks determined past trees, coffee shops, and bodegas. She will do it. This is what she wants. She walks a bit faster. Has been for weeks. She's been fooling herself to think that she and Leon will make it as a couple. One block left. Fifty sidewalk squares, a dozen brownstones with window boxes full of petunias like tiny purple lions looking curiously on the world. Eight blooming cherry trees and one majestic London plain wrinkling the sidewalk with its great plunging roots. If Leon had called her last night, maybe her choice would be different today. But then again, it might not. This is not about Leon. This is about her. A crow caws from its highest branches. Junie squints up into the tree to find the ominous bird portending her imminent fall from grace. Shut up, she thinks to the bird. I know what I am doing.

At Eliot's stoop she pauses, strokes the banana in her pocket for courage, then presses the buzzer and waits. Waits, rocking back and forth on saddle shoes. Waits, gnawing on the silky inside of her cheek. Waits, listening for his noises. Creaking stairs. Shadows in the hall. He is there opening the door, his hair a mess, his clothes wrinkled, his grin presumptuous. "Hey, Junie," he says.

Junie can't make her feet step forward or her lips pucker as he stands in front of her. "Hello," she squeaks, then stumbles into the foyer.

He kisses her on the cheek and pats her shoulder. She wishes he would grab her ass. "Come on up," he says.

She watches Eliot tramp up the crooked stairs. She berates herself for being such a wimp. She had her chance and let it pass. If she is going to be adulterous then she will have to do much better than tagging behind him with a pounding heart and sweating palms, wondering if he wears boxers or briefs.

Eliot fumbles. Eliot mumbles. Eliot is an imbecile, Alfie has decided, and therefore, no great competition. Junie has come, ostensibly to return the keys. She breezes through the door behind Eliot and smiles at Alfie. He winds himself between her legs, peeks up her skirt, and sees white cotton covering her delicate parts that she touched for him. She bends down and scoops him into her hug.

"Good morning, love," she coos and Alfie is frozen by the jolt of memory.

In the mornings he passed her as gulls circled and cried overhead. She smiled every time he went by. If she called out, "Good morning, love," then his skin contracted into a rash of gooseflesh and his pulse quickened to a canter. There was more to her words than that simple greeting conveyed. It contained a promise, one that he eagerly anticipated. As an answer, he tipped his hat to this fair lady. Her cheeks deepened to a glowing pink while crimson curls quivered wild beneath her bonnet. But he did not stop. Danger lurked nearby. All around them water. Sails slapping against the wind. The sound of men's voices and the smell of fish. Another man stood near, angry and protective. He scowled from behind a knife and bloodstained apron as he slopped entrails into the gutter.

Eliot interrupts Alfie's reverie. He lures Junie into the kitchen, promising lukewarm coffee. Coffee! Alfie shakes his head in disgust. The man knows nothing about the subtle art of seduction. Dark-red wine staining her lips and making her heart pound is what she deserves. A single thorn-stripped rose presented with a bow. Yet she follows, so easily led, that naive lass.

Alfie watches them from the doorway. When Junie sits at

the table, he hops into her lap and inhales her. Same smell, same taste, same caresses on his skin. So many lives and so many bodies. He has found her again. I would compose a ballad for you, Alfie thinks, if I weren't stuck in the body of a cat named Alfie, for God's sake.

Junie notices a new bunch of bananas, the severed paw of some great yellow ape, on the counter beside where Eliot pours their coffee. She hopes the missing one did not peep from her pocket when she slid off her coat. Eliot joins her at the table. He sits across from her and stretches his legs out, one foot on either side of her chair as if he were staking a claim. She could easily crawl into his lap.

"Thanks again for taking care of Alfie."

"Alfie and I are buddies." She pats the cat, who lies purring on her thighs. The vision of herself on Eliot's bed with her hand down her pants and Alfie on her stomach flashes through her mind. "Did I give Alfie the shot the right way and everything? Did he seem okay when you got back?"

"Everything was fine. Except my desk." Eliot laughs.

Junie sucks in a breath. She thought she erased it. She was sure she did. But she didn't double-check. The coffee tastes metallic, a penny against the roof of her mouth. She swallows and lays her hands flat on the table, ready to offer an explanation. Make it a joke. Pretend she was kidding!

"He messed it all up."

"Who?"

"Alfie. He walked all over my keyboard. There's cat hair on the screen and kitty litter rocks stuck in my keys. He shoved my papers onto the floor and batted my mouse around. I found tooth marks on the power cord."

Junie relaxes her grip on the edge of the table. "Alfie did that?"

"I'm pretty sure it was Alfie. Unless it was you messing with my stuff," Eliot says.

It takes a half-second for Junie to realize he's joking. She laughs uneasily and wonders if he caught the delay. "Maybe he was mad that you were gone," she offers.

"Probably. He does it every time I leave him. Once he knocked my phone off the hook. He destroyed my clock radio. He hates my Play Station and you know how he feels about the electric can opener. Now my computer."

"Maybe you should take him to the kitty shrink."

The phone rings then. Eliot says, "The machine will get it." Junie sips her coffee.

"Hey, monkey boy," a woman's husky voice echoes through the apartment. Eliot pushes his chair back and jogs past Junie into the living room. "Woof, woof," the woman says, then laughs. "I'm in town . . ." The voice cuts off. Eliot comes back into the kitchen with his hand tangled in his hair.

"Friend of yours?" Junie asks.

"It's nothing." He paces across the kitchen. She finds the momentary silence uncomfortable. He stands behind her and grips the back of her chair. "You have plans tonight?" he asks. "Is the boyfriend back?"

The skin of Junie's neck prickles. "He's still on the road," she says. She twists around to see him. "Virginia or North Carolina or something. College gigs."

Eliot's mischievous grin begins to form. Junie feels the prick-les crawl down her spine and into the small of her back, the pit of her stomach, the fleshy part of her thighs.

"That means I have you all to myself."

She nods and thinks about calling out, "I'm ready!" But she can't seem to form the words. The specter of Leon, the cawing crow, Barbarella's stare, and a cat that knows her secret.

"Let me buy you dinner. I owe you."

Dinner. Relief. A chance to work slowly. Besides, if she wants to spend the evening with Eliot, she can. It's not a sin.

"You pick the restaurant," he says.

"I know a great little Vietnamese place in Chinatown. You need a Sherpa to find it."

"I thought Sherpas were Tibetan."

"You're a smart-ass."

He grips her shoulders and massages, a little too hard. "It's nice to see you," he says. "Let's go now." He walks to the front of her chair and extends a hand toward her. "We could walk around Canal Street for a while."

She takes his hand, firm and thick. Imagines it cupping her breast, caressing the curve of her belly. He pulls her up from the chair and she dumps Alfie to the floor. Eliot lets go. In the living room, she walks directly to the desk and looks carefully to make sure the message is completely gone. The surface is a collage of kitty paw prints. No words. Beside his keyboard is a frayed copy of *Liberty Voyage.* Eliot picks it up and flips through the pages. Junie's stomach tightens. Is this the book that she had been reading in the bedroom? Does he know? Or is this another one? How egotistical (and confusing) to keep so many.

"You know," he says. "This book was quite controversial for a while." He taps the book against his palm. "A lot of women thought I was really sexist." He leans against the desk and watches her. The intensity of his stare makes her want to lie across the keyboard and invite him in. "Can you imagine?" he asks sarcastically.

"Sexist?" She looks up at Eliot. "I wouldn't say you're sexist." She is lying. She knows he sees her only as a piece of ass. Still, she doesn't care. Abandoning all pretenses of mutual respect in exchange for senseless passion in which she is merely an object to be desired is what she wants. She can't blame him for that. "I don't have a problem with it. Why?"

"Just curious. I like to ask hot chicks what they think." He grins.

"Charming," Junie says.

"We all have our little obsessions."

"Just as long as I don't have to tell you mine."

Eliot steps up close to her and says quietly in her ear, "Someday, I'll drag a deep, dark secret out of you."

The hair on the back of her neck rises and her nipples tighten into tiny buds. There's one lurking in my pocket, she thinks.

Alfie slinks out from under the kitchen table when Eliot and Junie leave. He leaps onto the counter, tiptoes carefully around crusty dishes in the sink, and then hops onto the windowsill where he can stare down into the neighbor's garden. A large oak tree shades the small patch of green. Three squirrels, the devil's minions as far as Alfie is concerned, chase one another around protruding roots, up the trunk, through crisscrossing branches and across electrical wires. They flaunt their freedom while he is sentenced to a lifetime indoors. Alfie cannot take it much longer. His past life love so blithely coming and going. How many lives and how many deaths to find her again? Only to be trapped in this hellhole with a rogue like Eliot leading her away.

Alfie watches the sky where little starlings flitter. He must remember who she was before. Pull from the dark and cloudy recesses of his mind what they meant to one another once. Perhaps if he can trip that memory then she too will remember and they will both be set free. That skin. Those eyes. The smile of desire. All so familiar yet different from before. He licks his lips and recalls the mackerel upon her fingertips. Yes, yes. It's coming back. The boats. The men. The marketplace each day. Blackpool, Lancashire, England. The scowling man with a bloody knife and fish guts on his apron. Of course. She was the fishmonger's wife!

At the market, she weighed and wrapped each day's catch. That casual morning greeting, "Good morning, love," she called out to passersby, luring them in for the freshest fish. Gulls circled and cried overhead. But for me, Alfie now remembers, those words were a signal. Her voice like rain on water made his soul float into his mouth because it meant that later she would meet him on the docks where, on bended knee, he would take her hands and extol her virtues in rhyming verse. Then put an arm around her waist and pull her close. Beg her to come away to his place, not far from the market. If her husband was out to sea, then she would agree to steal away to his room where he would slowly undress her, letting petticoats drop.

Each time, when they were finished, she cried into her pillow, bemoaning her fate. "It's you," she told him over and over. "You are my true love. My destiny. My soul!"

And he, a simple man, a weaver by trade, ousted from his job by new machinery, would curse the luck of loving this exquisite creature when he had not two pennies to rub together. How could he whisk her away to a new life?

Her declaration of undying love has strung him through so many unhappy lives. Searching for the comfort of his soul joined with hers again. Now finally they have been reunited. Oh, the joy and the heartache, for only one thing stands in their way. Alfie coughs a huge hairball onto the middle of the floor. Eliot. That knave. That wizard of technology. That stealer of women.

The cat hops down from the windowsill and prowls through the apartment. He will not let Eliot get away with this. He will fight tooth and claw for his love. Eliot will be sorry. Alfie jumps onto the desk and stands on top of the keyboard pumping his throat, working up hair and phlegm from his gut to spit onto the keys. Splat! Take that you damn rapscallion!

# CHAPTER
# SEVENTEEN

Eliot and Junie walk deep in the belly of Chinatown, where the McDonald's sign is written in Chinese characters and old women sell pork buns from carts on corners. They weave through the crowds on their way to the Vietnamese restaurant, passing noodle shops with crispy ducks and disembodied pig heads swaying gently in steamy windows. Drawing in chilly air, Junie notices the smell of fish, then tries to think of something to say.

"I love Canal Street!" she says like a too enthusiastic tourist and points to the fish market on the corner. Live crabs claw over each other, trying to escape their Styrofoam coffin. Red snapper stare straight up with never-blinking, red-rimmed eyes. A Chinese woman grabs a handful of shrimp, still in their armor. Next to the market is a fruit-and-vegetable stand with a mound of pale green and white baby bok choy. Bean sprouts overflow from a wooden crate and spiny fruit hang off the awning like distended blowfish in yellow net bags.

"Whenever I leave New York, this is what I miss," says Eliot.

"Me, too," Junie says but really it's a question. Do you miss me, too?

They stop at an intersection where cars crawl through the narrow street surrounded by mobs of people spilling off the curbs. Crabs in Styrofoam, Junie thinks. She notices a man, in the middle of the mass of people, selling tiny live turtles from a pink plastic bowl. She watches the little reptiles clamber over each other toward freedom. A song pops into her head. "One, two, three, four, five, six, seven, eight, nine, ten. Ten tiny turtles on the telephone talking to the grocery man." It was Jacob's song. "We would like some lettuce. Please bring us ten heads, please." From Sesame Street. "And ten ripe tomatoes and ten rutabagas with the dimples on their knees!"

After school. Jacob on the floor. Chocolate milk. Powdered Nestlé Quik stuck to the sides of the glass and grilled cheese on a paper towel in front of the TV. He loved Cookie Monster. Laughed with his mouth full of gooey yellow cheese when Cookie devoured everything on his plate. Felt a profound connection with Kermit the Frog and begged for a trench coat just like his. Junie lay on the red shag carpet and drew Crayola pictures. Glanced up occasionally at the show. They memorized songs and sang them together. Nobody else knows those songs.

"Do you know the one about the snail that got mugged by the turtles?" Eliot asks. It takes Junie a few seconds to realize that he wants to tell her a joke. She shakes her head and turns her attention to him again.

"So there's this snail, see," Eliot begins. "And he's walking home late one night. All of a sudden these three turtles jump him. They're roughing him up and going for his wallet. Luckily, the police come and break it up. They stand the turtles up against the squad car and pat them down, which is hard to do of course, because they're turtles. Anyway, while they're doing that, the police captain comes over to the snail and says, 'Calm down now. Everything is fine. I know you're shaken up, but just take your time and tell me in your own words what happened.' And the snail says, 'I don't know officer, it all happened so fast.'" Eliot waits with his eyebrows lifted.

Junie giggles uncomfortably. The joke is not funny. It's Eliot telling something so silly that it makes her laugh and dissatisfies her a little. A goofy Eliot trying to entertain doesn't fit in with her ribald notions of what they will have together. "I've never heard you tell a joke."

"I have all kinds of secret sides."

"I bet you do," Junie says and remembers the woman who called his apartment earlier.

The light changes, the cars stop. Eliot steps into the intersection and pulls Junie by the wrist with him. She likes feeling Eliot's fingers wrapped lightly around her forearm, leading her. She tries to maneuver her hand so she can weave her fingers into his. But he lets go when they get to the other side.

They walk side by side in silence, past a parking lot with a chain-link fence. Junie glances at him again and memorizes the whorls of his ear. She is in an alternate universe in which Leon doesn't exist and won't be hurt when she pulls Eliot close and presses against the fence until its diamond-and-twist pattern is

imprinted on her back. She can feel Eliot next to her. She imagines what his hair in her fingers would feel like and how his lips
would press against hers. How he would touch her.

Junie pauses by the fence. Eliot glances at her and raises his
eyebrows again. This time the question is, What? She wants to
tell him that she's ready. The words are forming on her tongue.
Before she can speak, Eliot looks away and asks, "Are we close to
the restaurant? I'm starving."

"Yeah," she says, letting her chance slip through the holes in
the fence. "It's right around the corner."

Inside Nha Trang, the smells of grilled fish, spices she can't
name, bunches of fresh green cilantro, and jasmine tea drift
through the restaurant and calm Junie.

"I thought I knew all the secret Chinatown dives," Eliot
says. "How did you find this?"

Leon brought her here on one of their first dates. Her decision to bring Eliot to the same place seems ridiculously
Freudian. Hey thanks, subconscience, she thinks to herself.
Nice to know you're still in the business of making me feel like
an ass. She doesn't want to invoke Leon's presence now. Nor her
guilty conscience. So she is here with another man. Where's the
sin in that? "A friend turned me on to this place," she says and
leaves it at that.

The restaurant is small and greasy, loud and chaotic. But
that's what Junie likes about it—that such delectable food can
come out of such disorder. "I love the chicken *phó* here," she
says.

"Good enough for me."

A young Vietnamese waiter seats them at a small corner table in the back. She and Eliot are perpendicular to one another. Their elbows and knees very close.

"We know what we want," Junie tells the waiter. "Two bowls of chicken *phó.*" He nods and rushes off, calling out their order in Vietnamese.

Junie watches Eliot and imagines feeding him. His head tilting back and jaws opening. Dangling purple basil over his open mouth and dropping tiny shredded carrot slivers onto his tongue. She pulls a pair of long plastic chopsticks from the stainless steel container in the middle of the table. "Can you use chopsticks?" she asks. Neither of her parents can. Maybe it's a generational thing.

"Of course," he says. "I used to live in Chinatown."

She huddles closer to him and looks down over the tops of her glasses. "What else is in your sordid past?"

"I'll never tell," he says and pulls a pair of chopsticks out of the canister.

Leon always drums with his chopsticks. Junie thought this habit charming when they first met. He'd do drum solos with his mouth but pretend to hit all the beats with his chopsticks. He would find the tones of different things on the table by hitting a chopstick against the metal canister, against the water glass half full, against the teapot, against the fish sauce bottle. Eliot holds his chopsticks like a pencil.

The waiter sets two bowls of soup in front of them. Bright green cilantro leaves cover the broth like lily pads in a murky pond. Junie drops handfuls of mung bean sprouts into the soup and mixes the hot sauce and plum sauce just right. Eliot fishes in his bowl and extracts long noodles. Steam covers his glasses so his eyes become invisible. He slurps his first bite. Watching him, Junie knows how it would feel to enter his mouth, to warm him, satisfy him, sustain him like broth noodles. She studies his face. She rarely looks at him long but this time she lets her look linger there deep in the belly of Chinatown so that she knows who is fucking up her life right now. Not just some man or any man, but this man whom she has chosen purposefully.

Junie is sure she is supposed to kiss Eliot now. Her shoulders ache and her hands twitch. Leaning forward, tilting her head and closing her eyes seems like the natural order of the universe. As she makes her trek across the space between them, Eliot looks up with his face as placid as the steaming broth, his glasses still covered with a layer of fog. "It's really good," he says and turns away to polish his lenses on his shirttail.

Junie stops short. This is getting old. "Eliot," she says. He squints at her without his glasses. His eyes are small and close together. "I missed you," she says.

He cocks his head to one side and puts on his glasses. "I was only gone one night."

Eliot's indifference stuns Junie. She realizes she's not breathing. She concentrates on pulling in a long, slow breath.

Eliot reaches under the table and rests his hand on her knee. "But thanks. That was very sweet."

Junie wants to call time-out then. Pull him aside to ask if he thinks her just some silly little girl he can flirt with mercilessly. Or if this hand on her knee is telling her to continue. The sinew in her deepest joints, her shoulders, her hips, her knees, coils tightly, ready to spring. She has to do something. Anything. Stand up on the table and perform a striptease to the Vietnamese pop music. Crawl beneath the table and slither into his lap. Jump up and run away. She is determined to act this time so she reaches down below the lip of the table and pulls his hand further up her skirt.

Eliot's eyebrows lift and the comma appears next to his grin. He wraps his hand around her thigh, pushes it up further beneath her skirt, and runs his thumb under the seam of her panties. "Actually I missed you, too," he says.

"You were only gone one night," she retorts, trying to sound unbothered by that thumb so close to the sudden dampness between her legs.

Eliot laughs. He pats her leg and withdraws his hand. "Want to go back to my place?" he asks.

"Yes," Junie says. "I do."

# CHAPTER
# EIGHTEEN

Junie and Eliot sit quietly side by side on the grubby F train back to Brooklyn. Their shoulders bump in time to the rhythmic jolts of subway wheels against rusty tracks. People enter and exit the car at each stop. By Delancey Street the Chinese faces have been replaced by Lower East Side hipsters. As they head into the tunnel below the East River only tired Brooklynites are left huddled on the seats. What assumptions do these strangers make about Eliot and Junie, sitting close and quiet? Father and daughter? Uncle and niece? Professor and student? Would anyone suspect the lewd fantasies she's considering?

In her mind, the train is stuck beneath the East River. The lights are out. Their car is empty. She gropes for him. Finds his leg. Hoists herself onto his lap. Knees straddle his thighs. Hands press into his shoulders. Tits shove into his face. Clothes fly off à la Erica Jong's zipless fuck. Or he makes the first move. Dives for her. Lusty lips on the side of her neck. He pushes her down so she's on her back across three seats. His hand up her skirt again, this time with a handful of her ass, while her legs wrap around his back. Or she is pressed against the door. Or hangs upside down on the handrail above him.

Junie is revved. Aroused and ready. Squirming in her seat, each bump of the train sends her thighs jumping. She rubs against Eliot's shoulder. Scoots her butt closer to his hip. Presses her knee into his meaty thigh. The banana in her pocket crushes between their legs. She basks in the heat his body emits and wiggles sideways to whisper her desires into his ear. But Eliot's eyes are closed. His arms are crossed. His chin buried in his chest. She draws back and looks at him carefully. "Eliot," she whispers but he does not stir. She elbows him lightly in the ribs and he grunts before resettling himself into a deep and sated sleep.

Outside the Seventh Avenue station Junie and Eliot walk side by side on the deserted streets of their neighborhood. The night has become overcast. Occasionally a bright, three-quarter moon shines brilliant between cumulous gray clouds drifting quickly across the black sky. Eliot walks beside her with his hands in his pants pockets and his head down.

"Did you have a nice nap?" she asks, then regrets the sarcasm in her voice.

Eliot shrugs. Seems pensive. She wonders if this will work. If he is even interested. How can she start? If she stopped under the moving clouds and spotlight moon and pulled his banana out of her pocket, then yelled, I fucked myself with this while you were gone, would he react? She wishes she were drunk enough to have an excuse for such a bizarre outburst. "Want to get some bourbon?" she asks.

Eliot looks up and nods. "A nightcap," he says. "Sounds good."

They duck into a corner liquor store and buy a flask wrapped in a brown paper bag. Junie totes it under her arm. She doesn't fool herself about its purpose. It's justification in a bottle. Something to point to and blame when she's caught. They walk toward his apartment, which is good. She can't imagine sipping bourbon while Eliot leers at her from among Leon's CDs and her dirty socks.

At his corner, he glances around furtively. Is he embarrassed to be seen with her? Is someone lurking behind the trashcans? "Everything all right?" she asks.

"Yeah, fine," he says, preoccupied with fishing his keys out of his pocket.

She stands behind him on the stoop as he unlocks the first door to the little foyer. Junie turns away from the building and looks into the sky. A break in the clouds reveals the moon for a moment and exposes them standing back to back. She with an illicit brown bottle beneath her arm. He with jingling keys. Eliot opens the door and they step into the tiny foyer.

The lightbulb has burnt out. She stands close to Eliot's back in the dark as he fumbles with his key to the second door three feet away. She moves her arm and feels the back of her fingers lightly brush Eliot's elbow. She wonders if it's really her fingers feeling him or just the thought of her fingers touching the thought of his elbow. In the dark just then her body feels lost. She knows all the parts are there but can't be sure where her arms become her hands and then divide into each separate finger. She remembers from a college anatomy class that a fourth of all human bones are in a person's hands. Hers feel heavy from this burden. She lifts her hand and lets her fingers rest on Eliot's upper arm like a bug dancing on a branch. Eliot pauses. She can hear him breathe. Feel his torso expand and contract under her touch. He says her name quietly like a question.

She doesn't want to hear his voice, reminding her who he is and what she is about to do. "Shhh," she whispers and gropes for Eliot's hand. She finds it hanging limply by his side. Weaving her fingers into his, she steps close and says, "Just don't think, Eliot. It's nice in the dark if you don't think."

Junie watches his silhouette against the glass window of the second door. Crazy spirals on his head protrude like exclamation points as he turns toward her. She imagines the comma, embedded in his cheek since childhood. A hesitation. The pause in his character. He lets go of her hand, then puts his fingers into her hair. She tilts her head into his palm and feels her breath leave her body in a quick exhale. Eliot leans forward and Junie freezes with Leon in the center of her mind.

"No, wait!" she says and hops away from Eliot's touch. "I can't," she sputters. "I'm sorry." She grapples for the doorknob behind her. Something heavy slips from under her arm. The bourbon. It thuds to the floor by her shoe. Her back is against the door. The knob is slipping in her fingers. Eliot stands mute with his hands outstretched. She flounders with the door, pulling it open, knocking it against her back, yanking it open again, muttering, "I'm so sorry. I just . . . I can't." Then she is on the stoop, hears the echo of the door rattling in its frame as she moves quickly down the sidewalk.

Junie stumbles up the stairs to Leon's apartment. Her hands are someone else's. Someone old. Someone who shakes and can't quite get the key in the lock. She kicks the door, tries again, inserts the key, and bursts into the kitchen. Redolent Moroccan stew mixed with an undernote of the rotting banana lingers in the air. She can never get away from Leon trying to nourish her. Soothe her with food. This makes Junie more furious. The way he gives and gives and gives. As if that's supposed to co-opt her love for eternity.

She stomps into the living room. "Idiot," she berates herself. "Jerk!" she yells. She marches from room to room in the dark. Pacing out her anger. Knows somewhere in her mind that she should stop. The neighbors will be angered by the noise. Fuck the neighbors, she thinks and then says out loud, "Fuck you all!" Hears her own voice echo off the walls and ceilings before being absorbed into the soft surfaces of her life. Couch cushions where she and Leon have had passionate sex. An easy chair with cigarette burns that his mother gave them. Their towels. Their sheets. The bushel basket with their soiled clothes. Leon is everywhere. Junie resents his intrusion. Always there. Always giving. Expecting her to do the same. As if it's that goddamn easy. Well it's not. What Leon doesn't get is that sometimes you can't love a person enough.

And Junie knows this because she sat beside Jacob's coffin on the padded seat of a folding chair. A short black dress with white Peter Pan collar and shiny Mary Janes. Snapdragons all around. Yellow, pink, and white mouths saying, Oh! Junie watched her Mary Janes swing. One-two-one-two. White socks inside the buckle part. Jacob liked the Mary Janes. Called them Minnie Mouse shoes. In his coffin he wore brown Buster Browns that tie. Junie knew he hated those shoes. Chucked them off in church. Toe to heel and push. His socks always bunched around his ankles like old lady pantyhose. He loved his cleats. Black with white stripes. They made him run faster. He whispered to her under the covers when he was sick and she crawled into his bed, "I want to wear my cleats to Heaven."

Junie promised to make sure. "Who dresses him for the funeral?" she had asked her mother.

"The mortician."

Junie imagined this mortician as the husband of the beautician who did her grandmother's hair every Tuesday afternoon. She wondered if they put Jacob's head under a dryer.

"How do they get his clothes?" she asked.

"I gave them clothes," her mother said and then began to cry, dabbing her eyes with a soggy, shredded tissue.

"What shoes is he going to wear?" Junie persisted.

"Oh, Junie," her mother said through a strangled sob. "What difference does it make?" She walked away.

Junie ran to the living room and rummaged through the mixed-up, kicked-off shoes tossed in the front closet everyday after school and left to mingle. Her mother stood outside the closet with hands on her hips. Junie peered out from behind overcoats, holding a rain boot in her left hand and a white summer sandal in her right.

Her mother yanked Junie to a stand. "Pick all of this up this instant." She shook her slightly, then released her arm. "Do not make any more messes. Do you understand me? We have people coming over here after the funeral." Before Junie could explain, her mother was gone, stomping up the stairs, slamming her bedroom door.

At the funeral, Junie looked over the edge of the casket. Jacob's mouth was shut and his purple lips were pressed together on waxy skin. In real life, Jacob's mouth was pink and always opened just a little bit because his nose was stuffy with a perpetual cold. "That's not him," she told her mother, who bit her lip and turned her head away.

Her father patted Junie on the shoulder. "You're right," he said. "That's just the body his soul used while he was on earth with us. Now he's in heaven with God and Grandpa."

"But what will happen to his body?" she asked.

Her mother sobbed into wads of tissues. Her father stood between them looking bewildered. "Junie, please stop," he whispered. "We don't want to upset Mommy any more." He put his arms around Junie's mom and led her to a side chair, leaving Junie peering at Jacob in the box. She wanted so badly to reach in and pry those lips apart. Make it look like the real Jacob again.

Swinging Mary Janes. Peter Pan collar. Snapdragons saying, Oh! People filed by to shake their heads, wipe their eyes, touch her hair, and say how sad and small Junie looked. Said Jacob took a piece of her with him. Then at home, they all came. Filled the house with their smells and sounds of rustling in uncomfortable clothes. Junie stayed in the closet with her eyes closed so no light could come in. She felt the hole, a perfect circle, between the bottom of her sternum and the top of her belly button. The piece of her that Jacob took. Like when Yosemite Sam got hit with a cannonball. Maybe all the people had seen through her. A clear shot. Like that tunnel through the giant redwoods she and Jacob saw in a book once and promised they would visit when they were old enough to drive.

How could Jacob leave her before they had a chance to take that trip? And why can't she let go? He's been dead for so long, yet she still pines away. Waiting for a Jacob substitute to make life jubilant again. As if she's got no gumption on her own. What she needs to do is prove her mettle to herself. Go somewhere. What's stopping her? Certainly not Leon. Clearly she has no business trying to make a life with him. She's only fucking it up. In fact, she could leave right now. It wouldn't be that hard. All she has to do is pack a bag.

What would she take? Which clothes? Which books? She tiptoes to the closet in the bedroom, as if she is making a secret getaway. She grabs blouses, skirts, pants, and shoes, an armload of herself gone slack, and dumps them on the floor. Books next. She runs her fingers over the spines. Picks out all of Eliot's loners. Makes a stack on the floor. Then she weeds through the CD collection to pick out the dozen that belong to her.

She has a mound of her belongings in the middle of the bedroom floor. Feels a tiny thrill at the thought of leaving with it all, finally allaying the persistent whine of guilt over always failing to love Leon enough. What should she carry all her stuff in? A suitcase? Too impermanent, too much like a vacation, implies that one intends to return. Cardboard boxes? Banana boxes are best. Most sturdy. Her mother taught her how to pack. Fold the clothes nicely, shoes in plastic bags on the bottom, disperse the books so nothing is too heavy. Maybe it's all too much. Too weighty and hard to carry. She should travel light and take only the necessities.

As she ponders her pile of things, she knows that she is bluffing. She can't take off. She has no car. No ticket anywhere. Probably only enough money to get her to Weehawken. But she can't stay here anymore. Where then? Katie's? No. She's tired of the human ping-pong ball act, bouncing between Leon and Katie. She needs a swift, clean break. So it's Eliot's again.

She abandons her pile in the middle of the floor. The precondition for a bonfire. She doesn't need a thing because this fling with Eliot will fail, she is certain, and there is comfort in that knowledge. This is the easy part, she thinks as she moves through the apartment, picking up her coat and keys. The part that she does best. The part where she finally gives up and leaves.

# CHAPTER
# NINETEEN

Eliot slowly climbs the stairs to his apartment with the bottle of bourbon in his hand. He is getting too old for these escapades. First, Twyla nearly gave him a heart attack with her antics in Montreal and now Junie wants him to chase her all over Brooklyn. He stops midway up the flight. His back is creaky from the lumpy hotel mattress and he did something funny to his knee during some weird foreplay with Miss Dominatrix. He bends and straightens his leg and rolls his head around a few times. He should start exercising regularly if he is going to get involved with women who expect spectacular performances.

He yawns and hobbles up the rest of the stairs. He should have rested for a day before he called Junie. But he'd left her that note and the boyfriend is out of town this weekend. He really did want to see her. She surprised him at the restaurant. He thought it would be several days, maybe even a week, before he got her into the sack. He hadn't even tried yet. Just bided his time. Oscillating between indifference and interest. Hoping to peak her curiosity before making any real move. When she pulled his hand up her skirt, he figured he had underestimated her. Taken her for a sweet young thing he'd have to coax into mischief. Not that that didn't have its own appeal. It was a beautiful moment, though, sitting in a crowded restaurant with his thumb stroking the crease of her smooth thigh.

He had thought about pulling his hand away and continuing to eat his noodles. Ratcheting up the tension between them. Making her wait longer. But he didn't have the energy for a prolonged pursuit. When he was younger he could have handled two women in two countries on one weekend. Kinky sex in Montreal on a Friday. Long, sultry seduction on a Saturday. No problem. Tonight, he fell asleep beside Junie on the train like some hoary old man. How embarrassing. He hopes he didn't snore. Truthfully, he hadn't expected things to go as far as they did tonight and in a way he is relieved that Junie left. Only he wishes it wasn't under such duress.

He stood on the stoop for several minutes after she disappeared, staring down the dark street, thinking that she would return. He even thought about going after her. Not running and calling her name or anything theatrical like that. He's never gone for drama. But slowly walking, a midnight stroll, expecting to find her on a bench somewhere, maybe even waiting for him. Then he decided not to bother. He's too old for cat and mouse games, especially if they involve traipsing all over Brooklyn near midnight.

And what is Twyla doing in New York anyway? Her film doesn't wrap in Canada until the end of the week. All night he has feared that she will suddenly appear. Part of him wanted it to happen. Twyla on one side. Junie on the other. His perverted mind could go in all sorts of directions if he weren't too exhausted to fantasize. He wouldn't mind seeing Twyla again sometime, but good God, he needs to rest first.

Inside the apartment, he smells the unmistakable stench of cat vomit before he even turns on the lights. "Christ," he mumbles. Not what he needs. All he really wants is to drop in bed and sleep until late tomorrow morning. He tosses the bourbon on the couch, then walks slowly through the apartment, turning on lights and sniffing the air. Sometimes he thinks it would be a huge relief to put the cat to sleep, or wring his little neck. Alfie gets crankier and more feeble every year. The vet bills are outrageous. Insulin, abscesses, stomach ailments. Eliot would shoot himself if he had that many health problems. But every time he seriously considers bumping off the cat, he feels hugely guilty. How could he kill the one stable thing in his life just because the cat has become inconvenient?

Eliot looks carefully at every corner, behind every stack of books, beneath the couch. Each space is covered with the fur of long-neglected dust but no sign of what Alfie spewed. The cat has a way of puking in hidden places. Little crevices that are nearly impossible to find and hopeless to clean. He can't be a normal cat that barfs in the middle of the floor and then looks a bit contrite. No, he has to lurk behind bookshelves or under furniture or in the sock drawer so that Eliot discovers petrified puke weeks later or comes upon the slimy remains when he least expects it. Sometimes he thinks Alfie does it on purpose.

"Alfie," he calls from his hands and knees in the middle of the living room. "Where are you, you little piece of shit?"

On the windowsill above the kitchen sink, Alfie fastidiously licks his front paw. The night is quiet. The squirrels sleep in their treetop nests. Every now and then, the moon reveals itself through midnight clouds and shines on Alfie's perch. He hears Eliot clomping through the apartment, cursing. Think, man, think! Alfie wants to say. It's not so hard to locate my sabotage.

In Blackpool, so long ago, his feelings had been quite similar, but the target of his ire was not some silly machine for writing. (What nonsense. Only the laziest of miscreants cannot put pen to paper.) He joined a group who called themselves the Luddites. They roved the city streets at night carrying clubs and singing rallying songs, ready to smash the machinery that stole the dignity of an honest living.

In this modern age, Alfie scoffs at the outcomes of rampant industrialism. Crime, pollution, disease, anomie. Ned Ludd and the boys may not have won the battle against machines, but at least they resisted. Now, once again Alfie will defy the tyranny of his master. Sedition for revenge. And in this life also, the love of a red-haired woman urges him on. Alfie may not be able to woo Junie, but he will be damned if Eliot gets off easy.

"Alfie," Eliot calls. As if the cat will happily run to his master. Gad, the man is such a buffoon. What could sweet Junie possibly see in him? Perhaps she sees nothing in him. She did not return this evening. That is a good sign. Maybe she has finally come to her senses and will soon find her way back into the arms of her one true love for eternity.

Eliot gives up his search. The cat is a wily one. The puke will dry and the smell will go away. Someday, Eliot will happen upon it. No need to spend the rest of the night on his hands and knees. He stands slowly, arching his back, rolling his head, trying to work out the kinks. The search has woken him up. If he goes to bed now, he will likely lie awake thinking about Junie and Twyla. Better he should get some work done. Jot down a few ideas for the Twyla article.

First he would like a drink. He retrieves the bourbon from the couch and carries it to the kitchen. Junie, Junie, Junie, he thinks. I should be sharing a glass of hooch with you. Oh well. He opens the cabinet for a glass. The shelves are empty. Every cup he owns is dirty in the sink. He roots around through the plates and bowls to uncover a coffee mug. As he rinses it, he sees Alfie poised halfway behind the filmy curtain in the window above the sink.

"There you are you son of a bitch," he says.

Alfie looks at him indifferently, then turns his attention to the night again.

Eliot breaks the red wax seal on the bourbon bottle. He pours himself a generous shot, adds two ice cubes from the freezer, then stirs the drink with his index finger.

"Aw, Alfie," he says. "I'm getting too old for all this bullshit." He leans against the sink and sips the cool bourbon. "What do you care, though?" He reaches out and strokes the cat, who continues to ignore him. "As long as you have your food and a place to crap. You've got it easy, old boy." He pats the cat's head but Alfie ducks away from him.

Eliot carries his drink into the living room and sets it on his desk. He turns on his computer and waits for the screen to light. Twyla Smart. What a nut. What can he possibly write? The computer beeps and the cursor blinks. He interlaces his fingers and stretches his arms in front of his body. He needs a good introduction. Something catchy. He closes his eyes to think and places his fingers on the middle row of the keyboard where they land in something sickeningly slimy. He jumps back and snatches his hands away. Looks down to see the mess.

"Goddammit, Alfie!" Eliot roars.

In the kitchen, the cat hops down from the windowsill, slinks across the counter, and jumps on top of the refrigerator. He curls into a self-satisfied ball behind several half-empty boxes of Corn Flakes and purrs loudly.

# CHAPTER
# TWENTY

Leon looks out at the crowd of people with baby smooth faces, full heads of hair, and wide open eyes. When, he wonders as he plays the backbeat, did college kids start looking like this? Surely they are from high school. But not everyone could have a fake ID. It's a college bar so some of them have to be in their twenties. So when did twenty-somethings stop looking like him and start looking like these kids?

As he watches the audience sway and dance, talk and drink, and flirt with each other, Leon is acutely aware that he is no longer young and hip. It's not the first time he has felt old, but the feeling is coming more frequently lately. Sometimes, he seems archaic to himself. He has no tattoos or body piercings. What's worse, he doesn't want any. And if being bald is slipping into passé, then he will be screwed. He'll have to go back to wearing a hat. Junie never liked the hat.

He plays through the songs like an automaton, pondering how age crept up on him. He's nearly thirty. But that can't be old. He knows plenty of people over thirty who are still hip. But hip within the crowd of people in their thirties. So that's the answer, Leon thinks. To be cool in your own crowd and not compare yourself to the young. Surely he is cool in his own age group.

Junie is not near thirty. Barely twenty-five. But she thinks he's cool. At least he thinks she thinks he's cool. Leon compares himself to other people who are thirty. His cousin Sam is thirty-two. He started an Internet company that flopped right after he bought a house in Westchester. Poor schmoe. Leon's old roommate Kenny was cool. But he quit playing the guitar two years ago and became a graphic designer. He's married now and has a kid.

The other guys in the band, they are all in their late twenties. Leon watches them sweating under the lights as they play the same songs for the thousandth time. The gig will end. They will load up the smelly van and drive to a Motel Six where Leon will watch VH1 and listen to Tim grouse about Steve until they fall asleep. Tomorrow they will eat greasy hash browns and runny eggs at Denny's, do the radio interview, then play some lame afternoon festival before loading up their gear and heading home again.

How long can they keep it up? Long enough to make all the hours of slogging for nearly nothing pay off? Leon has very little faith that Angeline, Ms. Epic A&R, will come through for them. More likely he will spend years playing fill after fill while Steve beats the mic stand against the stage and the crowd whoops and hollers between beers. At some point it will no longer be enough. At some point, soon, Leon will need a change.

Between sets, Leon and Tim head out to the parking lot for some air. Leon leans against the van and takes a long sip of cold seltzer water. "You know what I realized in there?" he asks Tim.

"That Steve is a fucking bastard who can't remember his own lyrics?"

"No," Leon says. He has grown weary of complaining about Steve. "I realized that I'm old."

Tim frowns. "You're the same age as me."

"Then you're old, too."

Tim shakes his head. "I don't feel old."

"Look at the kids in there, man. They're, like, twenty-one. They look like fucking teenagers. Compared to them, you and me, we are old men."

"Shit," Tim says. "Speak for yourself."

Leon crosses his arms and looks hard at Tim. "What do we have to show for ourselves? We're both nearly thirty. Neither of us owns a thing. We make shit for a living. We aren't married. We've got no kids."

"At least we do what we want."

Leon paces by the side of the van. "I don't know, man. I don't know. Is this really what you want? To be playing in some college bar in North Carolina? Didn't you think you'd be further along by now?"

"Goddamn, Leon," Tim says. "We're finally getting somewhere and you're depressing the hell out of me."

"I know," Leon says. He slumps against the van again. "Getting old is depressing."

They stand quietly side by side. "You think Epic will pick us up?" Tim asks.

Leon shrugs. "Not counting on it."

"Damn," Tim says.

"You ever think about quitting?"

"And do what?" Tim takes a long drink of his Heineken. "Sell insurance?"

"Plastics."

Tim laughs, then he sighs. "At least you have Junie." He peels off a corner of the beer bottle label. "I don't even have a girlfriend."

"Yeah, Junie's great." Leon misses her then and feels bad for not calling her yet.

"Now you made me depressed," Tim says. "I'm going to go score some weed. You want some?"

Leon shakes his head. Tim doesn't get it. Scoring weed and picking up girls at the gigs isn't what Leon wants. He might feel old but he doesn't want to be twenty again. Worried about how he looks. Grappling with who he wants to be. Looking for somebody to love him. At least he's figured those things out. But sometimes he's afraid of losing what he's got. Ending up old and bitter. Sunk in a recliner with a beer between his legs. His father. Smoking in some bar alone. His mother.

Leon paces the parking lot. He wishes Junie were here. When they first started dating she came to a few out-of-town gigs with him. She sat in the back of the bar and drank bourbon while he played. He loved looking out and seeing her there. After the gig, they'd go to the hotel, make each other laugh, and then make love slowly. He wants to hear her voice then and make her laugh. Wants to listen to her tell him stories about her day. Wants to confess that being on the road with this band has lost its luster. And that he'd rather be home with her.

He leaves the parking lot to find a phone. He should have never listened to those morons in the van. What do Tim and Steve know about having a relationship? A relationship takes work. Constant practice. Keeping up your chops. And Tim said it just now, at least Leon has Junie. So why not do everything he can to make sure it stays that way. On the corner he finds a pay phone and dials. The phone rings four times, then the machine picks up. He glances at his watch. It's eleven o'clock. Maybe she's out with Katie.

The machine beeps and he speaks. "Hey, Junie. It's me. Sorry I didn't call earlier. We got tied up. So anyway, we're here. It's in between sets and I just missed you and wanted to hear your voice." He pauses. "And, I can't wait to talk to you and . . ." He pauses again. "Well, I just wanted to say that I love you. See you tomorrow night."

Leon hangs up and walks back to the bar. He needs some way to show her how much he loves her and how profoundly happy he is that she moved in with him. Phone messages, compilation tapes, dinner and a play, none of that is enough. Especially because this has been hard on her. Junie has always been a little jittery. She needs reassurance to feel she is doing the right thing. Leon likes that bit of insecurity beneath her bold exterior. Women who are too self-assured scare him, because they will never really need him. He hates to feel expendable.

Once, months and months ago, Junie asked him if he ever thought about getting married. This was way before they talked about moving in together. It was one of those obligatory early-in-a-relationship conversations. Leon freaked out when she asked him. Said that marriage ruins good relationships. That what they had was better. Junie said she wasn't talking about them. She never brought it up again.

Leon walks slowly between the cars in the lot. Marriage. Of course, he's thought about it. Thought about it with Junie. Imagined them older and more settled. A few years from now, after he saves up some money and convinces Junie to leave the City. But why wait? He's nearly thirty. She's twenty-five. That's not too young. His mom had him by the time she was twenty-five. People get married at this age all the time and there is nothing to stop him and Junie. Moving in together is a silly substitute. He knows he loves her. Never intends to break up with her.

How would he ask her? On bended knee? No, too anachronistic. Junie would just laugh. He could stick the ring on top of a scoop of butter pecan ice cream. That's too cute. It should be something original and heartfelt. What kind of ring would she want? A diamond? Could he buy a ring at Domsey's? Or maybe a spy ring from a cereal box. Would she think that was funny or just pathetic? He could get something vintage. Estate jewelry. She'd like that.

Leon wants to call her again. Run the whole thing by her.

But he can't ask her what she thinks of the idea. Especially not on an answering machine. That would kill all the romance. He has to think it through. Come up with a plan. Work out all the details to make it perfect and meaningful.

Proposing to Junie seems so obvious now! Why didn't he think of this before? He's a little light-headed. Maybe it's the heat of North Carolina or the excitement of knowing what he wants. But he doesn't have to rush. He can take his time. It's not as if Junie knows what he's planning. He'll save some money. Buy her a nice ring. God, he feels so much better. Even looks forward to going back in the bar and playing. He may be nearly thirty and bald but none of those twits inside have anything over him. He's going to marry Junie someday.

# CHAPTER
# TWENTY-ONE

Junie stands on Eliot's stoop, working up her courage. The moon is hidden, seemingly for good as the clouds have covered the sky like a plague of locusts. Being here is different now because this time she has not come for harmless flirting before flitting back to her comfy life. This time she is here to make a drastic change in her status. No longer girlfriend. Now cheater, liar, strumpet, whore. She can live with that. It feels about right. She tightens the belt of her coat, then reaches for the buzzer.

In the two minutes it takes Eliot to descend the stairs, Junie's mind darts through scenarios, consequences, possibilities for her future and dismisses each one before it fully forms. She hears the steps groan beneath Eliot's feet before she sees him. Then he is there, standing between the doors, looking at her through the window with two lines of surprise, concern, amusement sprouting between his eyebrows. He swings the door open and says, "You're back."

Junie licks her lips. "Yep," she squeaks and wishes her voice were sultry or at least grown-up.

He stands on the stoop with his body between the door and Junie. "Do you want to come in?" he asks.

"Yes."

"Should I leave the door open in case you want to run away again?"

She shakes her head. "I'm not leaving this time."

He nods and climbs up the stairs. She follows. How will they start? Will he take her straight back to the bedroom or undress her in the living room? Should she begin shedding clothes on the stairs? Leave a trail so she can find her way out again? She stands in the middle of his apartment as he locks the door. She has no idea what to do. She's never been an adulteress before. There should be instructions. Maybe she will launch a website.

Alfie runs through the kitchen doorway and meows frantically as he coils around her calves. She bends down to pet him. The cat stands on his hind legs and presses his front paws against her forearm. He licks her nose.

"Can I hang up your coat?" Eliot asks.

"Please," she says. Alfie continues to mewl at her feet as she removes her coat and hands it to Eliot, the perfect gentleman. This is good. Small talk and pleasantries. "Poor kitty," she croons, then picks up Alfie. "Don't you pay attention to him?" The cat crawls from her arms to her shoulder and purrs into her ear.

"Yeah, he's so neglected," Eliot says as he sloppily drapes her coat across a hanger. Junie has never noticed the closet before.

She wrestles Alfie off her shoulder and cradles him against her chest as she steps closer to get a better look at the closet. It runs nearly the length of the room.

"Jesus," she says. "That closet is huge."

"I can store all kinds of crap in there."

"You could rent it out to a couple of NYU students."

Eliot laughs through his nose and Junie thinks, Ah, this is how we'll start. She steps closer.

"Let's get inside it," she suggests and knows an impish grin prowls across her lips.

"Together?"

"No, one at a time," she says and dumps Alfie to the ground. The cat lands on all fours, then whips around and winds himself between her legs again. Junie takes a step closer to Eliot. She reaches out and places her palm flat against his chest. She gives him a little playful push.

Eliot steps back, looking slightly confused with his eyebrows knitting together, but the comma sprouts in his cheek, so Junie knows that he is intrigued. She takes another step toward Eliot but her feet tangle in Alfie's body and she trips. Eliot reaches out to catch her. She regains her balance. Eliot's hand is pressed against her shoulder. Alfie stands on his hind legs and digs his front claws into Junie's kneesock.

"Ouch!" she cries and jiggles free. "What's wrong with him?"

"I don't know. I think he's sick." Eliot pushes Alfie away with his foot but the cat is relentless. He arches his back and hisses, then lunges for Junie's legs again, releasing a caterwauling plea.

"For Christ's sake," Eliot mutters. He lifts Alfie from the floor. The cat sinks his tiny fangs into Eliot's hand. "Ouch!" Eliot yells. "Alfie, you bastard!" The cat goes for him again but Eliot is able to change his grip and avoid the bite. He carries the writhing animal quickly to the bathroom, tosses him in, and slams the door.

Eliot returns shaking his head. "I should probably get him neutered. It might calm him down but it seems like such indignity to take away his manhood."

Junie steps backward into the closet. The coats give against her weight. "Come here," she says quietly. Eliot strides toward her. She holds out her hand for him, which he takes. She pulls him close and finally they kiss. This kiss is what she has imagined. His lips are soft and his tongue is searching. Tiny earthquakes shiver through her muscles. Her hands shake. She retreats, then bends down to the floor and tugs on his hand. Underneath the coats she crawls, pushing shoes aside until there is a space long enough for her to lie down. Eliot is on all fours at her feet. She pulls him on top of her body.

"Here?" he asks.

"Right here," she confirms. "And shut the door."

Every moment during sex with Eliot is unexpected. She never thought through all the mundane details. His hands grappling with snaps and buttons to loosen her clothes. Her body wriggling free from her sweater and skirt. Shoving them off to the side with his discarded pants and sweater. Each of them removing their glasses. Then the skin of her belly and her thighs touching his. His mouth against her breast and her open legs

181

permitting his fingers entrance. She even has a chance to rethink what she is doing. He says, "Just a second. I'll get a condom," and he leaves the closet. She could get up. Put a stop to the whole thing. But she doesn't. She waits for him to return. They begin again. The rhythmic motion pacifies her anxieties about right and wrong and Junie loses her body in the dark, conjoined with boundaries blurry. This is what she wanted. She allows her mind to be blank until they finish with Eliot's strange little yelp of pleasure.

He lies on top of her and she holds him around the base of his back. His head burrows into her neck and she can smell his hair, the perfume of shampoo mixed with the day's accumulation of oil. It is then that she notices the toe of a sneaker under her right thigh and something, an umbrella maybe, poking the top of her head. A plastic bag has stuck to her calf and when she moves her leg it crinkles. She looks up at the coats. The folds of fabric overhead. The smells of outdoors.

Eliot kisses the side of her neck, then extricates himself from her body and props himself up on all fours above her. He gropes for his glasses on the floor. "I'll go get cleaned up," he says.

He turns the knob and swings the door open. Junie closes her eyes against the sudden light. When she opens them, Eliot is climbing out of the closet. She squints to see his ass, the backs of his knees, his calves and his heels, which are dry and cracked. She realizes then that she hasn't seen *it*. His penis. She felt it, held it in her hand, guided it between her legs but she has yet to look at it and isn't sure she wants to. As if that would confirm the reality of what she's done. She wishes then she could pull

the door closed and stay hidden beneath the overcoats, perhaps all night alone or with Eliot beside her, holding hands.

After Jacob's funeral, she waited in the closet for someone to come and tell her what to do. When her father finally opened the door and crouched down to talk to her, she asked if she could sleep inside the closet. He said, "I don't think you'd be very comfortable in there." And she said, "Ya-hunh. Jacob and I used to make beds in here and pretend we lived in a cave. We were lost orphans running away from a bad man. We can get the blankets and pillows out of the bench and take out all the shoes. You can stay here too, if you want."

Her father laughed but not like his usual laugh, which was quiet and soft, more through his nose than out his mouth. This laugh sounded sad, as if someone had dropped it from a tree and it was going to crash. "I think we should all sleep in our own beds." He picked her up and carried her to her room as if she were a toddler again.

Eliot is back at the door. He has a towel wrapped around his thick waist. The hair on his chest is more gray than on his head. Something in his stature reminds her of a rhinoceros, stocky, firm, self-assured in his breadth, but just a little dumb.

She grabs her glasses and sits up against the closet wall with shoes and bags and other things she can't name sticking to her bare skin.

"You coming out?" he says, then laughs uncomfortably.

"Is it okay if I use the bathroom?"

"Sure. I put Alfie in the bedroom so he won't bother you."

She sits up and scoots toward the door. No one has seen her

naked in a long time except Leon and Katie. When she is in the light, Eliot opens his arms. She steps into his hug. "You are so beautiful," he says into her hair.

How trite, Junie thinks. Especially for a writer.

"Can I get you something to drink? Hot tea? Bourbon? Water?" he asks.

"Bourbon would be great."

She turns away and heads to the bathroom. "Junie," Eliot says. She glances at him over her shoulder. "I'm glad you came back."

This surprises Junie. It's the first remotely sentimental thing he's said. She's not sure she likes it. "Thanks," she mumbles.

In the bathroom, she runs warm water into the tub and squats above the drain to rinse herself. There is nothing messy. No sperm trickling down her inner thigh but she wants her body clean. Absolution. The walls to her vagina still pulse a bit when she washes with sudsy lather. She did orgasm in the closet but it wasn't all that great. Frankly, she had expected more. Something huge and explosive. Like nothing she'd ever felt. After all, she'd never had sex under such illicit circumstances or in such a weird place. Although she and Leon had gone through a phase of doing it in the back of the car at a rest stop in Pennsylvania, on the beach at Fire Island, and in his mother's bathroom when they visited her on Easter.

Leon. He seems so far away. Someone else. Someone from her past that she doesn't have to be concerned about. She wonders how that can be. How she can feel so numb about what she has just done? Maybe it will hit her later. The same way the sadness about Jacob creeps up on her at odd times. Or maybe this is what she really wants. It's too confusing to understand. She's too tired to try.

She emerges from the bathroom wrapped in Eliot's towel and calls his name softly. "In here," he answers from the kitchen. She finds him mixing the bourbon and soda. He is wearing navy-blue plaid pajamas. Such conservative and purposeful sleepwear is incongruous with her vision of him as her degenerate accomplice.

The phone rings. Eliot ignores it. The machine picks up. The familiar throaty voice from earlier in the day says, "Be a good puppy. Roll over. Play dead." Eliot quickly heads for the phone. The voice continues, "And call me, you bastard." The answering machine beeps.

Eliot stops in the kitchen doorway. He turns toward Junie. "Sorry about that," he says.

Goosebumps shiver across Junie's skin. She wants to ask but then again she doesn't.

Eliot steps toward her and rubs her shoulder. "You're cold. Do you want something to put on or . . . ?"

"Or what?" she asks.

"Are you planning to stay or go?"

"Do you want me to go?" Her stomach knots. She hadn't counted on all of this. Weren't they just supposed to fall into bed and bask in passion for endless hours? Instead they did it in a closet while Alfie wailed like a demon from the bathroom and now some strange woman is calling.

Eliot stands behind her, wraps his arms around her shoulders, and kisses the back of her neck. "You're welcome to stay," he says.

Where else would she go?

In bed beside Eliot, Junie closes her eyes for sleep. No more torrid sex that night. They have settled in like a couple, with perfunctory kisses and cuddles. She lies on her side with Eliot behind her. His arm is slung across her hips, his hand rests against her belly. His arm, she thinks, is like every other man's arm after sex. They all like to huddle you against their bodies. Lay claim to you. Perhaps it is instinct kicking in. Maybe the hominoids walking across Olduvai Gorge slept the same way before the volcano stopped them in their tracks.

Soon Eliot is breathing heavily against her neck. She hasn't counted on the details of life after sex with someone other than Leon. That this one too would have an arm to sling across her body or possibly would snore or hog the covers never crossed her mind. The sex was easy. Not even a big deal. She'd thought about it enough before it happened so why not go ahead and do it? What's the difference? Adultery isn't really about the sex or shouldn't be. So someone else has entered the part of her body that Leon thinks is reserved for him. (As if there were one of her mother's tiny pumpkin place cards with Leon's name in gold glitter stuck between her thighs.) And she found this encounter somewhat pleasurable but mostly indifferent. How does that matter? Was it cheating when she accepted Eliot's first banana? Or when she masturbated on this very bed with the second and had an even bigger jolly orgasm? At this point, the sex seems trivial. But this! This arm. This breath on her neck. These eight hours side by side while they each dream. This is the onerous burden she will carry back into her life with Leon.

Oh Leon, Junie thinks. Somewhere in the Southeast. Probably breaking down his gear by now and heading toward a motel with Mr. Whipple. Will he think of her when he drifts toward sleep? Would he ever suspect she'd fuck a man inside a coat closet? Damn, she thinks with her eyes wide open. I fucked Eliot inside a coat closet!

Alfie paces from the front door, down the hall, past the bathroom and stops in front of the bedroom door, then retraces his path. He saw the glint in Junie's eyes. Familiar lovelorn stare. Her temperature was up and she was ready. He knows that look.

He left her once, on a narrow bed with red hair splayed across the pillow like spreading fire and her cheeks pink from exertion. Her eyes glistened with tears but her voice revealed relief. "My husband knows," she said and sighed. "But I don't care. I will never go back to him. He stinks of rotting fish." She grasped his hand and held the palm next to her lips. "I want to be here, with you, forever."

"And you shall," he said. "I have a plan." He promised to be back. Promised to make her his wife. Promised her a garden, a maidservant, children, anything she dreamed. She smiled and closed her eyes to sleep.

He joined the blokes who called themselves the Luddites. Spurred on by the love of this red-haired woman, with whom he wanted to make a life, he marched to the factory, intending to reclaim the livelihood that was rightfully his. But something went wrong that night. As he lifted his club over an automatic loom, the door opened. A rectangle of yellow light with the shadow of four men lay across the floor at his feet. He looked up to see. Then loud voices. A scuffle. A crack across his skull. He left the world and his love lying on his bed.

Oh my beloved, Alfie cries in a sorrowful meow. What did I do? Defiled you in the name of passion and then left the world in a fury. All these lives and deaths spent searching to fulfill my promise to you. No wonder she went to Eliot this time. She can't trust Alfie yet. Perhaps she is trying to make him jealous. Well, it's working, Alfie thinks as he paces the floor with murderous thoughts about Eliot. How that scoundrel seduced innocent Junie. Spring blossom. Vulnerable and unsure. He will not let her slip away again. It has taken him these one hundred and eighty-eight years to find her. He will not let her spend another night beside that wretch of a man. But what can he do? Thwarted by merely a door.

If nothing else, Eliot must pay for this treason. Alfie stops in midstride and works up a great wad of phlegm and fur, then expels it onto the Play Station controls. He hops onto the desk and bats the mouse to the ground. Then he works another projectile into his throat and lands it inside the printer. Next he jumps from the desk to the couch to the open door of the closet. As a final insult and revenge upon his nemesis he squats and urinates on the closet floor. Take that! He spits, then trots off to the kitchen for a drink of water and to throw up in the sugar bowl.

# CHAPTER
# TWENTY-TWO

In the morning, when Junie wakes she knows exactly where she is before she opens her eyes. She knows Eliot lies beside her and that Barbarella stares down at them from her perch up on the wall. Junie doesn't want to open her eyes. She doesn't want to see Eliot in the morning. What if his hair is greasy or his breath is foul? She's not ready for those intimacies yet. The morning after is supposed to be fun. They are supposed to roll toward one another and smile, then make love again, this time tenderly since the urgency of sex the first time is now gone. That's how it happened with Leon after he shaved his head and she spent the night.

She rolls to the edge of the bed and faces the wall, then opens her eyes. She listens carefully for Eliot's breathing. It is even and smooth. Slowly she turns her head to peek. His eyes are closed and he is pretty with wild curls and a placid face. The panic coursing through her body lessens and she remembers how sweet and gentle he was last night, how quickly he fell asleep. Nothing like she expected. She is slightly disappointed.

She slips out of the bed quietly and tiptoes to the door. In the hall she steps on something squishy, it mushes between her toes and the ball of her foot slides across the floor. "Gross," she says aloud as she hops away. A line of orange kitty puke dots the hallway. The ammonia smell of cat piss hangs sharp in the air. "Disgusting," she mutters and hobbles toward the bathroom to clean her foot.

"What's wrong?" Eliot says sleepily from the bedroom.

"Sorry for waking you, but Alfie puked all over the hall and I think maybe he peed somewhere."

"Shit."

When Junie comes out of the bathroom, Eliot is on his hands and knees with paper towels mopping up the piles of vomit. "Here, let me help," she says.

Eliot looks up perturbed. "No, don't worry about it." He sits back on his heels. "I can't believe he did this. It's everywhere. In the living room. On the keyboard. In the kitchen sink."

"Have you found the culprit yet?"

"No and good thing, too."

While Eliot is cleaning, Junie slips into the bedroom. Her clothes are in a pile on the floor. She dresses and joins him in the kitchen. "Did you get it all?"

"Yes, I think. Unless he's strategically placed some for me to find later." He dries his hands on a stained dish towel, then turns to her. "Anyway," he says and smiles. "Good morning. Nothing like waking up to cat puke, huh?"

"Nothing like it."

"I don't suppose you're hungry?"

"I could eat."

"You want me to cook or you want to go out?"

"You can cook?" Junie asks.

"No." He laughs.

"We'll go out," she says and is relieved. Getting out, escaping, finding an excuse to leave. These thoughts are foremost on Junie's mind.

"I'll get dressed and we can go. Maybe the apartment will air out while we're gone." Eliot steps toward her and bends down to kiss her on the lips. She reciprocates. "It's nice to be able to do that, finally," he says.

Junie waits for Eliot in the living room, trying to think of a way to leave after breakfast. Of course, she will have to go sometime because Leon returns tonight. Leon. Leon. Leon. Her head aches slightly. A tiny pound inside her skull each time she says his name.

Alfie slithers out from under the couch. She looks at him and shakes her head. "You are in big trouble, mister," she whispers. The cat chatters deep inside his throat as he jumps to her lap and rubs his head against her chin. She strokes his back. "Big trouble," she whispers. "You and me both."

Alfie sits on her lap, facing her, and meows softly. His look is completely earnest. "I know you didn't mean it," she says. He meows again and reaches his paws toward her face. She laughs and bats him away. Alfie tries again. He lands his paws on her shoulders and puts his nose against hers, then purrs loudly.

"You are a weird cat."

Alfie answers with a meow, closes his eyes, and licks her nose with that odd smooth tongue.

"There he is," Eliot says from the doorway. Alfie turns toward him and hisses. "Damn," Eliot says, taking a small step back.

"I think he knows he's in trouble," Junie says.

"I'm going to leave him in the bathroom while we're gone. If he's still sick, I don't want to have to look for more puke."

Alfie dashes off and slinks quickly beneath the couch.

"Dammit, Alfie," Eliot says. He leans over beside Junie's legs to peer at the cat. She lifts her feet and tucks them beneath her lap. Alfie growls and spits when Eliot reaches for him.

"Do you want me to try?" Junie asks.

"I don't want him to scratch you."

"He seems to like me better."

"Yes, I've noticed." Eliot stands up and runs his fingers through his hair. "Let's just leave him. He'll be fine. He must have puked everything up by now."

Alfie cowers beneath the couch with Junie's taste lingering on his tongue. He hears the door open, then close and footsteps fade. He cries, deep and forlorn. He has tried, repeatedly since she first sauntered into his life again, to prompt the memories of their love. Even if she cannot remember exactly who he is, how can she not feel the inexorable passion pulsing between them each time they touch? It seemed for a while as if she were slowly surmising the magnitude of their bond. She came to him alone. Pleasured herself while he looked on. Made him promise not to tell Eliot of her secret.

But now she has gone. Left him brokenhearted. And for what? Some craven milksop who knows nothing of true love. Alfie beseeches the universe in a long, sorrowful meow, "Am I meant to pay? Is this retribution for leaving her the first time that we were lovers? Is this my punishment for transgressions of the flesh? For coveting another man's wife so long ago? I have repented!" Alfie cries. "In the body of a cat, tormented by the knowledge that my one love for eternity cannot be mine. Enough! I have had enough."

He slithers into the farthest dark corner beneath the couch. Lies in dust, decades of cast off skin and hair forgotten. I am nothing but a mote, he thinks. An insignificant speck blown about by the capricious winds of time.

The sky is overcast this morning and the lights are dim inside the diner, so everything seems dull as Junie sits across from Eliot. They eat scrambled eggs and buttery toast quietly while the waitress refills coffee mugs and couples in the booths around them eat thick stacks of pancakes. Have any of the pancake-eaters just cheated, Junie wonders? Can other people tell?

She and Eliot have eaten together before but now everything has shifted. They know things about each other that make small talk impossible. He probably thinks she's a weirdo for wanting to do it in the closet. She keeps picturing the way he bit his lower lip and squinted just before he came. That knowledge fills up the space between them and there is no room left for Junie to discuss a movie or comment on the home fries. So she sits silently while Eliot occasionally smiles at her between bites and she looks away.

When only empty jelly cartons and toast corners remain, Eliot sits back and puts his napkin on the table. He lays his hand on top of Junie's. She pulls away as if she needs both hands to lift her lukewarm coffee to her lips. His touch is too intimate, too revealing. The boundary between illicit and permissible is blurry now. Eliot leaves his hand on the table and stares into his empty coffee mug. Junie wants to tell him that it's tea leaves that portend the future, not coffee dregs.

"So, what do you want to do today?" he asks after a small silence.

"Oh, well, I," Junie searches for important tasks that must be accomplished today. "Errands. And cleaning. I really have to clean. My bathtub is, wow. You don't want to know. Mildew like you wouldn't believe. And I have to go to the library. I'm thinking about grad school. Did I tell you that? My career."

"Your career?" Eliot says with his eyebrows lifted high on his forehead.

"Lack of, I should say."

"Mm-hm." Eliot smirks. "So you're busy, is what you're saying?"

Junie stacks her dishes. Mug on top of eggy plate, silverware inside of mug. "Kind of. Yeah. I have stuff." She mops up spilled water and crumbs with her crumpled napkin.

Eliot crosses his arms and tilts his head to the side. "How about dinner later?"

"Dinner? Yeah. Maybe." She nods. Shakes her head no. Continues wiping up the table. "Let's see. I could call you when I get done with my stuff and . . ."

"Junie." Eliot says her name sharply causing her to swallow the rest of her lame excuses. He laughs a little. "You are not required to spend the day with me. I'm a big boy. I can entertain myself."

This time she reaches across the table. She wraps her fingers around his thick forearm. Bristly black hair tickles her palm as she squeezes. "It's not that I don't want to . . ."

"When's the boyfriend come back?"

Junie retracts her hand. "Tonight," she mumbles.

"You've never been in this position before, have you?" He asks this with what sounds like genuine concern.

Junie narrows her eyes and studies his face. He wears a half-grin of curiosity but his eyes crinkle around the edges with amusement. "What are you now?" she asks. "My mentor?"

He laughs. "I like it when you're a smart-ass."

"Going to teach me how to cheat?"

Eliot leans forward. His hands slip beneath the lip of the table and he finds her knees. "Nope," he says and massages her legs. "You seem to be doing fine on your own."

# CHAPTER
# TWENTY-THREE

Junie walks home from the diner through the park. A balmy breeze brushes through the trees. They sway like sea anemone. The smell is dirt. Good dirt from the thawing ground where grass is greening up. It's too warm for her coat. She takes it off and spreads it on the ground beneath a lofty tree. Remembers the banana in her pocket. Exhibit A. Evidence of her crimes. She could bury it in the soft, cool dirt. Would a banana tree grow with fruit that tempts young women to come and defile themselves in the middle of the park? Would she be some sort of cult hero to grrrls and reviled by various fundamentalist groups?

Once in the backyard, she and Jacob buried a dead baby bird, blue and veiny, fallen from its nest. Its little beak was open but the eyes were swollen closed. Its head looked too big and heavy for its bald body.

"Don't touch it. It might have lice," Junie warned Jacob, who squatted over it and stared. His intensity agitated her. She picked up a big stick to push the bird away so Jacob would stop looking at it. "How can a bird be so stupid to fall out of its own nest?"

Jacob put his hand on the stick to stop her. "Maybe another bird pushed it out."

"It's gross. I don't want to look at it."

"We'll bury it," Jacob said. "Go get a box and some toilet paper and dad's little shovel. I'll stay here and guard it."

Junie didn't have a better idea about what to do so she trudged into the house. Found an empty tea box in the trash and pulled several feet of toilet paper from the roll. She got her father's garden trowel from the back porch. "Here," she shoved them toward Jacob still squatting over the bird.

He carefully shrouded its tiny body, wrapping around and around until it was mummified in the flowery pink toilet paper. Junie stood off to the side gouging the dirt with her big stick. He placed the tiny corpse gently into the box and dug a deep hole right where it had fallen. Junie's stomach sloshed and she swallowed the urge to throw up.

Jacob lowered the box into the ground, then patted down the dirt. He stood and wiped his filthy hands on the seat of his jeans. "We have to mark it."

Junie began to cry. She swiped furiously at the tears with the backs of her hands.

"Don't be sad about the bird," Jacob said.

"I'm not. I hate that stupid bird. I'm crying because you didn't let me help."

"You can mark it then," he said. "Use some sticks or something."

Junie gathered ten twigs from the ground and poked them in a circle around the grave site. She put a pretty rock in the center. "We should pray," she said. They held hands. "Dear God, please let this little bird fly up to heaven with you."

"Amen," said Jacob.

"Amen," said Junie and hoped that they were finished.

Jacob wasn't done, though. He dug up the cardboard coffin over and over again for weeks. "The box is soggy." He always made Junie look. "See the maggots." She hated it but couldn't help peering inside the hole with him. "See its little legs and beak. That's all that's left."

Jacob had such a healthy fascination for his own immortality. He didn't wallow in the inevitability of his death. He played with it. Explored it. Accepted it as part of his life. Like a little seven-year-old Buddhist. Junie was never so carefree. She fretted over his illness. Created secret potions in the bathroom sink out of toothpaste and orange juice and Noxema. Rubbed her tinctures across Jacob's tongue with a bobby pin and then watched him closely for signs of recovery. And she tried to make deals with God. If she ate lima beans and brought down her own laundry and didn't step on any ants, then Jacob would be okay. Or she could take a little bit of sickness away from him. Trade off. If she got the measles, he wouldn't have as many bloody noses. Her final resort was flat-out denial. Jacob wasn't really sick. He was faking.

She has become good at denial over the years. Sitting with her back against the broad, rough trunk of this Norwegian maple, she can look up and lose herself in the patterns of the dividing branches and shimmering leaves until the details of her life seem arbitrary and easily rearrangible. Leon? Eliot? Who are they? What do they mean to her? She is just some person, sitting under a tree. In fact, she could be anyone. A lesbian waiting for her lover. The next great political philosopher, pondering her future Noble Prize–winning theory. Heiress to the Duncan Hines cake mix empire.

She tried that kind of casual modification when she went to junior high school. On the first day, she said she was an only child, loved to ride horses, and her name was actually Janie. The list must have had a typo.

"Didn't you have a brother who died?" some boy with pimples on his chin asked in front of the whole class.

"No," she said and felt like telling him to shut his stupid zitty face.

"Yes, you did. My cousin lives across the street from you. You had a brother who died from some disease."

Junie denied it but the next day the teacher handed her a pass to visit the school psychologist during phys ed. "I didn't lie," Junie told the shrink. "It's just nobody else's business."

Such transparent denial only lasts so long. In that case about forty seconds. But deeper denial can go on for years. Such is the sinew holding together Junie's relationship with her parents. The three of them have developed an elaborate system of negation in order not to deal with the most obvious problems in their lives. Jacob's death did not affect us. We will not discuss anything bad in our lives. To ignore something so big and overwhelming takes a lot of effort. Junie's not sure she has the energy to do it again. So at some point, yes, she will have to deal with her current predicament. Leon or Eliot?

Or both? She could settle into a life of duplicity. Eliot said himself that she is doing just fine at cheating. It wouldn't be so hard. Leon during the week. Eliot when Leon is on the road. Take what she needs from each of them. How long could she sustain it? Until some random Sunday, while she and Leon fold socks, the memory of Eliot in the coat closet that lurks in the back of her mind will surface and she will blurt out, "I had sex with someone else!" Or maybe not. Maybe she could will herself to forget about it. She could just go home. Actually clean the apartment and throw herself into finding a real job. Pretend nothing happened between her and Eliot. Promise herself that she will never speak to Eliot again. Everyone is allowed one mistake, right? One giant error. That doesn't make her such a bad person, does it?

At dusk she stops on Seventh Avenue and debates between bourbon and cigarettes. She needs something to soften the edges of her guilt. She ducks into a liquor store for another bottle of Maker's Mark. She hates the smell of cigarettes and if she's drunk it will be easier to face Leon.

Opening the door to their apartment, she is greeted by the aroma of moldering banana. She sees the answering-machine-light blinking and pushes the button. Leon's voice. Professing his love. Yesterday that was all she wanted to hear. Now it is too late. Was she with Eliot in the closet at the same time Leon called? The universe loves a good mean joke. In the living room, she tosses her coat across the couch. The banana flops from her pocket onto the floor and bounces out of Junie's sight underneath the couch.

"Goddamnit," she mutters and lays on her stomach on the floor. She gropes beneath the couch for the banana but can't reach it. The smell of the rotting banana in the trash is already strong, nearly intoxicating, as if the fruit has begun to ferment. The second one beneath the couch is badly bruised and will begin to smell soon. Junie doesn't care. It's too much trouble to take out the trash or root around under the couch anymore.

In the bedroom, Junie strips off her guilty clothes and adds them to the pile on the floor. She should pick everything up. Put it all away. As if nothing has been disturbed in the last twenty-four hours. Not now, though. Later. She wraps herself in a soft white robe, then draws a hot bath, dousing it with pink foamy bubble wash. She will pamper herself tonight. While the tub fills, she pours herself a small tumbler of bourbon.

After she finishes her drink and pours another, she eases herself into the bathwater and leans back against the cradle of the tub. It's nice to be alone. Maybe she should get her own place. Forget about Leon and Eliot. Or date them both openly. Make no commitments. Be her own strong, independent woman without definitive ties to a man.

In the warm water, with bourbon smooth across her lips, Junie imagines packing up her stuff, telling Leon she still cares about him but she has to do this for herself. She could rent a studio apartment over a deli. She would run into Leon on the street. Kiss him on both cheeks. Suggest they meet for a drink.

Sometimes she would see Eliot. She would make very clear to both of them that she doesn't want a boyfriend just now.

She drinks more bourbon. Wishes she had brought the bottle. The bathwater has become tepid. With her foot, she spins the hot water tap. The tub fills and her body flushes from the heat. She feels a little dizzy as she finishes off the bourbon. Then her ribs ache. It's a familiar feeling. As if there is an anomalous organ beneath her bones that no one has yet discovered. She presses her fingers against her sternum. The bubbles part. She imagines she could unlock this plate, spread open her ribs, and release whatever is inside of her like bats rushing from a dark cave. But the feeling moves as Junie tries to put her finger on it. Shimmies and quivers as she breathes. It falls, down through her stomach and into her guts. Changes shape and hides between her mucky organs.

A little whimper escapes her mouth. Tears that she's swallowed for weeks. She lets them come, roll down her cheeks, drinks more bourbon to coax them out. She cries silently in the bathtub and isn't sure why. She hugs her knees close to her chest. Most of the bubbles have popped and the water is murky. She releases her clasped knees and settles her body under the water again. Tiny bubbles nest on her skin, in her pubic hair. Her toes stick up out of the water. She and Jacob took baths together. His was the first penis she ever saw.

"It's a turtle!" he said and hid it beneath his palms.

"What's mine called?" she asked her mom, who soaped a washcloth from the edge of the tub.

"Vagina," she answered through tight lips.

"Gina, gina, gina, gina!" Junie and Jacob chanted.

"VA-gina," their mother corrected tersely.

"VA-gina, VA-gina, VA-gina," they repeated.

Junie laughs a little. Their mother was so uncomfortable even then, when they were both alive and healthy and happy. Junie thinks she should give her mother a break. Call her about the Walk-a-Thon. Humor her a little. For God's sake, the woman did lose her son. Her sweet perfect little son who was so smart and so cute and never had to go through puberty and get gawky and ugly and greasy and temperamental. Who never lied and never got turned down by all the good colleges and never lost a job or fucked up a relationship or got drunk in a bathtub and cried and laughed for no reason. Yes, yes, her poor tight-ass mother who was stuck with Junie for a daughter. Junie, who secreted Jacob away to hiding places while he was sick, then asked all the wrong questions after he died. Well, fuck her mother. Junie is not going to call.

She stands up in the tub. Her head spins. "Wheeee!" she says out loud. She wraps her warm body in her robe and pads through the dark apartment into the kitchen where she stands in front of the fridge staring at the stew, feeling guilty. She isn't hungry. Just a little queasy. She closes the refrigerator door. The blinking light of the answering machine catches her eye. Someone must have called while she was in the tub. Leon again? Eliot, maybe? Would he do that? She pushes the button and stands back a little ways, afraid to hear who it might be. Her mother. Again. Wondering why Junie hasn't called. Saying she really wants to talk about Junie's pledge. Junie should call her.

Wants to call her. Wishes she could tell her about the predicament she's in and ask for advice.

Junie dials her parents' number. Her mother answers, a breathless hello, as if she were in the middle of something more important. "Mom, it's me," Junie says.

"Junie. Oh good. I wondered when you would call. When I didn't hear from you, I thought maybe you and Leon had broken up."

"What?" Junie is immediately furious. "What is that supposed to mean? It's not like you've been looking for me for a week." Junie hears her voice creeping up and up to a shrill and hostile pitch. "And why would you assume that we broke up?"

"Well I don't know Junie. It's just what I thought. Don't you think you're being a little sensitive?"

Every conversation this happens. Her mother drops some snide remark and then claims Junie takes offense at nothing.

"Anyway," her mother goes on. "I'm just on my way out the door. Have you decided how much you want to pledge?"

Junie can picture her mother in a smart sweater set and coifed dyed blonde hair. She is standing in the kitchen, next to the microwave, gathering her keys and checkbook. The pledge list is hanging on a clipboard next to the phone.

"That's not why I called." Junie picks at the edge of the dancing lobster magnet on the fridge.

"I do need to know. I have to turn in my pledge list at tonight's meeting."

"Would you forget about the stupid Walk-a-Thon," Junie

snaps. There is a pause. A hard little silence. Like hitting the stone of a peach.

"I hardly think it's stupid." Her mother's voice is tight. Junie sees her face when she says this. How her perfectly plucked eyebrows raise and her mouth purses.

Junie thinks about hanging up. Never calling again. It would be easier than these strained conversations where nothing ever really gets said. She can't do it, though, because abandoning her mother means being abandoned herself and that is more terrifying than enduring her mother's subtle scorn. "Fine," Junie says. "It's not stupid. How much do you want?"

"I know you're not working."

"Jesus, mother. I am working." She pulls the magnet off the fridge and squeezes it in her palm.

"Temping."

"You know what? Forget it," Junie says. "Forget I called." But she is bluffing. She doesn't put the receiver down. She keeps it pressed against her ear.

"All I want is some support," her mother says quietly.

Junie closes her eyes and leans her forehead against the cool refrigerator. "So do I."

"For what?" her mother asks incredulously.

What should Junie say after seventeen years of silence? Surely there's a moratorium on how long she can hold her parents accountable for the shitty job they did. And what would she say anyway? Spew a laundry list of needs unmet and current problems. Even the thought of such an endeavor is exhausting. "How's twenty bucks?" Junie asks.

"Two dollars a mile. I'll put you down. Anything else?"

There is nothing more to say, but Junie would gladly stay on the line and listen to her mother breathe. "No," she says. "Good-bye."

Junie walks slowly to the bedroom, more tears creeping down her face. She hates this bitter, salty water cried over her mother. Wipes angrily at her eyes and bunches her fingers into two tight fists. It is futile to expect anything from this woman who dealt with grief by packing Jacob's stuff away in neatly labeled cardboard boxes. Junie found a purple magic marker and wrote "See ya', Mel!" in tiny script on the sides. Her father created perfect flowerbeds surrounded by even brick walls in the yard. Beneath the hydrangea bushes and day lilies, Junie buried Jacob's treasures, seashells, polished rocks, green-plastic army men. Then she lay in the storage bench, waiting for Jacob to float through the lid and tell her what death was like because his death was different than she had expected and no one was explaining.

No one even noticed when Junie went missing for hours. She lay inside the bench, waiting for her mother or father to realize that she was gone and to call her name, frantically pleading for their daughter's safe return. Junie vowed to stay inside the bench until one of them had to retrieve a blanket. It could take days or weeks. She could picture it so clearly. Her mother would lift the lid to find Junie lying there nearly dead from lack of air and food. Her father would pick up Junie's limp body and they would sob over her, finally seeing how wrong they had been not to miss their daughter.

Junie never carried out her childish fantasies of revenge

against her parents. And now she's way too old to hatch such schemes. Her urge for vengeance has gone underground, become the resistance movement, and created a disenfranchised daughter who lurks around the periphery of her parents lobbing stones at them. Tonight, though, she's too exhausted to plot a counterstrike against her mother's indifference. What Junie needs is sleep. She takes off her robe and slips between the cool sheets, naked. Too tired even to find pajamas. The soft fabric of the sheets is lovely against her skin.

From the shadows across the room, she makes out the shapes of Leon's possessions. Through the bedroom doorway she can see the outline of the sofa. The lump of a Thai throw pillow he bought her last Christmas. And by the kitchen doorway, Leon's tower of CDs, the sound track to his life. She misses Leon then. Misses his smell. Running her finger along the soft skin behind his ear that has never been exposed to harsh life. The hair on his belly that gets wet and slick like an otter when he comes out of the shower. The strange indentation on his chest where his sternum dips toward his heart and makes a perfect pillow for her head.

Every time she hears a car door shut, Junie's muscles contract, ready to spring, fly away, pounce, and cling to the ceiling like a cartoon cat. But no one comes up the steps for the hour that she lies in bed and she begins to worry again. It would be just her luck if fucking someone else was the last thing she did before Leon dies in a horrible head-on collision with a Mack truck. At least he would perish thinking that everything between them had been fine.

No. Junie rolls to her stomach and buries her face into her pillow. This line of irrational thought has gotten old. Her real fear is not Leon dying. It is that Leon will keep coming home and she will continue to feel like a complete fuckup. The girlfriend who could never love him enough. The daughter who could never pull it together. She is afraid that she will live up to all her lowly expectations of herself. She squeezes her eyes shut and wishes she could take it all back. Erase time. Pick herself up and carry herself across some timeline, then plop herself down at the last moment when she and Leon were happy. Maybe right before she met Eliot at the vet's. Or the first time she wore the *Charlie's Angel* tee shirt to bed. She would work so much harder this time if she had another chance.

# CHAPTER
# TWENTY-FOUR

Empty thunks bang along the hallway walls. Junie wakes with drool pooling on the pillow beneath her cheek. Leon is coming up the stairs. The sounds of drums are unmistakable. Then Leon is at the door, jingling his keys. Everything he does has melody. How could she forget that he is music? How could she forget to love him? She hops out of the bed and runs around the floor, kicking her pile of clothes to find some kind of pajamas. Nothing appropriate surfaces, then the door opens and Leon steps inside.

She can see his shadow against the door. He lifts one drum at a time over the threshold. Bass drum, toms, snare, and cymbals lined up against the wall. Leon locks the door and turns toward the living room. She hears him sniff, a quick little inhale through the nose. That nose that ponders herbs in oil now considering the odor of rotten fruit. She runs and jumps back onto the bed, hoping she can feign sleep, but the squeaking of their old box spring gives her away.

"Junie?" he calls.

Junie knows that she should answer. Roll call response, Here! Instead she sits up and watches him walk through the kitchen and living room. "Junie? Is that you?"

She tries to speak but phlegm has collected in her throat and no sound can get past. She huddles against the headboard and pulls the sheet tight around her body before she clears her throat and tries again. "Yes," she says.

Leon leans against the bedroom door frame. "Hey, what are you doing?"

"Sleeping."

"Sitting up?" he asks with laughter in his voice. His words float across the room to stick against her clammy skin.

"I heard you."

"Did I wake you?" He stands above her. A wall of Leon.

Junie reaches out and grabs his belt buckle, then pulls him down into a kiss. "I missed you," she says.

He laughs between her kisses. "I missed you, too." Junie opens the sheet to reveal her body. Leon smiles and says, "Damn, it's good to be home!"

Leon breathes smooth and easy, sprawled naked across the disheveled bed. The man is nearly narcoleptic after sex. Junie sits up and hugs her pillow while she watches him in the half-dark. The sex was good. So good, in fact, that Junie is freaked out. They haven't been so strenuous, so inspired, so noisy and willing to give themselves over to each other since Leon went out on the road with Mr. Whipple for the last three weeks of

February. When he got back, Junie nearly orgasmed at the sight of his shining head. No sooner was he in the door than he had her perched on the kitchen counter, panties around her ankles, his tongue reducing her to frothy ecstasy.

They'd planned dinner out that night but they never made it past the couch, then the armchair, then the bed. It was that night that Junie decided she could try a long-term thing with Leon. Not just because of the sex. But because she had been so desperately happy to see him again. Tonight guilt was the only fuel for her passion. She lies beside him with her pillow clamped tightly to her body and she matches her breath to his.

After Jacob died, she crept into her parents' room every night and lay on her belly beside the bed to listen to them breathe. She had to hear that gentle swish of air in and out before she could sleep because suddenly she knew, death could kill anyone. Her mother. Her father. Her grandmother. The neighbor's cat. Even her own existence seemed precarious. To comfort herself she would match her breath to her parents', find the rhythm of their inhales and exhales in her own body, certain that if they could just stay together, breathing, no one else could slip away as easily as Jacob had.

She hugs her pillow tighter and wishes she could roll on top of Leon. Press down on him until her ribs would open up like cage doors and the strong suck and pull of her blood surging would drag him in to scrub out all the muck that keeps her from loving him enough. Maybe it's your fault, she says silently to Jacob. If you hadn't died, maybe I would be capable of having a decent relationship.

She played that game all the time when she was growing up. If Jacob hadn't died, her grandmother wouldn't have moved to Florida. Her father would have remembered to pick her up from piano lessons more often. Her mother would have been home when Junie had strep throat and started her period for the first time. But the game is not fair. Who knows what would have happened? She'd probably be just as screwy and in the same exact mess. She can't blame Jacob. He wasn't the one who crawled inside the closet with a pervert like Eliot.

Junie watches Leon slumber peacefully, as if nothing has happened to ruin his happy life. Her remorse is immense. Not just because she will hurt him so badly when she confesses—and she will have to tell him because Leon deserves more than her infidelity—but because of what she's lost. No longer will she be privy to the way he sees the world and how he makes it all so terribly funny. Or see his eyes open a bit wider when she comes in the door. He won't greet her with a hug, with his arms gathered at the small of her back, or squeeze her so that her body fits his perfectly like Lincoln Logs. She has lost the privilege of dancing to his perfect rhythmic grooves and of tasting the food he makes with love. She has thrown away all of these things. And for what? Absolutely nothing.

Junie rises from the bed. She finds some clean panties and pulls Leon's tee shirt over her head, then pads into the living room. She curls into the armchair and tries to summon the courage to tell Leon the truth. A few minutes pass and she hears Leon stirring. The bed squeaks as he lifts himself. She hears the fabric of his boxer shorts slide against his skin. Then he is in the living room, standing over her and smiling.

"Can't sleep?" he asks.

Junie has no words just then. Leon bends to kiss her on the lips. She turns her face and he catches her on the cheek, then runs his fingers through her hair.

"Hey, I forgot. I brought you something." He goes into the bedroom and returns with something in his hand.

Junie extends her fingers to accept his gift. It's small and rubbery. She bends it between her fingers.

"It's a magnet," Leon says. "Elvis."

Junie holds it up to catch some light against its surface. She can make out the shape of a person with his hips swung forward but no details are apparent.

"I thought he would look good with Billy Ray and the others," he says. "Do you like it?"

Junie puts the magnet on the table beside the chair. "Leon," she says.

He moves to the couch, sits at the end so his knees are close to hers, leans forward so he is near. "What, babe? What's the matter?"

Junie shrinks into the chair, curls her legs in tight against her chest, and rubs her eyes. "I have to leave," she says.

"Where are you going?"

"I'm not sure. Maybe Katie's."

"Why?"

"I can't stay here now."

"Oh, Junie," he says gently. "It'll be okay. We're going to

make it. Everything will be fine. Don't you see? What just happened in there?" He shakes his head and smiles at her. "That
was phenomenal!"

"I have to go."

"Why?"

Junie shrugs. The question seems funny to her. She wonders
if it matters. Of course she should tell him why but it seems so
trite. "I've been seeing someone else and I slept with him while
you were gone," she says simply and is surprised by how easy it
is to admit.

Leon doesn't move. She watches him out of the corners of
her eyes. "Are you joking?" he asks with an uneasy laugh.

Exhaustion settles over Junie. She wonders if she even has
the strength to leave. Maybe she could stay in the chair. Shrink
down to a dust mite and crawl between the fibers to lunch on
dead skin and lint.

"No," she says. "I'm not."

"What the fuck?" he whispers.

"I know," she says. "I'm going to go. I just have to get some
stuff together." She places her feet on the floor and her hands at
the end of chair arms. The distance between her body sitting
and her body standing seems enormous. "I should have done it
before you got here, but I couldn't. And I know I shouldn't have
done that," she waves toward the bedroom. "But I couldn't help
it. I should have told you first, but I couldn't find the words."

Leon holds out his hand to stop her. Panic contorts his face.
His eyes are wide and searching. His mouth unsure what to do. A
tiny twitch in his left cheek. "You can't just say that, then take off."

Junie pulls herself to a stand. He steps to her and wraps his arms around her shoulders. "Look. I'm sorry I didn't call you from the road. I just thought that maybe I was smothering you. Or maybe we were taking each other for granted and I needed to back off a little."

Junie can't believe that he is touching her gently and taking the blame. She wants him to handle her roughly. To kick her out. She wants to fall to her knees and repent, be punished, like some Biblical character cast out and smote. She squirms away from him. "I'm the one who fucked up, Leon," she says.

"You can't just leave me, though."

"I think I should, don't you?"

He steps away from her. "I think you should explain!" His outburst startles Junie. She's rarely heard him shout. "Why the fuck you did this. Who it was. What you want." He growls his words. Anger makes his consonants snap.

Bile creeps into the back of Junie's throat and she swallows. "I'm not quite sure."

"That's not good enough, Junie," Leon snarls. He paces the floor in front of her. "You're going to have to do better than that."

Junie can see the pulse at the side of his neck and his cheeks are suddenly ruddy. He is beautiful in his anger.

"You're at least going to have to tell me who," he demands.

"Eliot," she says.

Leon stops in front of her. He narrows his eyes and his nostrils flare. "Who the fuck is Eliot?"

"The guy with the cat."

"The cat?" he says bewildered. "The fucking diabetic cat?" June nods. "You slept with the moron who keeps a diabetic cat?" Junie nods again. Leon shakes his head over and over. "I don't get this," he mutters. "I don't get this at all. I come home and you are in bed naked, then you pull me into the bed and we have the best sex we've probably ever had and now you tell me you slept with some asshole with a fucking diabetic cat while I was gone." He leans down and stares into her eyes. "It's a cat, Junie. A cat. Not a person with diabetes. He keeps a cat with diabetes!"

Junie steps back a bit. "I don't see what Alfie has to do with this."

"Who the fuck is Alfie? Did you fuck him, too?"

"Alfie is the cat."

Leon's chest rises and lowers. "I'm not talking about the cat!" he yells. "I'm talking about you. The person who had sex with someone else while I was gone, then comes home and does it with me as if everything is fine."

"I didn't mean to," she says meekly.

Leon stops and stomps one foot against the floor as he tosses his hands up in exasperation. "You didn't mean to! What the fuck is that supposed to mean?"

Junie feels the heat coming off of Leon's skin. She wants to touch him then.

"Answer me!" he orders her.

"I mean I didn't have sex with him because of you. And I didn't have sex with you because of him." Slowly she backs up to the bedroom door to escape before she makes things worse. "Look, it's a lot more complicated than that. And yelling at each other won't help. I did it. It was fucked up and I should leave." Junie steps into the bedroom and closes the door behind her before Leon can say anything.

She stands with her back against the door for several seconds to catch her jagged breath. Then she slides down the door onto the floor where she crosses her arms over her knees and buries her head between her legs. She sucks in air, trying to stop her head from spinning.

When she feels more stable, she thinks about what to take with her. What is in that pile on the floor? She can't lug it all with her now. Then she thinks, underwear. Always take extra underwear. The one piece of advice her mother gave her that has stuck. She lifts herself from the floor and walks to the dresser. She takes out a handful of panties and tosses them on the bed, then does the same with socks. A few tee shirts, some pants, a pair of shoes. She starts to pull Leon's tee shirt over her head and change into one of her own, but she stops when she catches his scent in the fibers. She shoves the wads of clothes on the bed into her backpack and slings it all across one shoulder. Then she kicks her pile farther into the corner.

Junie opens the bedroom door and sees Leon sitting on the couch. He has turned on a lamp and tears sparkle on his eyelashes. She walks silently to the bathroom for her toothbrush. In the mirror she sees herself. Ravaged. As if she were staring at an older stranger whose eyes are bruised beneath the blue glasses. Whose lips are dry and skin is sallow. Whose hair has faded back toward auburn and is brittle with random pieces levitating off her scalp.

Junie wishes she could shave it all off. Make baldness the mark of her deception. A penance. The same reason she wanted to shave it when Jacob lost his hair. Contrition for her sorrow or punishment for not being the one who would die. But her mom said no. Junie remembers now. Her mother reached out for Junie's head and smoothed her hair across her scalp. No, she said. You have beautiful hair. That is the last time Junie's mother touched her with pure affection. After that, there was a hesitation and a distance in her mother's touches, as if she were patting a stray dog.

As Junie walks back into the living room, Leon holds out his hands to her. Tears roll down his cheeks. "I'm sorry I yelled at you," he says. "I'm calm now. I won't get angry again. I promise."

"Oh, Leon," Junie says and wishes she could comfort him but she doesn't know what to say. "I should go."

"Why are you leaving?" he asks.

"Because what I've done is unforgivable."

"I get to decide what's forgivable. Not you."

"Well," she says. "I can't forgive myself and I don't know how to make it right."

"Just stay and let's talk about it." He reaches his hand out to her. She weaves her fingers into his. Familiar fingers. Talented hands. She always did have a thing for drummers and the secrets their fingers hold. "Come here." He tugs on her hand and she follows his lead to stand between his legs with his thighs squeezing against her knees. Staying is tempting. Curling into him, pressing her ear against his chest. Forgetting the whole damn thing happened.

"Don't you want to work this out?" Leon says. "Don't you love me?"

Junie thinks for a moment about the truest answer she can give him. "I don't even know if I know how."

He drops her hands. "That's such bullshit. It's just an excuse." He grinds his teeth together so that the muscle on the side of his jaw makes a knot. Junie feels defeated. She tried to be really honest and he doesn't believe her.

"You're going to him, aren't you?"

"No," she says. "I'm going to Katie's." She bends down for her backpack and slings it over her shoulder again.

"Well, fuck you, Junie!" he yells after her. She nods and closes the door quietly behind her.

# CHAPTER
# TWENTY-FIVE

At the bottom of the stairs, Junie pauses and looks at her name beside Leon's on the mailbox, announcing some vague commitment to be together. How long will it take for him to remove her name? To purge every reminder of her existence from his life? Has he started erasing her already? Tossing out pictures, clothes, books. Would he light a fire to her pile or give it all to the Salvation Army? Could she buy back her life at a deep discount?

The night is clear and warm. It has been the first day without a whisper of winter in the air and this feels like some false promise. As if spring and baby chicks and daffodil blossoms will bring with them a happier life. Junie walks toward Katie's apartment and wishes she had brought the bourbon because now her head is pounding and she could use another drink. At Katie's stoop she presses the buzzer and waits. She hasn't called to see if Katie is home. She might be out with the boy. She might not come home at all tonight. Junie begins to mutter, "Come on,

Katie. Come on." Katie doesn't answer after the fifth buzz and Junie collapses to the steps.

She tries to keep her head clear and lists her options:

1. Go back to Leon and tell him she has changed her mind. Stay up all night trying to explain why she slept with Eliot, why she can't love Leon enough, why she is such a failure as a girlfriend. All of which will be impossible because she hasn't figured it out for herself yet. At some point he will either become very angry and kick her out or he will forgive her and expect her to stay. Neither of which she wants right now.

2. Go to Eliot's. Tell him she changed her mind and decided to leave Leon for him. He might not want her there. Or he might and then he will expect her to have sex with him. She can't deal with either of those outcomes.

3. Sleep in the park, where she might be maimed or murdered.

4. Sit and wait because there is nothing else she can do.

Option four makes her cry. Then she sobs. Lets torrents of tears streak down her cheeks. She rubs her nose against her shoulder, trailing snot across the fabric of Leon's shirt, and this makes her cry harder.

"Junie?" Junie looks up to see Katie walking toward her. "Is that you June Bug?" Katie is not alone. She is with a very tall man in horn-rimmed black glasses and a Count Chocula tee shirt.

"Hi," Junie squeaks.

"Oh my God," Katie says and climbs the steps to her side. "What's wrong?"

"I fucked it all up." Junie sobs.

Katie wraps an arm around Junie's shoulders and hugs her close. "It's okay," Katie says. She looks at the tall man, then back to Junie.

"I'm sorry," Junie says, trying to stop herself from crying. She wipes her face on the bottom of the shirt. "I didn't know that you'd be on a date."

"It is a rare occurrence," Katie says. "This is Mike."

"Hey," the tall man says and lifts a hand limply toward Junie.

"Hi, Mike," Junie says, then mutters, "Sorry."

"No problem," he says.

"Come on." Katie squeezes Junie's shoulders and begins to lift her. "We're going inside for some tea."

Katie speaks to her like she's a child or an invalid and this tone feels comforting to Junie. She wishes everyone would whisper around her like they did when Jacob died. Junie looks up at her friend. Beautiful Katie on a date interrupted.

"No," Junie says. "I'll go."

"Shut up," Katie says and puts her key in the front door lock. "You'll come up. We'll have tea."

Junie looks at the tall man. He seems uneasy. Katie glances over her shoulder at him.

"I think I'll head home," he says.

"Bye," Katie calls and opens the door for Junie.

"Oh, Katie." Junie sobs again. "I'm so sorry. Was that the guy? He's kind of cute."

Katie holds Junie's hand and pulls her up the steps. "He's dull as shit. All he talks about is sampling street sounds and programming them in his keyboard. Thinks he's writing an urban soundscape symphony. I probably would have had sex with him just to shut him up."

Junie lays her head against Katie's shoulder. "You are so very good to me."

"Somebody has to be." Katie squeezes her hand and leads her inside.

# CHAPTER
# TWENTY-SIX

Junie left. Maybe hours ago. Leon has no idea how long it's been. He sits on the couch and cries and curses and beats his fists against the dusty cushions. He can't even think of someone to tell that she slept with someone else, packed a bag, and walked out the door. The guys in the band will just say, Fuck her, man. They have no clue about relationships. They were the ones who told him not to call her and look what it has gotten him. He certainly can't call his mother or father. What advice could they give him? Smoke up. Have a drink.

He picks up the phone to call Katie. Sits with it clutched in his sweaty palm and stares at the numbers on the push pad. He tries out several beginnings in his mind:

Katie, please let me talk to Junie.
Katie, I know she's there so put her on.
Katie, put that bitch on the phone now!

But he doesn't dial. What if she isn't there? What would he do then? The thought makes him pace the floor again. He lumbers from the kitchen through the living room into the bedroom. Racks his brain to figure out what has gone wrong. To pinpoint the moment when things began to change between them. Tries to remember every detail he knows about this asshole Eliot.

Leon wonders if Junie has been sleeping with Eliot all along. She has vaguely mentioned him over the past couple of weeks. Plus she was always reading. Curled on the couch, tucked beneath the bedcovers, huddled over a book at the kitchen table. Leon would ask her what she was reading and she would say it was some book that guy Eliot gave her. Leon feels so stupid now. How could he not have grasped that all her attention on the books was just a substitute for her interest in the man? But he trusted her. Of course he didn't think that. Surely there are clues in the novels about who this guy is and what Junie sees in him. Leon never looked closely to see what books the jerk gave her.

He goes to the shelves and starts pulling down random books. What would they be? *Madame Bovary?* He rips it open, expecting to find Eliot's name and an inscription inside the front cover. Nothing. No, too obvious. Even Leon knows that. Dumb, stupid Leon who never went to college. Poetry? A guy with a name like Eliot would probably love poetry. Sylvia Plath? Merwin, Keats, or Yeats? William Carlos Williams? Nothing. *Middlemarch?* But wasn't George Eliot a woman? Leon kicks the books he's thrown on the floor.

What he really needs to do is call the fucker. What is his last name? Surely Junie said it once in passing. Surely that name is lurking in the recesses of Leon's brain. He picks up the phone and punches in 411. James Earl Jones welcomes him to local and national 411 and then a prerecorded operator asks in her lovely voice, "What listing?" Leon huffs into the phone. Good fucking question. What listing? How the hell should he know? What's he going to do? Ask for every listing with the first name Eliot in the neighborhood. He jabs the Off key and tosses the phone to the couch. Then he grabs the phone book and begins skimming through the A's, looking for any Eliot. But how does this jackass spell his name? Eliot, Elliot, or Elliott? Why couldn't he have a normal name that's only spelled one way? Leon slams the phone book closed and throws it aside as well.

Then he remembers that Junie kept some books beside the bed. The room is a mess. Her stuff streams out of drawers and is kicked into the corner. The bed is unmade and there are dirty cups on every flat surface. On the floor, on her side of the bed, Leon finds a stack of magazines and some sci-fi books. He never knew she liked sci-fi. He crouches down to shuffle through the pile of fusty old paperbacks with dark comic book covers. What was she doing reading this crap? Since when was she such a geek? What else will he discover about her tonight? That she's secretly played Dungeons and Dragons since high school and has an on-line persona for fantasy games? Does he really know anything about her?

Buried in the center of the pile, he sees a cover with the name Eliot in big bold letters. He lifts up the book. *Liberty Voyage* by Eliot Bloom. Is that him? Junie never said he was a writer. Leon turns it over, looking for an author photo, but there is none. He skims the back cover blurb. An all-female planet. A sexual amusement park. What the hell is the Lap of Luxury? Sounds like some kind of sci-fi sex romp. Junie read this in their bed? Beside him while he slept? Or worse, while he was gone? Is this whole thing about sex? Leon drops the book, sits back against the edge of the bed, and holds his head in his hands. That hurts. He knew they had their problems but sex is one thing he thought was okay between them.

He's got to call the fucker. He carries the book to the living room and finds the phone book between the couch and the end table. Bloom, Eliot. He traces the invisible line between the name and the number. He picks up the phone and holds it against his head, the persistent buzz of the dial tone like an alarm warning him to stop. He has no idea what to say if he gets hold of the guy. Threaten to kick his ass? And then what? Ask him why? He puts the phone down again and slumps back onto the couch. He throws Eliot's book against the opposite wall as hard as he can. It ricochets, then flies across the room with pages fluttering like many wings. Lands opened and wounded on the floor.

Sitting on the couch, he can think of nothing else to do so he turns on the TV. Carol Brady and Alice make sandwiches for the kids. Six white bread sandwiches with creamy mayonnaise and cold cuts Alice bought from Sam the butcher. Leon feels certain Carol Brady would never wait for Mike to come home from a business trip, fuck him, then confess her infidelity, pack a bag, and leave. And even though Sam and Alice weren't married, they were faithful. Lucy wouldn't leave Ricky no matter what mistakes she made.

Why couldn't Junie be like that? Why did she have to leave? Like his father, who packed a bag and left at four o'clock on a Sunday. His parents hated each other toward the end. They stopped even pretending to get along. Sneered at each other over breakfast. "Do you know what your problem is?" one would say and the other would yell, "You! You're my problem," like a scripted fight off a bad TV show. Then they'd launch into a litany of complaints, dislikes, and petty digs while Leon banged out a rhythm on anything he could find.

Leon always figured his parents just didn't try hard enough. Let things slip until it was impossible to remember what they had liked about each other to begin with. But hadn't he loved Junie? Loved her when she was late coming home? Loved her when she was grouchy for no reason? Loved her even when she confessed that she had cheated? He asked her to stay. She left anyway. Leon closes his eyes and cries silently. Well fuck her, he thinks. He deserves better than that.

Warm air wafts in from the window. A faint trace of rotting fruit lingers in the air. The smell is sickening but Leon is too tired to get up and close the window. He stays on the couch, feeling the tears dripping beneath his chin as he drifts toward an angry sleep.

# CHAPTER
# TWENTY-SEVEN

Eliot shuffles around his apartment. It's too bad that Junie never called. But it's always this way when he's involved with someone who is involved. The remorse. The guilt. The back and forth. Sometimes those emotions are a great aphrodisiac. Other times they kill the romance quickly. Which way will Junie go? If the closet is any indication, things will be just fine.

He runs his finger over the spines of his books. She still has a lot of his loaners. But she will be back. All Eliot has to do is wait. He should write. Start the article about Twyla, that lunatic, but he's not in the mood. He still has a few days until it's due. He'll get to it when the inspiration strikes. For now, he turns on the TV, fires up the Play Station. A few rounds of *Grand Theft Auto* will take his mind off things, then he'll write.

He loses two lives quickly. He isn't concentrating well. Junie at his door. Junie in the closet. Junie in his pajamas, next to him in bed. He never imagined it would happen like it did but that's the fun of Junie. She is unexpected. Where else would she like to have sex? Does she have a thing for enclosed spaces? Is she the kind of woman who stops elevators between floors or pulls men into toilet stalls? He hasn't had sex like that in years. Twyla was fun, too. More aggressive. But he preferred Junie's sweetness and liked that she stayed the night. Had a drink with him. Slept with her body tucked into his. He enjoyed waking up and not immediately screwing again but going to breakfast and basking in the postsex warmth. Until she left. Now he misses her. It's been a long time since he's been in love or even had a crush on someone. This makes him feel old.

Alfie struts by. He stops and watches the screen. "Move it, Alfie." The cat looks at Eliot, then drops down and gnaws on the joystick cord. Eliot swats at him. The cat hisses, then runs away. Eliot's player is dead. "Damn cat," he mutters and turns off the Play Station.

The kernel of a story has lodged itself in Eliot's mind and he actually feels like writing. He wiggles the mouse on his computer and opens a new file. It won't hurt to get a few ideas down before he works on the article.

A bright blast of light seared the midnight blue sky across Kansas wheat fields. A farmer plowing rows of grain stopped and wiped a handkerchief across his forehead. He assumed it was just another shooting star. But one hundred miles away, in the desolate grasslands, the spaceship from Liberty came to a bumpy rest.

•　　•　　•

The hatch opened slowly. The inhabitant carefully climbed out, surveying the surroundings with attentive green eyes. Her grandfather was right. No humans were nearby. Red hair flashed under the beam of a single moon as Ju Ni 1 moved silently across the plains toward the lights of a highway.

The phone rings. Eliot ignores it. It rings again and he picks it up, hoping it will be Junie.

"You're home," says a low, gravelly voice.

"Twyla?" Eliot asks.

"Expecting someone else?"

Eliot paces the living room. "What's going on?" His palms are moist.

"You're a naughty doggy. You've been ignoring me."

"I've been busy."

"Down boy," she says. "I'm coming over."

"This isn't the best time. I'm writing the article about you."

"I'm bringing the leash with me."

Eliot stops. The leash intrigues him. Twyla hinted that she had accessories. And he needs to actually interview her. Besides, Junie left him. She went home to her boyfriend. Who knows what she is doing with Baldy or if she'll ever come back? Anyway, he won't get any work done now. Twyla might even be an inspiration.

"The leash, huh?" he says.

"Let me hear you bark, monkey boy," Twyla growls.

"Woof," he says into the phone.

# CHAPTER
# TWENTY-EIGHT

**K**atie takes Junie upstairs and installs her in the futon under twisted covers and layers of discarded clothes. She puts the cat in bed, too, as if Junie were an invalid or an elderly woman whose life would be extended by caring for some furry beast. Junie thinks it is a cheap reminder that the world does not revolve around her.

"I'll make some tea," says Katie.

"Can I have bourbon in mine?"

"A hot toddy?"

"What is a hot toddy, anyway?"

"No idea," says Katie. "But I'll make you one."

Junie burrows down into the covers seeking warmth and comfort in the smell of Katie. She snuggles the cat close to her side. "This whole thing is your fault," she tells the kitty. "If you hadn't needed shots, I would never have gone with Katie to the vet's and I would never have met Eliot and I wouldn't be in this predicament." The cat looks at Junie and licks his own nose.

Neat trick, she thinks, and wishes she could show such indifference when being accused of ruining someone's life. She lays her head on his soft belly and tries to match her breath to his. She finds herself panting to keep up.

Katie comes into the room with two steaming mugs. "Try this," she says.

Junie blows across the hot liquid. Fumes of alcohol fill her nose. "What the hell is it?"

"Secret potion." Katie pushes clothes off the bed and sits at Junie's feet. "It'll make you forget all your troubles."

Junie takes a sip. Chokes and sputters. "Jesus. It'll make me forget my name. It's awful."

"Old family recipe. Rum, vodka, honey, lemon, and a tiny splash of orange juice." Katie sips her drink. "Perfect," she says through a grimace. Then she shimmies under the covers beside Junie. The cat curls into a sleeping ball between them. "So. What happened?"

The steam swirls off Junie's drink in delicate curlicues. The warmth of the mug seeps into her hands. "I've made such a mess," she says quietly.

"The sci-fi writer?"

Junie nods.

"Leon knows?"

"He does now."

"How'd he take it?"

"He got really angry," says Junie. "That's the first time I've ever seen him truly pissed off."

"What's he like when he's mad?"

Junie sets her drink on the floor and pulls her knees into her chest. "Actually, he's kind of sexy."

Katie chuckles. "You're so twisted."

"He wanted me to stay."

"You left anyway," says Katie.

"He didn't really want me there. He just didn't want to be alone. Didn't want to see the problem. Thinks we can sweep it into a corner and live happily ever after."

"So what *is* the problem, Junie?"

Junie buries her face into her knees and crosses her arms over the top of her head. She groans then looks up at Katie. "What the hell is my problem? I have this perfect guy who loves me but I can't handle it. So what do I do? I go off and have sex with Eliot in a coat closet."

"A coat closet!" Katie guffaws and snorts. "What the hell were you doing in a closet?"

"I don't know," says Junie. "It turned me on. It was so big and dark and . . ." She stops. Remembers lying in the bottom of the quiet closet. First with Jacob. Then waiting for her father after the funeral. More recently holding Eliot around the back. "My brother and I used to hide in the closet together," she nearly whispers. "I felt so safe in there. Like none of our problems could get in. Then there I was again last night, only this time . . ." She bangs her head against the wall. "God, I'm so fucked up."

"You're not that bad," says Katie.

"Don't you think it's kind of weird?"

"You've always been a little weird."

Junie slumps down into the pillows. "It's all my parents' fault."

Katie shrugs. "Isn't it all," she mutters.

"No. I'm serious. They changed so much after Jacob died. They kept forgetting me. At piano practice. I would just sit there on the teacher's steps, waiting. Sometimes, I would hide behind the bushes so that the teacher wouldn't know they had forgotten me again."

"No offense, Junie," says Katie. "I know you're upset, but that hardly sounds like the worst thing that ever happened. Plenty of parents do that who never had a kid die."

Junie hops off the futon and paces across the floor. "It wasn't just that, though. Things got really fucked up in our house. My mom became such a freak." She huffs around the room, gesticulating wildly. "She packed up everything Jacob ever owned. Stuck it all in boxes and closed the door to his room as if we were never supposed to go in there again. Like we were supposed to forget he ever existed. All she did was clean. All the time. Vacuuming at midnight. Repotting her stupid ferns. Dusting until you could see your reflection in everything. Until she started volunteering for the Leukemia Foundation and was never home."

Katie scoots down to her side. Props her head up on her elbow. Settles in for the story. "What about your dad?" she asks.

"He got quiet. Totally withdrawn. I haven't seen my father get mad since Jacob died. Not even raise his voice. Hell, he doesn't even state strong opinions anymore." Junie shakes her head. "Just like Leon."

She stops and leans against the wall. "Sometimes I feel like I've spent my whole life fucking up so my parents would notice me. It's like I'm jumping up and down waving my arms, screaming, 'Hey, look at me!'" Junie bounces on her toes and flaps her arms above her head. "'I can't hold a job! I can't stay in a decent relationship! Look at the loser you raised!'"

"Give yourself a break," says Katie.

"The awful part is, that they don't know how much it affected me. How sad I was. Sometimes I wonder how all that sadness fit inside my body when I was a kid. Where on earth did I keep it?" She jabs a finger into her belly. "Behind my spleen?" Jabs into her chest. "In my lungs? And it's still in there. Festering. Bubbling up at the worst moments."

"So you'll never be a Mouseketeer," says Katie with a shrug.

"Or a motivational speaker," says Junie.

"Maybe you should purge."

"What? Primal scream therapy?"

"Kick-boxing classes."

Junie imagines pinning her parents to the ground and pummeling them with angry fists. "Maybe if I got it all out of me, I could take remedial emotional bonding classes. Learn to love without fear."

Katie looks at her with a sappy grin. "Junie," she says in a whispery voice. "Can you say, 'I love you'?"

"Ee wub shu," Junie blubbers.

Katie laughs. "You're a regular peace-loving earth goddess now."

"Hardly," Junie snorts. She stomps across the floor again.

"You know what I should do?" She stomps back. "I should go home."

"You just got here."

"Not to Leon. To Indiana. To my parents." Junie stands with her fists on her hips. "I've never told them how pissed off I am at them. Not even when I was a snotty little teenager. They always seemed too fragile." She sneers.

"Maybe this isn't the best time to do anything," Katie says gently. "You're pretty upset."

Junie collapses to the futon. "Actually, I'm fucking exhausted. Besides, I wouldn't know what to say."

Katie pats Junie's leg. "Sleep on it. Decide in the morning what you want to do. There's no hurry right now."

Junie crawls beneath the covers and sinks her head into the pillows. "Do you think Leon is okay?"

Katie gathers the mugs from the floor. "I'm sure he's really sad, Junie. But he'll get through it. So will you."

"I suppose you're right," Junie says.

"Can I get you anything else?" Katie asks from the doorway.

Junie shakes her head.

"Want me to turn off the light?"

"Okay."

Katie flips the switch.

"Hey," says Junie to the dark.

"Yeah," says Katie.

"Thank you."

"Any time," says Katie and quietly closes the door.

Junie feels like a child again, left alone, sad in her bed while the grown-ups move about. She listens to Katie's sounds. Water running. Dishes clinking. Ice cracking. The television on low. After Jacob died, she counted on those night sounds to lull her into sleep. Otherwise, she lay awake thinking about how Jacob was really gone. How he would never creep into her bed again and they would never tell stories or sleep with their legs intertwined.

She understood what death meant then. A huge gaping hole in her life. Not just the absence of Jacob. But the absence of everything Jacob. Every moment she would have spent with him. Everything she would have said to him and shown him. All of that was gone and would never come back again.

Sometimes on those sleepless nights, she shoved her pillow into her mouth to hide her sobs, but her father always heard her. He sat on the side of her bed and rubbed slow circles around her back. "Shhh," he would whisper as she cried. "Shhh. Jacob wouldn't want us to be so sad." His voice sounded small. Far away. Inside a room with no windows. Inside a coat closet. Waiting for someone to come and get him, too.

Junie woke up one night not long after they had buried Jacob and saw her mother beside her in bed. Hair fell across her face like a soft brown curtain. Junie reached out carefully to brush those strands away. Her mother's face was creased in sadness and silent crying. It was her mother but it wasn't her mother. It was someone wearing a mask of her mother. She wondered if this woman put the pillow in her mouth, too. Junie leaned close to her face, inhaled her smell, indefinable yet eternally recognizable.

"Jacob loves you Mommy," she whispered. "And I do, too." Her mother's face relaxed for just a second and Junie recognized her again. She kissed her cheek. Felt a moment of relief. As if really, nothing had changed and Jacob was healthy in bed down the hall and this woman with the happy face and familiar smell was her mother, forever. Then her mom's face twisted in anguish again and Junie remembered all the hurt swirling unchecked inside her own body. It felt too big. A wave that would carry her away before anyone could swim out and rescue her.

Junie sits up in bed. How could her parents have abandoned her like that? Left her alone so sad and small to grieve all by herself. She grabs the phone from the nightstand and sits with it in her lap, working up the courage to dial her parents' number. The cat looks at her and chortles deep in his throat, then hops off the bed.

"Chicken," she says to him and punches in the number. The phone rings once. Junie glances at the clock beside the bed. It's nearly midnight. The phone rings again and she hangs up quickly, her finger pulsing hotly on the cancel button.

She can't call them this late. They've probably been in bed for hours. Besides, if she is going to really confront them she doesn't want to do it over the phone. She wants to see their faces. Wants to watch them gnash their teeth and rent their clothing into shreds over their red scratched skin when they realize their mistakes cost them not only their son but their daughter, too.

She could hitchhike back to Indiana. Jump out of a big rig

in front of their shuttered house. Stand on their porch, unwashed and defiant. The opposite of a runaway. A run-back-to. Her mother in all her politeness would invite filthy Junie in to sit on a towel draped neatly over the upholstered furniture and discuss her feelings calmly. But Junie will become the Tasmanian Devil. Whirling, dervish style, slobbering and enraged, through the house until the furniture is overturned, the curtains are in tatters and both her parents understand just how devastating their apathy has been.

All these thoughts of confrontation exhaust Junie. The truth is, she's not even sure that confronting her parents would help. It could make things worse. The easiest thing to do is nothing. Keep on the course she's set in life. It hasn't been so bad. She can stay with Katie for a while. Visit her parents on major holidays. Fool around with Eliot when she's lonely. Find another Leon.

Leon. Poor sweet man. He didn't deserve any of this. Junie feels the tears coming. The aching sobs gathering in her throat. How could she have been so horrible? She pictures him at home on the couch. He'll probably sleep there all night. When he wakes, there will be creases on his cheek where the cushion and his clothing cut into his soft skin. She wants to press her fingers into those marks and smooth them out. She wishes she could call and make sure that he's okay. How can she do that after making such a show of leaving? She lifts the bottom of Leon's tee shirt to wipe the tears from her eyes. Traces of his scent fill her nose and she breaks. The sobbing starts. She shoves a pillow in her mouth so she can recklessly weep herself to sleep.

# CHAPTER
# TWENTY-NINE

**K**atie has been great. Tells Junie to stay as long as she wants. Even offers to take out all the paint and easels from Junie's old bedroom so she doesn't have to sleep on the couch for another week. But Junie says no. Insists she will get her shit together very soon. Although truthfully, she doesn't know what shit it is she should be getting together. Should she find her own apartment? Try to patch things up with Leon? Carry on with Eliot? It's been easier not to think about the mess. Just get up every day, borrow some of Katie's clothes (because she's too chicken to go back to Leon's and gather any of her own belongings), schlump off to work where she despondently licks envelopes or answers phones for corporate giants, then come home and park her ass in front of the television. Every night she goes to sleep in Leon's tee shirt. The one she wore when she left their apartment. It's dirty now but she can't bear to wash away his smell.

When Junie does venture out, she prowls around the neighborhood, ducking into stores with her head bent low, her eyes furtively darting, fearing she will see Leon gallivanting about town with a fine new lady friend. A better version of Junie. Someone taller. Thinner. With raven tresses cascading down her back. She will be smarter. With an important job. Bitch will be a lawyer who does pro bono work for Hungarian orphans when she's not pulling down six figures for suing big tobacco. And she will be funnier. Junie will round a corner, sniveling into her smelly tattered coat, wearing mismatched socks and she will see Leon, head tossed back, mouth wide open, bellowing a massive laugh over some hilarious anecdote Ms. Fabulous has told. Junie already hates the woman's guts.

On Thursday afternoon, Junie comes home from work and sees a yellow Post-it stuck to Katie's answering machine. "Listen to me!" it says in Katie's slanted script. Junie unbuttons her coat and pushes the play button on the machine.

"Hey."

It's Leon's voice. She doubles over as if someone has punched her in the gut. She hovers over the tiny speaker as if by getting closer she will be able to smell him, touch him, feel his body heat.

"Junie."

Her name from his lips. How does it sound? Is that the way he usually said it? He rarely said her name. Always called her babe or honey or sweetie.

"Your mom called."

She listens carefully to each word. Tries to decipher his state of mind from the length of every vowel.

"I didn't tell her anything."

Does he sound sad or just annoyed?

"I said you'd call her back."

Then he pauses, takes a breath. She waits for something else but all he says is "Good-bye." Not "bye" or "see ya'" or "talk to you later" or even "take care." She listens to his voice over and over. Is his tone forlorn or full of forgiveness or verging on complete indifference? That pause near the end. What does it mean? Is he trying to find a way to express some deeper emotion? Or is he just breathing. "Good-bye," he says and it sounds so final.

Junie picks up the phone and sits on the armrest of the couch. Thinks about calling Leon back. Thanking him for the message. Asking him if he wants to get some coffee and talk. She is sweating and realizes she is still wearing her coat. She wrestles it off and drops it on the floor. A wad of green-and-white checks. She wishes Katie were home so they could listen to Leon's message together and figure out what he might be thinking. Katie has been gone a lot lately. She works long hours and takes painting classes downtown. Junie knows she can't expect things to be just like they were before she moved out.

She holds the phone away from her head. She is lonely and would love to hear Leon's voice. She punches the first three digits of his number. It won't hurt to call him. He called her first. But just to give her a message. He was obligated. There was no indication he wanted her to call him back. Katie's cat tiptoes through the room. He rubs against Junie's shins. She reaches down to stroke his fur. The phone waits for the next four digits. She punches in Eliot's number instead.

"Hi, Eliot," she says when he answers. "It's me, Junie."

"Well, well," he says, then chuckles. "Long time. Wondered when you'd call. Boyfriend back?"

"Uh, sort of. Yeah," Junie stammers.

"I know. I called you once. He answered. I said I had the wrong number."

"Please don't call there," Junie says quickly.

Eliot laughs again. "Nice of you to get in touch. Is there something you want? Something you need?"

Why did she call him? He's so clearly a putz. "Just hadn't talked to you since . . . I mean, I just figured I should, you know."

"You want to come over?"

Junie is completely consternated. She has no interest in seeing him but how can she extract herself. She's the one who called him. "Actually, I can't," she says and feels very proud of herself.

Eliot snorts. "I get it. When Baldy goes away again, you know where to find me."

"It's not like that," Junie says. One step forward. Forty-seven back.

"It's any way you want it, toots. I'm around."

"Really I called to tell you that I'm going to be gone for a while."

"Where you going?"

Junie hesitates. Where is she going? Hawaii? On a fabulous all-expenses-paid trip she won in the Girlfriend of the Year Contest. "To visit my parents," she says and wonders what the hell she is talking about. Surely she will pay for this very stupid lie. Every time she leaves the house for the next week, Eliot will be on every single street corner she passes. "It's a family thing. Reunion. Grandparents. Cousins."

"So sorry," Eliot says. His phone clicks. Call waiting. "Listen. I'm going to let you go now, okay?" It clicks again.

"Alright," Junie says and the line goes dead. Good riddance she thinks and slumps sideways on the couch.

The weekend spreads before Junie like a big, empty pool. Dive in and crack your skull. She doesn't have a temp gig on Friday and Katie is going upstate to paint at a friend's cabin in the woods. She invited Junie to come, but Junie said no. She doesn't want to be a total pain in the ass, whining about her miserable life while Katie tries to find inspiration in decomposing vegetation. So she lies on the couch, staring at the ceiling, thinking about the crappy existence she has carved out for herself. Working meaningless jobs. Mooching off her best friend. Hiding from her boyfriend because she's afraid he is happier without her. And now she has to avoid Eliot because she told such a stupid lie. Of course, she could actually go home. Or at least return her mother's call. She probably wants to know where Junie's check for the Walk-a-Thon is. She picks up the phone and dials quickly before she loses her nerve.

Her mother answers on the third ring, breathless as usual.

"Hi, mom." Junie says and realizes that her heart is beating fast. She is nervous. Afraid that her mother will be able to deduce from the first five words out of Junie's mouth that she has ruined her relationship and is sleeping on someone's couch.

"Junie, what a surprise. I only called three days ago."

"I've been busy," Junie mumbles.

"Doing what?" Her mother sounds incredulous.

"I don't know, Mom. Just stuff. Why did you call? Is it about the check for the Walk-a-Thon? I'll send it this weekend."

"No, actually I called to tell you the walk had been postponed until this Sunday. We had tornado warnings here. Maybe you saw it on the Weather Channel. Your father and I are fine, by the way."

"We don't have cable."

"Right. So anyway, don't worry about the money, yet. You can send it next week."

"Okay," Junie says quietly. They sit in silence for a moment. Wasn't there a whole lot more that Junie wanted to say to her mother? She's lain in bed every night going over the conversation she'd like to have with this woman.

"Hey Mom."

"Yes?"

"Can we talk for a minute?" Junie hears the wobble in her voice.

"About what?"

Junie takes a deep breath. Hears it echo back to her through the phone. It's now or never, or maybe later, but now is better. "Jacob."

Her mother is silent. Junie debates hanging up. Forgetting the whole thing. Or pretending she really said *giblets*. I want to talk about making gravy! Then having a good laugh when her mother says, Oh, I thought you said Jacob. Who would want to talk about him, Junie would ask. He's dead! We've all moved on.

"Jacob," her mother says slowly. "What about him?"

Yes, Junie thinks. What about him? What was it that she wanted to say about him? It was something important. Something about how her parents didn't do things right so now Junie is a loser but all she can remember is that image of her mother beside her in bed with the hair across her face.

"Well," her mother says.

Junie can't picture her mother just then as she must really be on the other end of the phone. What color is her hair exactly? How has her face changed since Junie saw her last. And what about her father? In her mind he is young, his head full of hair. He is crouching in front of her in the closet. Who the hell are these people? And how could she intend to crush them under the load of all her problems? She is too small to do any damage.

"Can I come home?" Junie blurts.

Her mother pauses again, then she chuckles. "Junie, is this about the Walk-a-Thon?"

"Yes," Junie says quickly. "It is. I want to walk with you." Junie feels tears dropping from her eyes. Something has gone terribly, terribly wrong.

"It's this Sunday."

"I can get there tomorrow," Junie says. "For dinner."

"Well this is just such a surprise. Are you sure?"

Junie hears clear delight in her mother's voice. Something she has not heard in a very long time. She hesitates. Realizes this is her chance to set the record straight. Tell her mother that no, of course she doesn't want to walk in any stupid Walk-a-Thon. She wants to talk about her life and how her parents have messed it up. But she can't do it. "Yes," she squeaks. "I'm sure."

"Would you like fish or chicken for dinner?"

"I don't care."

"Because I'd planned to thaw a chicken, but if you'd like fish I could run out to the market."

"I really don't care."

"Junie," her mother says. Junie waits. Her mother takes a deep breath. "I'm really looking forward to you being here."

Junie can't remember a time when her mother has said that. "Me, too," she mumbles, then says good-bye. She hangs up the phone. Her body is melting into the couch. She's a blob. Reduced to a quivering mass of emotions, oozing in all directions. She is going home to eat chicken and walk ten miles in matching tee shirts with her mother. Oh God, Junie thinks, I am such a coward!

# CHAPTER
# THIRTY

The Bottom Line is one of the nicest clubs to play in New York. Great load-in. Good sound system. Plenty of time to sound-check. Nice private backstage area. And they don't cram six bands in one night. Two acts. Two shows. A break in between. Tonight's gig should be a good one. Mr. Whipple is opening for the Garden Gnomes, who just signed a development deal with Sony. *Time Out* gave the gig a star and the *Voice* ran a short article on the Gnomes. Steve claims the first show is already sold out and when Leon peeked out from backstage, he saw that the room was nearly full. Many of the usual Mr. Whipple groupies were there, including the girl named after a car, Austin Healy, who spied him and waved with a big smile.

Leon could have cared less. He could care less about the crowd, about the Gnomes, about Angeline, who sits on the ratty couch backstage with one hand on Steve's knee and the other dangling a smoldering cigarette. He could care less whether his snare drum head is tight enough or whether his hands are warmed up. For all he cares, Steve, Randy, and Tim can go out and lip-synch Milli Vanilli songs while he slouches at the bar slugging back stiff bourbons. If he drank, that is. Since he doesn't, his only choice is to sit backstage on an uncomfortable stool until the show starts and watch Tim make an asshole out of himself.

Leon has never seen Tim so agitated. He already broke a string at the sound check and now works a new E into place on his bass as he tries desperately to engage Angeline in a conversation. She could not be less interested.

"Who are some of the bands you've signed?" Tim asks, twisting and turning the tuning key on his bass.

"No one you've heard of, yet," she says as she drops ashes on the floor, then turns to Steve and says something quietly to him. He squeezes her knee.

"Try me." Tim laughs nervously. "I check out a lot of music around town. I bet I know at least one band you've signed."

"Most of the bands aren't from New York," she says.

"Where then? Do you travel a lot?"

Her cell phone rings from inside her tiny beaded bag. She removes the silver phone and with a snap presses it against her ear.

Tim goes on cranking on the string. "I bet I know someone she's signed," he says to no one in particular. "Not that many bands in New York. I've probably played with half of them."

Angeline nods and says, "Uh-huh. Uh-huh, yeah," into the phone.

"Hey man," Tim says. "Hand me that pick." He points to

the tortoiseshell pick on the table beside Randy. Randy doesn't move. When he's nervous, he shuts down. Clams up. Sits as if he were catatonic. He hasn't even taken a sip of the beer sweating in his hand. "Hey." Tim nudges Randy with his foot. "The pick. Hand me the pick so I can check this string." He kicks Randy a little harder.

"What? Huh?" Randy looks around, blinking as if someone just turned on the lights.

"God," Tim says. He reaches over Randy's legs and grabs the pick himself. "This. A pick. Ever seen one?"

Angeline stands up with a finger in her free ear. "Hang on. Just a sec," she says and leaves the room.

"What's that all about?" Tim asks.

"It's about you being an asshole," Steve says.

"Shut the fuck up," Tim says. He pings the E string with the pick.

"Flat," Steve says.

"You wouldn't know flat if it bitch-slapped you," Tim says but he tightens the string anyway.

"Now, it's too sharp," Steve says.

"Go to hell," Tim says and keeps tightening. The pitch creeps up too high as Tim plucks and before he can loosen it, the string snaps. "Motherfucker!" Tim yells and wings the pick against the wall.

Steve shakes his head and laughs as Tim stomps out of the room. "Hope he has another one," Steve says.

"Lay off him," Leon says.

"He deserves it," says Steve.

"Whatever." Leon doesn't feel like embroiling himself anymore in their petty animosity.

Steve stands up and checks himself in the small mirror hanging beside the door. He tousles his hair and retucks his shirt. "Junie coming?" he asks.

The question catches Leon off-guard. He hasn't told anyone that she left because he is unsure whether she is gone for good. What is there to say anyway? That she is temporarily missing. Her clothes still hang in the closet and her socks and underwear continue to mingle with his in the dresser. (How jealous he is of his own socks!) A pile of her stuff remains in the corner of the bedroom. He hasn't touched anything. Just left everything where she left it. What's he waiting on? Her to come breezing back through the door and put her books and CDs back on shelves, hang up her wrinkled skirts and blouses. Is that what he wants? He has no idea.

"No," he says finally. "She's not coming."

"Why not?" Steve asks. "I thought she was our biggest fan."

"Maybe she just got tired of hearing us play the same shit over and over," Leon says.

Tim comes back into the room carrying another E string. "Don't say a fucking word," he says and shakes the string at Steve. Steve holds up his hands as if he has been wrongly accused.

Then Angeline peaks her head around the doorway. "Psst," she whispers to get Steve's attention. He looks her way and raises his eyebrows. She grins and nods quick but definite. Steve begins to smile but then checks himself. Drops back down to the couch. She disappears into the hall.

Tim stops stringing his bass. "What the hell?"

Everyone remains quiet.

"What was that all about?" Tim says again.

Steve busily reties his shoe.

"Yo, Steve. What's going on?" Tim demands.

"What?" Steve asks.

"That whole thing." Tim waves toward the door. "The call. The looks."

"Jesus, man," Steve says. He stands and smooths his green velvet pants down his thighs. "You're really getting paranoid."

Tim looks at Leon, then at Randy. "Am I the only one who saw that?"

Leon would rather not get involved but even Randy has perked up and now sits forward with his elbows on his knees.

"Something is definitely going on," Tim says.

"She was just looking at me, man. Isn't she allowed to look at me?" Steve says.

"Only if you're fucking her," says Tim.

"Hey!" Steve snaps. He steps close and points a finger at Tim. "I'm just about sick of your bullshit. That's none of your business and you know it."

Tim leans into Steve and says close to his face, "It is my business when she might be paying my rent."

"You don't need to worry about it," Steve says.

Leon hops off the stool and steps between them. "Come on. Enough."

Tim reaches around Leon and pokes Steve on the shoulder. "You better be straight with us."

Steve steps back and holds up his hands, again the gesture of innocence. "Have I ever not?" he asks and grins before he leaves the room.

The stage manager sticks her head in the door. "About five minutes, guys," she says.

"Yeah, alright," Leon says. He grabs Tim's shoulder and massages it hard. "Just put your string on and forget it. Nothing you can do about it right now."

Tim shakes his head. "He better not screw us."

"He wouldn't," Randy says and gulps half his warm beer in one drink. "He's just jacking with you."

# CHAPTER
# THIRTY-ONE

The land between the airport and Junie's hometown is flat and the highway seems to go on forever in a straight line in both directions. A time line. Past, present, and future all happening at once. Junie is going backward. The low buildings of Indianapolis fade quickly and are replaced first by new houses on the outskirts of the city, then by old barns and farmhouses as her father drives her home. Indiana has a particular smell to Junie. As if tiny particles of hay have infiltrated the air. At first she sneezes, then her nose remembers how to breathe in the sweet farm smells and she cracks the window of her father's Cadillac.

"I can turn on the air conditioner," he says.

"No, I'm enjoying this."

After forty minutes of small talk and silence, they coast into her parents' tiny town. The yards are meticulously manicured. Baskets of impossibly large and colorful geraniums hang above porch railings. Lawn geese greet pedestrians from front-yard flowerbeds. The streets are clean, the air is fresh, and nothing is out of place. Couples power-walking for exercise wave heartily to the car as they pass by. Junie already misses the chaos and grit of New York where she can remain unknown. She is a pariah here. An infidel and a slut. The antithesis to all this good, clean wholesomeness. No wonder she is such a disappointment to her parents.

Her father pulls into the driveway that wraps around their old white Queen Anne house. Black shutters. Trim hedges. A welcome mat on the regal front porch. She and Jacob sold lemonade there and waved to cars driving by. Her father pulls into the garage behind the house where every item has a place. The lawn mower goes on top of the cardboard square to catch leaking oil. The rakes hang on nails beside the ladders. Even nuts and bolts have special tiny drawers. And her mother labels everything. One-inch nails. Thumbtacks. String. Junie pictures a smooth white label, hidden on the metal frame of her childhood bed, just below the lip of the chenille spread, the word "Daughter" written in her mother's even script. What would Jacob's room be labeled? "Son, deceased."

"I guess Mom's not home yet," her father says, nodding to the empty side of the garage.

Junie is not surprised, but her mother's absence needles her in the side. She flew all this way, after all. The least the woman could do is be home to say hello.

"She had a meeting," her father explains. "But she'll be home for dinner. She's making chicken. I'm going to mow the lawn."

Junie looks across the yard, as short and precise as a new cadet's crew cut. "Are you kidding?" she asks.

He moves toward the mower. "Why would I joke about that?"

"You wouldn't," Junie says. "It just looks so short to me."

"You rarely see grass," her father points out. He bends down stiffly beside the mower, takes his glasses from his shirt pocket and unscrews the gas cap to peer inside the tank. He looks old. Junie is sure she could knock him over with just a loud noise. She can't possibly say hurtful things to this gentle man.

"Do you need any help?" she asks.

He shakes his head. "No, no. You go rest up for the big walk. It won't take me very long. And Mom will be home soon."

Junie tiptoes through the house as if it were a museum exhibit. "Modern Families in the Late-Twentieth Century." Linoleum in the white-applianced kitchen. Beige carpet through the downstairs. Wallpaper and paint, silk-flower arrangements, and framed reproduction prints. All lovely and tasteful and unmistakably her mother.

She stops in front of the coat closet and opens the door. The smells of shoes and coats greet her. Jacob with a flashlight, her father in the doorway, Eliot's hand against her breast. She shuts the door. There is no place left to hide and she is embarrassed by how transparent she is sometimes. She lifts the bench lid. It seems so small now. Was Jacob's real coffin that little? It had seemed so big. The lining so puffy. She had wanted to try it. Crawl in beside him and hold his hand. She shuts the bench quietly and walks slowly up the stairs.

Junie's bedroom was redecorated the minute Junie went to college. The once white walls covered in collages of rock stars and hunky actors were stripped bare, then painted butter cream with a cabbage rose wallpaper border. The frilly furniture and deep-pile carpet are new, too. Junie is a guest now in this place. She looks out the window for the witch in the tree trunk that only she could ever see. As a kid, she thought it was that witch who made Jacob sick until her father explained in hushed whispers about leukemia and then Junie felt sorry for the witch. Knew that an evil wizard had turned her into a tree and the noisy squirrels were her only friends. Junie decided to be her friend, too. Talked to her when there was no one else to listen. There is a knot higher up than she remembers. She squints at it. It could sort of look like a face.

Down the hall is Jacob's room. She pauses in front of his door. Only seven years in this house. His life was a blink, a breath, a sigh. She opens the door that usually stays shut. His room is stuffy. The back of the house gets a lot of sun but no air with the windows always closed. Boxes, clearly labeled, are stacked on the dresser and under the stripped-bare bed. Junie scans some titles, "Grandmother's China," "Exercise Equipment," "Junie's Dance Recital Costumes." The room is a palimpsest. Layer after layer of Junie's life covering over Jacob. She looks out the window to the backyard where her father walks in straight lines, pushing the buzzing power mower across the grass.

She pushes boxes aside. "Canning Jars," "Picture Frames," "Macramé." She wants to find the "See ya' Mel" boxes, his cleats, his Cookie Monster tee shirt. That little trench coat he used to wear. The drawings he made, the stories they wrote, and the games they loved to play. *Ants in Your Pants. Cooties. Operation. Chutes and Ladders.* Nothing is there. No evidence of his existence. How could her mother keep Perry Como LPs but erase her only son? Fill his room with the flotsam from their meaningless lives. She is such a bitch and Junie's anger swells inside her body. Not home ten minutes and already she is furious. What the hell is she doing here and how is she going to Walk-for-a-Cure without pushing her mother over the edge of a deep and jagged ravine?

She hears the mower rumble across the driveway. Through the window she sees her father cut the power, then wheel the mower into the garage. Her mother's car is there, too. Junie imagines throwing boxes through the window and screaming, "I will not let you forget him!" All the memories her mother tucked away so neatly would be scattered across the concrete. Neighbors would peek through their eyelet curtains at the crazy daughter returned. But we don't make scenes, Junie thinks. We control our anger and our sadness. We squish it down down down down into our toes and we put on a happy face because if you look happy, you are happy. What matters is what people think. How could she, deranged daughter of the poor bereft couple who lost their only son, dare to question this tried-and-true philosophy of Midwestern WASPy living? Marching in from New York City where she has mingled with cultures that beat their breasts and wail at the least provocation. In her dark clothes and brightly colored hair. Thinking that after nearly twenty years she can dredge the depths of her family's emotions.

Ah, Junie thinks. This is not what we do. We mow our lawns and eat baked chicken and walk miles and miles and miles to keep our rage in check. And who is she to try to change that? Angrily she restacks the boxes, slamming one down on top of the other, making the contents rattle. Good, she thinks, and hopes everything turns to dust. The room is sweltering. Her mother is home. She will expect Junie to come downstairs, fresh and ready to eat soon. What are her other choices? Stay up here digging through the past? Run downstairs screaming like a lunatic? It isn't worth her time and anger. She has to simply get through the next few days and then she can leave again. Slowly, she backs out of the room and shuts the door behind her.

As she turns to go down the hall, she sees her mother at the top of the stairs. Age has snuck up on her and hidden in the crevices of her skin. Who is this person with wiry gray strands weaving into her thick dyed-blonde hair? And how did she get that bruised skin under her eyes, like apples going bad? She stands with her hand lightly on the banister in her perfectly creased khaki pants and a sweater set. Her hair is sprayed into place and her lipstick is a tasteful color of coral.

"I thought I heard you up here," her mother says.

"I was just . . ." Junie points to the room but can't think of how to finish her sentence.

"I'm glad you made it," her mother says and opens her arms. Junie steps up dutifully and lightly hugs her mother. "How was your flight?"

"Fine," says Junie.

"Your hair." Her mother reaches toward Junie's head, then withdraws her hand.

"I colored it."

"Mm-hmm," her mother says. "Hungry?"

"Not really."

"Dinner will be ready in an hour."

"Do you want some help?" asks Junie wearily. She can't imagine standing next to her mother just now with a sharp object in her hand.

"No. You rest up," says her mother as she descends the stairs. She stops midway down and looks back at Junie. "I'm glad you're here," she says. Junie nods uncertainly.

For the next hour, Junie hides out in her bedroom. Exactly as she did in high school. Only this time she is ensconced in flouncy throw pillows that perfectly match the wallpaper in her room. She rereads junior high and high school diaries stashed in the bottom drawer of her old dresser. She used to be mortified at the thought of anyone else, especially her mother, reading them. Now she sees they are merely a catalogue of every boy she ever liked, disliked, kissed, and thought about kissing. What she wore to dances held in sweaty gyms redecorated with balloons and crepe paper. Who said what about whom at football games. She skims these entries looking for any insight into her teenage psyche. She knows that Jacob's death insinuated itself into every relationship she's ever had, so why didn't she record any of that history instead of itemizing each insipid detail of her adolescent love life?

Her father raps lightly on her door. She can tell it is his knock. "Dinner's ready," he says through the door. Since Junie hit puberty he's never entered her room, even when invited.

"Be right down," she says. She gathers the diaries and begins to put them back in their hiding place, then decides there is no use. She tosses them in her trash can and goes downstairs.

Her mother has set the dining room table with place mats and the good crystal goblets. Her father pours them each a half-glass of a chilly Chardonnay. A perfectly golden-baked chicken surrounded by baby carrots and pearl onions is flanked by a bowl of creamy mashed potatoes on one side and grayish green beans flecked with bacon on the other. Junie knows from experience that looks can be deceiving at this dinner table. Her mother's food is notoriously bland. The one time that Leon came to visit he snuck out and bought a jar of jalapeño peppers to nibble on at night just so his taste buds wouldn't atrophy.

"Did you mow the lawn?" Junie's mother asks her father as he carves a wing and part of the chicken breast for himself.

"Yes," he says. "Would you like dark meat?"

Her mother nods and hands her plate across the table. He serves her a thigh and leg, then turns to Junie, carving knife and serving fork raised and ready for action. "For you?"

"Anything is fine," Junie says, lifting her plate toward him.

"What would you prefer?"

"I don't care."

"Surely you have a preference," her mother interjects.

"Not really. Whatever's easiest."

"Carving a chicken isn't hard," her father says.

"It really doesn't matter."

"White or dark?" her mother asks, just a little exasperated.

Junie sighs. Wrong choice. Her mother frowns deeply at her. "A little of both?" Junie says but her inflection makes it sound like a question.

"Breast or wing? Thigh or leg?" her father asks, still poised in the ready position.

Junie hesitates.

"Just make a choice, Junie," her mother says.

Junie is ready to slam her plate to the table and rip the chicken apart with her hands. Two hours home and already she and her parents are in a stalemate over chicken parts. No wonder she can't make any decisions in her life. Her parents stare at her as she waffles. "Breast," she says finally. Everyone seems relieved.

"How's work?" her father asks once they've all tucked into the food.

"Fine," Junie says.

"How's Leon?" her mother asks.

Junie falters. Lying about work is easy. Leon is another matter. "He's GREAT!" she says with way too much enthusiasm. "Just fine. Things are good. We might take a trip." She shoves chicken into her mouth to shut herself up.

"Where to?" her father asks.

Junie chews and chews, then shrugs. She swallows and says, "I don't know. Maybe we won't. He's really busy."

Silverware clinks against the china. Leon would have to tap his fork against each dish. Check this out, he'd say and get a rhythm going. Her mother and father would chuckle uncomfortably but be charmed anyway. Or in the silence he would meet Junie's eyes across the table so she would know that she is not alone.

"We were surprised to get your call," her mother says.

"Why's that?" Junie asks defensively.

"You haven't been home in a while and . . ." her father says.

"Then I'd think that you'd be glad," says Junie.

Her parents exchange flummoxed looks across the table. "We *are* happy that you're home, Junie," her mother says. "We're not criticizing you."

"We just wondered if there was anything special bringing you home," her father says.

Junie sits back. Tries to calm herself. Stop from acting like a rabid raccoon cornered in the garage. "I just . . ." She stops. Why is she home? To castigate, fume, and pout? She already gave up on that big idea. "Needed to get out of the city for a while," she says. She stands and stacks her dishes. "I'll wash up," she offers.

Usually her mother doesn't let Junie help at all, which Junie takes as an insult, as if she can't even be trusted with dishwashing. Leon has pointed out maybe it's something much less sinister. Maybe her mother just wants Junie to relax and feel like a guest.

"Okay," her mother says and hands Junie another plate.

Junie is surprised. This sudden change of heart is a bit perplexing. Is Junie more trustworthy now or is she no longer considered a guest? She cradles dishes carefully in her arms and carries them to the kitchen.

As she stands over the sink, considering whether she has been demoted or promoted, she tries to conjure up Jacob. Where would he be in all of this? At twenty-four. Her co-conspirator. The only other person who would know her parents the way she does. The two of them could have sneaked behind the garage for beers after the dishes were done. Dissected the dinner conversation. Jacob would have commiserated when Junie complained about their mother. They would have laughed about their father's idiosyncrasies. Found shadows of their parents in themselves and groaned with mock horror at turning out so much like them. The thought makes her smile. She catches her reflection in the dark window above the sink and it makes her sad.

The reality is that Jacob isn't here and Junie has no one to empathize with her. She dips each plate into the sudsy water and realizes how lonely she is in this house and always will be, no matter how much she and her parents can repair their fragile relationships. This heartache, she knows, is as much a part of her as the connective tissue between her bones and muscles. It makes her who she is, but it will never be less than agony when she probes her sadness because at every moment in her life, Jacob is not here and that is unforgivable.

Junie finishes the dishes and dries her hands. She finds her parents in the den, watching a *Seinfeld* rerun for the tenthousandth time. Junie lingers in the doorway, watching them laugh before the punch line of every joke. This is not where she wants to be. Pretending things are fine. But, she's already missed her chance to confront her parents. In the car with her dad. Upstairs with her mom. Then at the dinner table with both of them. Clearly, she's too much of a chickenshit to carry out her plan of attack. Now the cause is lost. She'll have to retreat. Stick it out for a few more days, then go back to New York and pick up the pieces of her life.

# CHAPTER
# THIRTY-TWO

On Saturday morning, Junie wakes early. The sun streams into her bedroom and birds sing in the trees outside. She had forgotten how gorgeous and peaceful this part of the country can be. She tries to think of something productive to do today. Her mother offered to take her shopping in Indianapolis today. Said Talbot's is having their semi-annual sale. Junie understood this proposal as a backhanded way of stating that Junie's clothes are deplorable. She politely declined but urged her mother not to miss the sale on her behalf. She could offer to help her dad around the yard. Trim hedges, weed flower beds, graft orchid trimmings together, or whatever occupies him for hours and hours outside in that immaculate green space. When she asks him what he does he just shrugs and says, "I putter."

Maybe she should go to the library in town and research a new occupation. Read some career reference books. Dig up a Meyers-Briggs personality test. Figure out whether she is an introverted judging hoo-haw or an extra-crispy sentimental ying-yang. Perhaps today is the day to determine just what color her parachute might be. And then what? What does one do with that information? Walk into a random place of employment and demand a good, satisfying job? At some point she will have to write a résumé and the dismal truth will be told. She has absolutely no experience doing anything worthwhile. But, she is going to have to get it together soon because when she returns to New York she will have to make rent by herself.

In fact, it will be good for her. Junie is getting tired of assuming her prospects are nil. She's not an idiot. She has a college degree. In anthropology. Which isn't exactly useful, but she's just as smart as any other above-average learner. She's just never applied herself. At least that's what all her teachers said. Plus she's creative. She might not have a passion for a particular art like Katie or Leon or Eliot, but she's got flare. That should count for something. Really, all that's standing in her way is a little self-confidence and resolve. Do they sell that at Talbot's?

It's not as if Junie never had ambition, though. At some point, like every good American middle-class child raised in the eighties, Junie believed that she could be anything she wanted. When she was five or six, her mother asked what she wanted to be when she grew up. Junie said she wanted to be a stripper but if that didn't work out, she would be President of the United States. When did she stop believing in those possibilities? When did she stop believing in any possibilities? Who was that kid who thought she could be President? Or a stripper for that matter. Junie would like to find her. Get reacquainted. Figure out what her aspirations were before she stopped dreaming.

If there is any evidence left of that girl, then it is in this house because that is where she flittered away. Junie looks around her room. Nothing of her is left in here. Except her journals in the trash can. What a disappointment to find no traces of herself beyond a record of silly high school crushes. But neither her posters nor her diaries go back far enough anyway. What she needs is buried deep. In the back bedroom. Where the past has been hermetically sealed.

Junie presses her ear against her bedroom door before she opens it to ascertain the whereabouts of her parents. The hallway is quiet. The stairs are quiet. She hears no television or conversation. They are probably both out, doing whatever it is that they do. Junie tiptoes from her room to the back of the house. The trek is familiar and still at twenty-five, she fears she might get caught and reprimanded for sneaking out of bed and into Jacob's room. She goes undetected and quietly opens his door.

She excavates through strata of old clothes, school pictures, and dance recital costumes. She rummages through her old piano books, report cards, grizzled stuffed animals and one-legged Barbie dolls. Sweat blooms across her forehead and rolls down her forearms. She wants to know who she was before Jacob died. What she really wanted to be. And why she let his death squash every ambition she ever had. Was the loss of him really that devastating or has it simply been an excuse for her shortcomings?

She uncovers dried-out grade school art projects made from macaroni and glue. Disintegrating paper dolls with their features rubbed away. The *Little House on the Prairie* series. These artifacts of her childhood tell her nothing but that she was happy until she was eight. All her life she's used that as a measuring stick. In her mind, her life is divided into two sections, Before Jacob Died and After Jacob Died. Now that comparison seems terribly lopsided. Who but the most enlightened yogis and idiot savants retain the blissfulness of their early childhood? She pushes aside what she has uncovered, then ducks down to retrieve more boxes.

The door to the room opens and Junie whips around, an excuse already faltering on her tongue. Her mother steps in the room. She is wearing Lycra stirrup pants, a Walk-a-Thon tee shirt, and a baseball cap squished down on top of her head. Junie drops a handful of Lincoln Logs into a box.

"What are you looking for, Junie?" her mother asks. "Maybe I can help."

Junie rubs the back of her wrist across her forehead wet with sweat. "I don't know," she says and feels contrite, as if she should apologize.

"You don't know what you are looking for or you don't know if I can help?"

"Both."

Her mother steps further in the room and lifts the flap of a box marked "Photographs." She peeks inside, then closes the flap again. "First you call and say you want to do the Walk-a-Thon with me. Now I've found you twice up here digging through old boxes."

"Sorry," Junie mumbles and begins closing the flaps. But she stops. Stands up straight. Turns to face her mother. Why is she stopping? It's her own stuff. She can look at it if she wants. "What's the problem with that?" Junie asks.

Her mother stands perfectly still with one arm crossed against her midriff. "I didn't say there was anything wrong with it."

"Yes, you did," Junie says. "Your tone did."

"My tone?" her mother says doubtfully.

"Yes. Like that. That tone says a lot more than your words."

"Well, that's not what I meant. It's just such a surprise. That's all." Her mother fakes a grin. "I'm trying to understand you, Junie."

These words grate against Junie's skin like a rash. She snorts an angry little laugh. "You are trying to understand me?" she says. "That's rich."

*Rich,* Junie thinks. *Rich?* I just said *That's rich.* I don't say *That's rich.* Who is this person talking?

"You seem upset," her mother says.

Junie tosses her hands into the air and makes odd little noises in the back of her throat, too frustrated to form words. She takes a big breath and says too loudly, "You are just now noticing that?"

"I knew that your coming home was about more than just spending time with us," her mother hisses. She steps back as if she is going to leave, but she stays.

"I'm trying to figure out what happened to me," Junie says.

"What do you mean, what happened to *you?* Nothing happened to *you. You've* had a very nice life."

"For God's sake, mother." Junie is nearly shouting, but she

doesn't care. "I can't hold a job or keep a good relationship. I mess up everything. Doesn't that strike you as odd? Don't you think something must be wrong?"

"You're a very bright young woman. You just don't apply yourself." Her mother waves her hand in the air like a magician finishing a trick. Ta-da! "I've been saying that for years."

"There's more to it than that, but you refuse to see it."

Her mother sighs an exasperated huff. "I don't know what you want from me, Junie."

There is a long pause as Junie tries to work out how to tell her mother. Should she make a list? Unroll a very long scroll that trails through the hall and down the stairs, out the front door, into the street. Try to sum it all up in one very pithy phrase. Forget the whole thing and clam up like she usually does. But words gather in the back of Junie's throat, press against her tongue, and then she is shouting.

"I wanted you to show me how to get over him! All the stupid fund-raisers and grief support groups but you couldn't bring an ounce of it back to me!"

"You wouldn't listen," her mother snaps as if they've picked up on a conversation they've been having for years. And in a way they have. A silent conversation inside each of their minds, spoken for the first time now. "I tried to take you. Tried to get you involved with sibling groups, but you wouldn't do it." Her mother leans heavily against the dresser and turns her face away from Junie. "You've always thought that you were the only one."

"I did feel like I was the only one!" Junie shouts. "I felt so lonely." She kicks a box. "You stopped playing with me after he died. You stopped talking to me. You shut yourself off and left me completely alone. I didn't want a support group. I wanted you but you weren't there and it's fucked up my entire life."

Her mother whips her head around to face Junie again. "You never once thought about how hard it was for me." She pokes at her own sternum. "Trying to be a wife and mother when I was so terribly depressed. At some point I had to take care of myself or I wouldn't have been any kind of mother to you."

"And what kind of mother do you think you were?" Junie says. She knows the words are pernicious, but purposefully hurting her mother is not as exhilarating as she had imagined.

Her mother shakes her head. "That's not fair, Junie. That's not fair at all."

Junie's stomach churns and her head pounds. The tiny muggy room feels like the inside of someone's mouth. She needs air and space. She wants to push past her mom, leaving all the stupid boxes to rot. Get the hell out of the house, the town, the state. Go back to New York where she can start over again. This time without dragging every childhood calamity behind her like a palsied leg. She'll just get over it. Put all this drama about Jacob's death behind her because obviously, standing in a sweltering room full of boxed-up memories, screaming at her mother is not doing her any good.

But her mother lowers herself to a box, takes off her hat, and runs her fingers through her limp hair. The dim light of the room accentuates the deep lines running from the side of her mother's nose to the corners of her mouth. She looks defeated and Junie can't abandon her just yet.

"You know, I lost my first baby," her mother says.

Junie releases the fists her fingers have created. "I didn't know that," she says but she feels confused. Is this sudden confession a trick? A red herring to throw Junie off track. Still this disclosure is eerie and it would be terribly heartless of Junie to discount its importance. She stands quietly and waits for her mother to continue.

Her mother turns her hat over and over in her hands and talks quietly. "We'd only been married about three months when I got pregnant." She smiles a little, but it's not a happy smile. "I thought I was something else with my perfect little life. A husband and a house and pregnant on top of it all.

"That's all I really wanted, a family," says her mother. "I didn't know anything else. I was so young. Younger than you are now." She looks up at Junie with an expression near disbelief, as if this sudden confession is surprising to her as well. "I wasn't like you, Junie. I never wanted to go off to some other city and find myself or have a career."

Junie steps backward and knocks into a box. She is amazed that her mother has given her enough credit to be someone who is actually trying to find herself or a career. She plops to the bare mattress on the little twin bed. The old springs squeak.

"I always thought it was a boy. I don't know why. It's silly really." Her mother stares hard at the inside of her hat, as if the story is inscribed on the seams. "We didn't have sonograms and things like that to tell us. I just had a feeling."

Wait, Junie wants to say. Hold on. Stop. She wipes her hands across her face, mopping up beads of sweat gathered in her hairline. Just when she was beginning to understand the effect of losing Jacob, there's another dead brother to contend with? The possibility seems ludicrous and she thinks maybe she is confused. Maybe her mother is talking about Jacob.

"It's hard to describe," her mother continues. "But when you're pregnant you get so attached to that little life inside of you. You love it from the first instance that you feel nauseous or dizzy. And you make all sorts of promises to that little soul. About what his life will be like. And how wonderful he'll be. You can't help but start planning out his life. I was so young. It never occurred to me that . . ." She shrugs, then sighs. Closes her eyes for a moment, then opens them again and stares at the ceiling.

"But I lost it. Going into my sixth month. A lot of people lose their first one, especially early on. But no one talks about it. So I thought by the sixth month, everything would be fine. One day I was pregnant with a happy kicking baby and then the next day there was no movement." Her hand rests on her stomach. "You find ways to explain that to yourself. Maybe he's sleeping. Maybe I ate something that pacified him. But then I started bleeding. The doctors told me it was over. I didn't believe them of course. I was sure they were wrong but there's nothing you can do anyway. Just sit and wait out the inevitable.

"People around me said the stupidest things. That it was for the best because the baby would have been deformed. Or God didn't intend for me to have that baby. Or I would have another baby. But what they didn't understand is that I wanted *that* baby.

"I used to wake up in the middle of the night terrified of what happened to him. Maybe he hadn't really been dead. Maybe no one checked carefully enough. I didn't know where he went. What they did with him. I was afraid that he was floating in a glass jar of formaldehyde in the basement of the hospital."

Her mother draws in a deep breath and leans back against the wall. She is silent for a long time and Junie doesn't know what to do. She is unaccustomed to a mother who shares deep secrets, so the story of this dead baby seems like someone else's. Some mother that Junie never knew.

"After that it took me a long time to get pregnant again." Her mother closes her eyes. "We almost gave up, you know." She shakes her head. "It was just too hard to try every month and have nothing happen. Your dad was great, though. Took me on long weekends away. Tried to protect me from seeing our friends who'd just had babies. Two years of that and then." She looks at Junie and smiles. This time it's her real smile, the one Junie rarely sees anymore. Like any child reveling in the story of her own birth, Junie smiles back at her mother, encouraging her to continue.

"The whole time I was pregnant with you I was a nervous wreck. I was so afraid of losing you, too. But you were a strong little thing." Her hand flutters to her side. "I was so sick in the first months. Every time I threw up I thanked God because that meant you were okay. Then you kicked me until my ribs were sore and I loved every minute of it. I always knew that you would be fine. Then Jacob came so fast after you." Her eyes are wide and she sits up taller. "And there I was, with my perfect little family. One girl and one boy. Sometimes I look back at how smug I was in my happiness. As if nothing could touch me. And whenever I thought about that little one I lost first, I would think it was okay now because I had you two."

She looks around at all the boxes and she laughs. "The two of you were so cute together. Your dad and I would stay up after you went to bed and laugh about the stuff you two did. I just never thought . . ." She stops. Her chin quivers and she chews on her bottom lip. "I just never thought I would lose another one." Her mother knots the hat in her hands. "It was so fucking unfair."

Hearing her mother curse sends a little jolt through Junie's body.

"All the people around us had babies and healthy children. I'd see people in the K-Mart yelling at their kids. People who had no right . . ." She trails off. "You were so good with him when he was sick. Jacob would have rather been with you than anyone else in the world. Part of me was so grateful for that. And part of me . . ." She stops. Seems to have trouble locating the words. "I'm not proud of it, but honestly, part of me was jealous." She blinks up at Junie. "I know I didn't do everything right or well, Junie. But I did the best I could. I never did anything to hurt you. I've always loved you. I still do."

"I know you love me, Mom," Junie whispers. "I've always known you love me."

"Sometimes that's all you can do," her mother says. "And sometimes even that is not enough." She stands and straightens the stack of boxes in front of her, making sure each corner and edge line up perfectly. "That's all I could do for Jacob," she whispers. Her face is worn with creases and wrinkles tucked permanently beside her eyes and mouth.

Junie stands on shaky legs and walks toward her mom. "I think about him all the time," she says.

"So do I."

Junie hears a wail in the room, then realizes that it's her own voice. A tiny fissure has erupted across her sternum and the heavy sadness draping her organs pours out in howls and yelps. She knows this cry. It is familiar. She is crying for everything that has happened and everything she misses. She is crying for Jacob. For her mother and her father. For how devastating loving someone so much can be. For the futility of their attempts to protect themselves. But this time the crying is different because she finds herself wrapped in her mother's hug, face pressed against her collarbone.

Pointing an accusing finger for everything wrong in her life no longer seems like an urgent task to Junie. Because it won't make things easier or better. What she wants just now is to stay intertwined in her mother's arms and cry. And after that she wants a chance to talk. Time to compare their stories, their sadness and to understand. To say, I know just how you feel. She steps back from her mom's embrace ready for a heart-to-heart. A spilling of guts. A mother-daughter moment.

But her mother puts the hat back on her head, tucks her hair beneath it, and walks toward the door. Junie is left with her arms extended. That's it, she thinks. That's all I get? Fly several hundred miles, dig through old boxes, scream at my mother the things I've needed to say for years, hear her confess the deepest sadness of her life, and a two-minute cry-and-hug is the sum total of our interaction?

"You can't just drop all of that on me, then walk away," Junie says. "There's so much more for us to talk about."

Her mother pats a few loose strands of hair back into place, then checks her watch. "I have to set up the course for the Walk tomorrow."

"And that's more important than this!" Junie yells. She grips her hair with her hands and squeezes her eyes shut. "It will never change."

Her mother reaches out and lays her hands gently on Junie's shoulders. "It's not more important than this," she says firmly. Junie lets her arms drop to her sides. She opens her eyes. "It's just easier right now." She gives Junie a weak smile that says *forgive me.* "I know there is a lot for us to talk about, but you'll have to be patient with me. Can you do that?"

Junie swallows gathered tears and inhales deeply. She doesn't want to let her mother go. She is afraid of losing this tiny foothold they have carved. Their relationship could so quickly slip back into banalities if she simply nods and lets her mother walk out of the room. "Can I come with you?" she asks. "And help."

Her mother raises both eyebrows and purses her lips. "I don't want you to feel obligated."

"I don't. I'd just like to spend some more time with you, Mom." Maybe they can start slow and small. Find tiny patches of common ground. Learn to like one another. Work up to a relationship that can bear the weight of their fury toward one another.

"I'd like that," her mother says.

"Can you wait for me to get dressed?"

"Yes," her mother says, then she pauses. "But . . ." She stops and closes her mouth tightly.

"What?" Junie says defensively. She knows where the conversation is likely to head. Will anything ever change? "I'll put on something respectable," Junie offers.

Her mother shakes her head quickly. "No," she says and grins. "I'd rather you put on something Junie."

"You sure about that?"

"Well, maybe a little bit respectable would be okay."

"I can do that," Junie says.

As her mother leaves, Junie slowly returns the boxes to their places. Neat and orderly stacks. She can do that for her mother. She will find something nice to do for her father, too. Maybe trim the hedges. She stacks the boxes and surveys the room, then sees one short tower of boxes in the corner by the closet. "See ya' Mel" is written on the side in her uneven eight-year-old loopy letters. She squats in front of them. Only three little boxes. His entire life. She gingerly opens the top one. There are drawings and broken crayons. Dusty cans of Play-Doh. A *Highlights* magazine with scribbles across the cover. She opens another. Digs through layers of rusted Hot Wheels and green-plastic army men. In the third box, near the bottom, she finds clothes. Small tee shirts, bell-bottom jeans, little boy tube socks. Then Jacob's cleats. Tiny shoes tied together at the top. Black with dirty white stripes down the side. They made him run faster. She pulls them out and holds them up. Wants to show them to Leon. Little boy shoes. He would understand.

She wants to talk to Leon then. Tell him about the bench, the boxes, the witch in the tree, her father mowing the lawn. How just when she was ready to indict her mother for every problem in her life, she stopped short, shut up, and listened instead. Leon used to listen to her. Held her hand and stroked the inside of her arm when she needed to be heard. That's what she's been craving all these years. Another best friend. Another person to love entirely. What she really wants to do is press her lips against Leon's head and tell him that she's sorry for how she's hurt him. That she could be a better friend and lover for him now because today she got her ass kicked more firmly into adulthood. And it felt good. And she wishes he would forgive her and let her try again.

Junie hears her mother rattling her keys downstairs. She knows she has to get through today and tomorrow as the daughter, then worry about herself as the jerk who left her boyfriend. She replaces the boxes and takes the cleats to her room to stash them in her backpack before she goes downstairs. Remember to seem interested in the Walk-a-Thon, she tells herself. Tell Dad the yard looks nice.

# CHAPTER
# THIRTY-THREE

Leon sits behind the drum kit at Montana Rehearsal Studio and paradiddles while he waits for the rest of the band to show up. Steve and Randy are usually five or ten minutes late and Tim sometimes shows up half an hour after rehearsal starts. Leon doesn't really care. He uses the time to practice since the room is already rented out for three hours. These biweekly rehearsals have completely lost their focus anyway. Steve hasn't brought in any new songs for the past few weeks so they've spent their time arguing about the set list and watching Steve figure out new ways to pummel Randy during raging guitar solos.

The show at the Bottom Line went well. It was one of those rare gigs when Leon felt the thrill that addicts rock stars to the music business. There are few things more satisfying than having a packed room scream for more while loitering backstage, waiting for the stomping and clapping and whistling to crescendo before running out for the encore. Of course, the one thing that could have made it better for Leon was to have Junie beaming up at him from the front row.

The door opens and Tim comes in with his bass slung over his shoulder. He is eating a donut and listening to his Walkman so loudly that Leon can make out the AC/DC guitar riff from "Back in Black."

"Going back to your roots?" Leon asks.

Tim pushes the headphones off and says, "Huh?"

"I said, going back to your roots? AC/DC?"

"Yeah, man. Angus Young was one bad-ass mother. Think we could get Steve to wear a schoolboy uniform?"

Leon speeds up his paradiddles while Tim unpacks his gear. A few minutes later Randy comes in smoking a cigarette and carrying a Styrofoam cup of coffee.

"Where's Steve?" Tim asks.

Randy shrugs. "How should I know?"

"You guys are roommates," Tim says as he plugs into an amp.

"He hasn't been home much lately."

Tim snorts and shakes his head. "Angeline?"

"Don't know." Randy sits on a speaker. "I don't ask."

Leon stops playing and stands to stretch his legs and arms. His ass is sore from sitting on the drum throne so much lately. They've got three more festivals coming up. All in the Midwest. Five days in the van. He's not looking forward to it, but then again, being away might be a nice distraction from the lack of Junie in his life.

The door opens again and Steve comes in, Angeline in tow.

"Hey guys," Steve says. He puts his arm around Angeline's shoulders. She leans into him and grins. "We've got some news for you."

Tim stops noodling on the bass. Randy crushes out his cigarette in an overflowing ashtray and Leon puts his sticks in his back pocket. They all assume the news is about a record deal with Epic. Either that or those crazy kids have run off and eloped. Fat chance Steve would limit his prospects with commitment to one woman. So it must be the record deal. They've been waiting five years for this, but Leon feels ambivalent now.

"Do you want me to tell them?" Angeline says.

"No. I should." Steve withdraws his arm from her shoulder and claps his hands together. "Look, here's the deal. Epic has offered Mr. Whipple a development-and-distribution deal for the next CD."

"Yes!" Tim yells and pumps his fist in the air. Randy smiles broadly. But Leon watches Steve's face shift from his usual gratuitous grin to a shaky frown.

"There's a catch, though," Steve says.

"What?" Tim asks. "What kind of catch?" He glares at Angeline who crosses her arms and looks blankly back at him.

"The deal is, Angeline has a producer she would like Mr. Whipple to work with."

"Great," Tim says.

"Except," says Steve.

"Except what?" asks Tim.

"The producer wants to bring in his own rhythm section."

Everyone is quiet. Angeline's cell phone rings. She pulls it from her bag and excuses herself into the hallway. Cool trick, Leon thinks. How did she time that?

"For the recording?" asks Tim.

Steve nods.

"But not for the live gigs, right?" Randy asks.

"Look, guys. I can't pass it up. You've been so great. I love you guys. You know that. I love this band. But if I say no then there's no deal. There's nothing else I can do."

"Wait, wait, wait, wait." Tim shrugs off his bass and stalks across the room. "Are you dumping us? Are you fucking dumping us?"

"It's not me." Steve steps backward and holds out his hands. "It's them. It's Epic. It's the way things work. I have no choice."

"You sure as hell do have a choice!" Tim yells. "Tell them it's no deal without the band!" He looks desperately at Leon, then at Randy. Randy stands mute with his mouth open and his hands in fists by his side.

"I can't," Steve says.

"Fuck you, man!" Tim yells. "This isn't your band. You don't own this music."

"Actually," Steve says. "I wrote the songs. They're all copyrighted under my name."

Leon shakes his head and laughs a little. Being sold out isn't that much of a surprise. And frankly, he's not all that bothered by it. He slowly gathers up his sticks and brushes while Tim screams and turns red. Leon unscrews his cymbals and slides them into his bag. Randy paces, opens and closes his fists. Angeline is probably hiding out in the woman's toilet until the coast is clear. It could get ugly. Leon loosens his snare drum and zips it into the soft case. Tim and Randy have backed Steve into a corner. Tim screams about all the time they've put in, all the shitty-paying gigs they've done. He threatens lawsuits and bad press and boycotts. Leon's heard enough. There really isn't a reason to stick around for the messy ending. He slips out the door while they hash out their hatred. He disappears into the elevator before he is missed.

The F train is nearly empty on the way back to Brooklyn. Leon sits in the corner seat and stares out the window as the train goes elevated over Carroll Gardens. Junie loves this part of the train ride. She told Leon once that it took her months to notice the Statue of Liberty in the bay. When she noticed it for the first time she nearly cried. Not out of patriotic sentiment, but because it was the moment when she realized that she was making a life for herself in New York City. She felt awed and overwhelmed by the accomplishment of simply getting through a day here. It was in that same conversation when she said that falling in love with Leon had made New York seem ten times smaller and more manageable.

He knew exactly what she meant. And now, traveling around the city without the knowledge of where she is, makes the place seem vast and empty. The train ducks into a tunnel again. The thing that really sucks is that even though he is so angry with her, he still misses her. She fucks somebody else and he sits around missing her. That's just pathetic. It's been nearly two weeks since she left and she hasn't made any effort to contact him. She's probably with that prick Eliot. A writer, for God's sake. Leon knows he should accept the fact that things are over. Just like he did with the band. Time to move on.

He remembers then the card that Austin Healy gave him at the Mercury Lounge gig. He wonders if she is seeing Randy. Not that it matters so much. She was always really friendly to Leon. If he wants to call her, he can. He opens his wallet and searches through the receipts and stamps and five-dollar bills. He finds her card and holds it in his hand. She lives in Williamsburg. Figures. He tries to picture her clearly. Her hair was striped blue and she wore baggy clothes. Nothing like Junie, but isn't that the point? The train pulls into Leon's stop. He exits and climbs the stairs to the familiar street. Each time he scans the people milling around, half-hoping and half-dreading to catch a glimpse of Junie. The card is still in his fingers. He can't date someone named after a car. He crumples the card and drops it in a trash can.

As Leon walks home, he realizes that there is virtually nothing holding him in New York anymore. The band has dissolved. Junie is gone. He could make a clean break. Pack up his crap and get out for good. No more hauling drums up three flights of stairs and sitting in traffic jams at one A.M. No more smelly vans and smoky bars. He could find a little town somewhere. Get a job in a restaurant and learn the ropes. Start testing recipes. Save up money until he can put a down payment on a place. Maybe even ask his father for a loan. There is nothing stopping him from pursuing this dream. Nothing except that in this dream Junie was supposed to be beside him.

# CHAPTER
# THIRTY-FOUR

So, what are you going to do?" Katie asks.

Junie hugs the couch pillow to her chest. "I don't know," she says.

"Well, I'll tell you one thing," says Katie. She dangles a string in front of the cat, who dances on his hind legs and swats at it. "You keep mentioning Leon."

Junie falls to her side on the couch. "I know," she whines.

"I haven't once heard you talk about, what's his name, Grandpa."

"Eliot," Junie groans and covers her head with the pillow.

"Why don't you call him?"

Junie sits up. "Eliot?"

"I meant Leon. But maybe you should call Eliot." The cat snags the string and yanks it from Katie's hand.

"You think I owe him an explanation?"

"Do you actually have one?"

Junie pulls the end of the string. The cat follows it stealthily. "I've been trying to figure that out."

"Did you come up with anything?" asks Katie.

"Yeah." Junie lifts the string and the cat pounces. "I think that ever since Jacob died, I've been sabotaging the good things in my life because I'm afraid that if I'm happy and love someone it will hurt too much when that person's gone." The cat loses interest in the string and struts away.

Junie lies back on the couch and covers her eyes with one arm. "I also think I've been re-enacting parts of my childhood. Things that happened with Jacob. Asking Leon to shave his head. Having sex with Eliot in the closet. It's like I thought I could change the outcome this time around rather than deal with the fact that Jacob's dead." Junie shudders.

"Yeah, well, we've all got our oddities," Katie says and chuckles. "Some more odd than others."

"God, it's all so fucked-up," Junie says between nervous laughs.

"You are a freak."

"You'd make an excellent shrink," says Junie.

"That'll be a hundred dollars."

Junie sits up. "Put it on my tab."

"So," Katie says again. "What are you going to do?"

"I don't know," says Junie. She stretches her arms above her head. "I think the first thing I'll do is take a walk."

Junie meanders through Prospect Park with no plan about where to go. It has rained most of the night and through the early morning but finally there is a reprise and the sun shines down, mopping up the puddles. Everything has become very green in the park. The grass is a plush carpet, the trees are heavy with yellow and chartreuse leaves. Slender stalks of grape hyacinth and tiny narcissus bloom along the borders of the walks. She passes the pond where wild ducks prattle at the heron. Crows sit silently in the trees. She turns right to cut through a trail in the woods.

The Walk-a-Thon was not so bad, although her ass is still sore from marching up the hills behind her mother. Those hours of movement together gave them time to begin a different kind of relationship. One in which they could share tidbits about their lives like two friends. Junie wonders if other daughters have that relationship with their mothers. If it's normal or if it's an outgrowth of missing significant early parent-child moments. Maybe all they have left is a friendship. And maybe that's okay.

She told her mother about some of the jobs she's had. Found her mother laughing at her impersonations of the crazies she has worked for. Her mother gossiped about other parents walking for the cure. Mostly sad stories of people who had so much loss in their lives that Junie couldn't believe they put one foot in front of the other any more. But some of it was juicy and really quite disturbing. The voodoo parents practiced to save their dying children. Vitamin therapies. Enemas. Magnets. Religious zealots. Then the stories of the ones who couldn't take it anymore. The zombies. The ragers. The paranoids. And a good old-fashioned smattering of sordid affairs between grieving parents that tore entire families apart at the seams. Junie's parents seemed relatively normal and well adjusted after she heard some of those sad stories.

Junie even intimated to her mother that things were not perfect between her and Leon, but spared her the gory details. She was surprised by her mother's sympathy and confession that she really quite likes Leon. Thinks he is good for Junie and hopes they can work it out. Junie returned to Brooklyn feeling at least remotely optimistic.

Her shoes crunch tiny pebbles along the cinder path. A small stream runs beside her. She imagines building herself a boat of leaves and floating away. The urge to avoid is still potent. An undertow dragging her down and out to sea. She could sail away like a merchant marine. Maybe go to Coney Island to become a hot dog vendor on the boardwalk. Or Williamsburg to marry a Hasidic man. Or Chinatown to start a torrid affair with a fishmonger. Or she could stay in the park and become a wild woman hiding in the bushes.

What would she leave behind? Eliot, who crash-landed on her planet. Katie, who would go anywhere to meet Junie for a drink and a laugh. And Leon, for whom she continues to hold a pristine place, below all those layers of skin and bones and muscles and connective tissues, behind her organs, deep within her mind and heart. A little shimmering space that they could share if he would have her back. Fleeing is not the answer. Junie has come back to Brooklyn to make things right. Or at least, a little bit more right than they were when she left. She leaves the park and walks to Eliot's apartment before she loses her nerve.

Junie rings the buzzer and forces herself to stay on the stoop and wait. Eliot descends the stairs and when he sees her through the window, erupts into a huge grin. Junie feels thick and heavy, as if she will be unable to lift her feet and walk into his apartment. Couldn't she have skipped all this making-amends crap and sent him a postcard? From Dubuque. Where she could go and become a telemarketer. Marry a high school football coach. Have ugly kids and a show dog.

Eliot swings the door open and smiles broadly. "Return of the red-haired woman!" he nearly shouts. Was he always this loud?

"Hey." She tries to sound cheerful, to recall the banter they had before she crawled into the closet with him but she knows her voice is sober. "Can I come in?"

"Are you kidding?" He reaches for her, pulls her close to him for a hug. She slings one arm over his solid shoulder and momentarily embraces him before she lets go. Eliot looks down into her face. Concern in the lines around his eyes. "Come on up," he says quietly.

She trails him to the top of the stairs. Shaving cream. Cinnamony toothpaste. Hint of a cat. She watches his feet in front of her. Remembers his cracked heels. Just what did she find so attractive about this man?

"It's been a while. I thought you disappeared."

"I went away," Junie mumbles.

Eliot stops on the stairs and looks over his shoulder at her. "Somewhere exotic and romantic with Baldy?"

Junie frowns at him. "No," she says. "I visited my parents. Remember? I told you."

Eliot continues up the stairs. "Alfie will be happy to see you," he says as he opens his apartment door. "He's been in a snit since you left."

She steps into the living room. Books and typewriters all the same. His computer screen glows. So many trapped words. "Were you writing?" she asks.

Eliot grins and nods.

"Did you finish that article about the actress from Montreal?"

"No. The girl is up for some award so the editor wants a longer profile. I have a few more weeks. More interviews." He steps closer to her. Talks down into her face. Did he always stand this near and did she really find that invasion of personal space intriguing?

"But who cares about that? I started something new," he says. "Sci-fi." He puts his hand on her shoulder, leans in more. His muggy breath against her neck. "It's about the granddaughter of Doyle Hane and Ro El 3 who comes to earth and falls in love with an old burnt-out sci-fi writer. I named her Ju Ni 1. Want to see it?"

Junie takes a step back, out of Eliot's reach. This is getting creepy. The guy can't move on from his one-hit wonder and now he's writing about her. Yikes! Alfie careens around the corner. Junie bends down on one knee and catches him in her arms. Cradling him against her chest, she murmurs into his ear. "Missed you, kitty." Alfie purrs.

Eliot reaches for her again. Tucks a lose strand of her hair behind her ear. "Did you miss me, too?" he asks. Junie can't find anything to say. She scratches Alfie's belly. Eliot leans back against his desk, crosses his arms, and lets his head droop to one side. "So?" he asks.

"I'm sorry, Eliot." Alfie perks up and licks Junie's cheek. She wipes away his kitty spit with the back of her hand. "I came to tell you that I can't do this." She gestures between the two of them.

"Why not?" Eliot asks. "Baldy?"

Junie looks at her shoes. Saddles. Giddy up.

"You wouldn't have screwed around with me in the first place if you were really happy. Don't get caught up in conventions, Junie. Do what you want. Leave him."

"I already did."

"Then what's the problem?" Eliot asks. Junie is quiet. He nods. "I get it. The problem is me." She shakes her head. "Oh, right, right. The problem is not me. It's you," he says sarcastically. "Junie, don't be so trite. At least give it to me straight."

Junie imagines trying to explain it all—Jacob, her mom and dad, everything with Leon. No, giving it to him straight is not an option. She stays quiet.

"You want the bald guy back?" Eliot asks.

She likes his explanation better. She nods, then dumps Alfie from her arms. The cat coils between her legs.

"Well, I'm disappointed," Eliot says. He begins pacing and pointing at her. "Frankly, I expected more from someone who spent so much time flirting with me and then seduced me the way you did. That may not mean anything to you, Junie. You probably do this kind of shit all the time. Maybe it's some kind of little game you like to play. Maybe you feel some sense of power with such sexual conquests. But I'm not young, Junie, and this meant something to me." He stops in front of her, too close, crosses his arms against his stocky body, and stares down at her. A face-off with a temperamental rhino. Whatever you do, don't stare or make sudden moves.

"Sorry," she says meekly.

He drops the stance. Cups her elbow in his palm and says into her ear, "Well, you know, when you change your mind . . ."

She shrugs her shoulder to gently squirm her arm away from his loose grip. "Thanks," she says.

He holds out his hands. "Hug good-bye, at least?" Feeling obligated, she steps forward. He pulls her in, wraps his arms across her back, and kisses the top of her head. She holds her breath and really wants to go.

"I should leave," she says.

Eliot walks her to the door with his hand pressed into the small of her back. He leans against the jamb. Wild spirals of hair over sad eyes. Alfie cries at Junie's feet. She bends and rubs the cat behind his ears one more time. "I'm sorry, kitty," she says.

Eliot scoops the cat and holds him tight against his chest. Alfie thrashes in Eliot's clutch but Eliot doesn't seem to notice or care.

"I am sorry," Junie says.

Eliot shrugs. "You'll be back, toots."

It takes all of Junie's self-control not to roll her eyes and blurt something equally obnoxious. But it's not worth it. She simply shrugs and walks slowly down the creaking steps. She hears Alfie wail as she leaves the building.

# CHAPTER
# THIRTY-FIVE

A lfie writhes in Eliot's grip until he is dropped to the floor. Eliot shuffles away, his hands buried in his hair. Alfie hears him sniff. He knows that Eliot has chased Junie away with his boorish pawing and uncouth propositions. Rage pulses through the cat's body. His one chance. His past-life love. So many years. So many bodies. She was here! Alfie tried to tell her. Pleaded with her one last time to remember. He has tried all along to win her back. But what chance did he have? Now she's gone. And it's Eliot's fault.

Alfie prowls around the apartment. He is too small to kill and eat Eliot as he would his other enemies. Revenge, thinks the cat. He spots the glowing blue screen of that evil writing contraption. Stealthily he slinks across the rug with his eyes squinting at its long tail. He squats, readying himself for the pounce. Alfie leaps, lands on the cord, and begins to gnaw away at the carcass, digging deeper for its entrails.

The sting of cold water against Eliot's face eases the burning sensation in his cheeks. He looks into the bathroom mirror. He is getting too old for this bullshit. But still, he tries to think of what else he could have done to make Junie stay. Pointed out what they have in common? Is there anything beyond both liking his cat? What about listing all his attributes—I'm your father's age, I don't own any property, I have virtually no money, and I've never had a successful relationship with a woman. He could have praised everything he adores about her. Your ass, Junie! Your ass is so exceedingly sweet.

Why did he think this thing with Junie could last or be any different than all the other nebulous unions he's had with women? Because she's not a loony like the others? Just quirky and sweet and somewhat naïve, which makes her terribly charming. A person not just to have sex with. (Although that short promise of kinky couplings in closets and other small spaces did really turn him on.) But someone he could imagine sitting across from in a café on Sundays reading the paper or holding hands with in a movie. Maybe that was the real problem. What sane and centered woman would want a relationship with him? At least there's Twyla. With her, things will be easy. She will call when she wants to see him. Tell him what to do. She will require little effort. He can cut his losses. Finish the article before his new deadline. Appease Margaret and keep his job.

Eliot lies down on his bed, closes his eyes, and thinks about Junie for a while. He wants to purge the memories of conversations about his book, Junie's wide-eyed stare when he said something clever, and her body in his bed. He does not want to linger on someone who so quickly came and went. But she is hard to get out of his mind. She might be back. They often return. He is always ready for them.

Eliot hears a loud zap, then pop and a piercing screech coming from the living room. "Christ!" he yells as he jumps up from the bed and jogs through the hall. He smells something burning. Is the apartment on fire? Are things exploding? Is Twyla here? On the floor is Alfie, lying limp with the shredded computer cord in his jaws. The screen is blank and a thin line of smoke trickles out of the hard drive.

"Alfie?" Eliot says quietly. He bends down. "Alfie?" he says again and reaches for the cat.

The soul floats. Free again. Looks down upon a man crouching over the body of a cat. Not again, the soul thinks as it rises above the earth. But those first few moments after death are bliss and the soul is relieved to be out of Alfie's body.

Time stretches and bends as the soul floats away. It is a slippery thing. A fish through the fingers. A breeze past the cheek. A word floating on air. How long has this soul been searching for its mate? Perhaps forever. Since they were both trees or bird songs or ideas. Or maybe it was five minutes ago that they first encountered one another.

Time expands. Collapses into one long line. Past, present, and future all happening at once and the soul is going forward. Another life. Another chance. Endlessly searching for that moment when everything in the universe will line up right and the two souls will reunite.

Good-bye, the soul calls, as it slips away. Good-bye, my love. Until we meet again.

# CHAPTER
# THIRTY-SIX

Junie stands on the stoop and peers up at the window. We should have had flower boxes, she thinks. On the mailbox, her name still stands next to Leon's. But that doesn't mean much. Leon is the kind of person who would leave Christmas lights up all year. Should she buzz him or use her key? If she buzzes, he could tell her to leave. But using her key seems like an intrusion. She decides to unlock the outside door, then knock at his apartment. That way he can't turn her away so easily but she won't be barging in.

Skid marks on the wall. Steps that creak. Nothing much has changed. When she decided to leave, the walls should have mourned her departure by becoming gray, the steps should have melted into a slide. And upon her return the walls should color themselves bright orange and the steps become an escalator. She trudges through the inconsiderate structure to the third floor and feels cheated by the building's indifference. In real time she's been gone less than two weeks. But her hiatus can't be measured by a calendar or ticking second hand. If she could calculate who she was when she left and who she is now, the difference would span years.

At their door she smells nothing. Not even toast. Has Leon stopped cooking? She hears no music. Maybe he's on the road. She's not sure what she wants. For him to open the door in a ratty bathrobe and be a broken man without her. To light up when he sees her and beg her to come back. Or for him simply not to be home so she can sneak in and abscond with her belongings and never have to face him again.

She knocks. Lightly at first, then realizes he'll never hear. The man is already going deaf from all that banging on the drums. In thirty years she will have to shout to say "I love you." She knocks again with force, then steps back and waits with her heart pounding like her fist against the door.

His footsteps echo through the living room and kitchen. She considers fleeing. Jumping down the steps three or four at a time and running out the front door so he'll never know that she came by. But he'd know. He'd guess. Or she would drop a shoe, trail paper from her pockets, pluck her driver's license purposefully from her wallet and set it on the bottom step, anything to let him know that she tried. Would he follow her?

The locks are turning and the knob clicks, then Leon is standing in front of her. Clean-shaved head and a red-gold goatee. The little silver hoop dangling off the top ridge of his left ear. Rhythm emanating from his soul in concentric circles. He is beautiful, this man she left and Junie must squash the urge to jump. Wrap her arms around his shoulders, her legs around his hips, kiss the top of that bald head he shaved for her. She expected him to be a stranger by now. He is not. She knows him intimately. How he runs his hand over the top of his skull and draws in a breath while he looks at her silently for a moment, which means he's surprised. How he bites at the inside of his cheek and shakes his head a little bit, which means he's still angry. How he puts his hands deep into his back pockets and turns his feet over so he stands on the outside of his shoes like a little boy, which means he's nervous. Anything they do or say is mired in the context of a life together. Junie proceeds carefully.

"Hey," she says and raises her hand in a flaccid wave.

"Hey," he answers.

"Can I come in?"

He stands, blocking the door, unmoving, unspeaking. Junie feels dizzy. She may keel over and topple down the stairs, but before she tumbles he steps aside for her to pass. She treads lightly, trying to make no sound. Inside the apartment, every-thing is the same. There has been no purge. Leon shuts the door and leans against it. Junie stands uneasily in the middle of the room. She puts her backpack on the floor beside her feet.

"Where you been?" Leon asks sarcastically.

"I went home," she says. "To my parents."

He walks across the room, not looking at her. "I thought you were with him."

Junie shakes her head.

"You still seeing him?"

"I'm not," she says. "And I don't want to."

"Where are you staying now?" he asks.

"Katie's."

Leon shrugs as if he doesn't care but there are tiny hints of relief on his face that Junie sees. How his jaw relaxes just a little. How the corners of his eyes are less drawn.

"I can get my stuff out today. Or tomorrow. Whenever you want," she says.

He moves to a kitchen chair and she leans back against the sink. These places are familiar. After dinner. After the dishes were done. Her against the counter with a glass of water in her hand. Him perched in a chair with his long legs splayed before him. The talks they used to have in this position. The way they made each other laugh.

Junie sees the magnets on the fridge. "I see Elvis has joined Billy Ray and the others," she says quietly. "I miss the boys." She looks down at her shoes.

Leon says nothing.

"I was wondering if we could talk."

He crosses his arms and stares at her, unflinching.

Her head spins. The room reels. She holds onto the lip of the countertop to balance herself. "Look," she says. "I know I really fucked this up. . . ."

"Yeah, you did." His voice is flat, devoid of all emotion. She's never heard him speak this way. He will never forgive her.

She bows her head and knows that she will cry. "Do you want me to go?"

Leon stands up suddenly. To get the door? He wastes no time. She reaches for her backpack.

"At least have the decency to tell me what happened," he

says. "You just dropped this bomb on my head one night and disappeared. I don't know if I did something to piss you off or if you are in love with this guy." He glares at her. "I read his book," he says in a fierce whisper. "Was this all about sex?"

"It had nothing to do with sex," Junie says honestly.

"Then why?"

She gnaws on her bottom lip as tears glide down her face. "I got scared, Leon." She pauses. Wonders how that sounds. If he will accept it as a good enough reason. "I really love you and that's scary for me." He says nothing and she feels compelled to go on. To talk and talk and talk until she can make him understand. "Because the first person I ever loved died."

Leon looks at her puzzled. "Who?" he asks.

"Jacob," she says.

"Your brother?"

She nods. "I pushed you away because every day of loving you was another day of dredging him up. It was just too damn hard. So I walked away."

"You didn't walk away, Junie," he says. "You had sex with someone else behind my back and then you took off."

"I know. It was a horrible thing to do," she says. "And I'm not blaming what happened between us on my brother dying. I'm not saying that I should be forgiven just because I had some tragedy in my life. I know that I'm an adult and I have to accept responsibility for myself. I know that what I did hurt you terribly and for that I'm truly sorry, Leon."

She stops to breathe. Wishes he would open his arms and let her step into his hug so she could press her ear against his chest.

Maybe synchronize her heartbeat with his, then shrink to a microscopic speck and embark on a reconnaissance mission to his left ventricle where there might still be a corner dedicated to her. But he stands away from her and clenches his jaw.

"I'm really pissed off at you, Junie," he says through gritted teeth. "Just walking in here and talking about it isn't going to change that."

Junie doesn't know what to say. I'm sorry? She has a feeling that she will say that a lot but it won't make a difference. "I know you are mad at me and have every right," she says. "Maybe you won't ever forgive me. But couldn't we just . . ." She stops and searches. "Just . . ." The room again is topsy-turvy.

"What do you want, Junie?" Leon demands.

"This." She motions to the wobbly room. The tilting walls. The tipping furniture of their lives. "I want to be here with you. I want to eat your food and tell you about my day. I want to hear you drum with your mouth and listen to you complain about the guys in the band. I want to wait for you to come home from gigs, then curl up beside you in bed." She wipes angrily at the tears soaking her face, dripping from her chin, moistening her neck. "I want you to say that we can try again. And I want you to know that I will never ever do something so hurtful because I love you, Leon. I really love you."

The task she has set them seems huge and overwhelming and she feels very tiny. Leon looks around the room. Everywhere but at her. She should have known this wouldn't work. Failure is something she is so very good at. But then, he sits in the chair again.

"The thing is," he says and Junie holds her breath. "Things are different for me now. I'm not sure I want the same things that we had."

Junie bows her head, lets the teardrops fall onto her shoes. "I see."

"The band broke up," he says.

She looks up at him and sniffs, rubs her hand beneath her running nose. "God, Leon. When? What happened?"

He shrugs. "Epic signed Steve and he dumped us."

"I'm so sorry." She reaches out for him but then stops. Her hand hangs in the air between them, awkward and silly. She withdraws it to her side.

"It's not such a big deal, really," he says. "In a way, it's good. I was sick of being on the road and playing the same shit for five years."

"What are you going to do?"

He looks at her. Quietly studies her for several seconds. She stands up taller, lets his eyes roam. "I used to have this little fantasy," he says. "Of you and me leaving New York. Maybe going upstate to a little college town or even down south on the coast somewhere and opening our own restaurant." He laughs. "I thought that maybe we would get married and you would help me and we would have kids."

She smiles a little. "You never told me that."

"I think there is a lot of stuff we didn't tell each other," Leon says.

He leans back in his chair and rubs the top of his skull. Junie wants so badly to feel the surface of his head, too. So familiar.

Every bump beneath her fingertips. To never feel that head again is unacceptable. She will not give up so easily. Not when she has him here. Sitting down. Considering whether to let her back in. Even just a little. She will not let silence fill up the space between them. She has to say something. Anything. Even if it is unimportant.

"I did the Walk-a-Thon with my mom," she blurts out. He glances up at her. She won't let that little opening slip past. "We actually had a good time," she says quickly. "Can you believe that?"

Leon is quiet for a few seconds, then he says, "Things are not okay with us, Junie."

"I know," she says quickly. "But that doesn't mean that we can't try. Maybe we could just . . ." She steadies herself against the cabinets and takes in a deep breath. "Just start slow. You know, small things. Like having coffee. Or talking on the phone. If we could just try a little bit to be friends and see if maybe, I don't know, if maybe we could find a way to be together again because I can't lose you, Leon. I can't lose another person that I love. Not like this."

Leon pulls in a deep breath. Junie tries to match her inhale to his. Waits for him to exhale and lets her breath go, too. At one time, she wanted Leon to be her soul mate and hoped that that would be enough to carry them through a lifetime of love. But who knows if soul mates exist? Even if they do, there is no guarantee that a relationship between two would be as effortless as breathing because love is not merely a feeling. It is an action. Something to be done. Like walk-a-thons and cooking chickens. Planting gardens and burying little boy treasures. Or saying yes to leaving a place because your lover wants a change.

"Anything, Leon," she says. "Just any little thing."

He nods slowly. "Okay," he says. "I'll try."

Junie thinks that she might drop, prostrate at his feet. Wail with relief and moisten his toes with her tears of gratitude and joy. But that's not a way to start. She wants them on equal footing. Side by side. She squats down beside her backpack on shaky knees.

Jacob died and left her here alone to find her way. She wonders what he would think of Leon. "I have something I'd like to show you." She unzips her bag slowly. Leon watches her curiously as she pulls out Jacob's cleats. Black with white stripes. They made him run so fast. "I think you and Jacob would have liked each other very much," she says.

Leon smiles, just a little from the side of his mouth. "I'd like to know about him," he says.

"He was wonderful," Junie says and hands Leon the shoes. "Just like you."

# ONANISTIC Q&A
## WITH HEATHER SWAIN
### by
### HEATHER SWAIN

On a recent Sunday morning, I sat down to talk with myself about my book *Eliot's Banana*. It was a bit exhausting, what with running from one chair to the other. And I'm saddened to report the interview ended rather badly (I'm still nursing a black eye, two broken ribs, and I think I may walk with a limp for quite some time), but I hope you'll find this transcript worth the effort. By the way, if you want to know more, please come down and visit us at HeatherSwain.com.

## HS: HOW LONG HAVE YOU BEEN WRITING?

hs: I started writing when I was twenty-six and living in Japan. My husband and I had been married for six weeks when we moved to a small rural city two hours outside of Tokyo where I taught English in several public junior high schools. My job was very cushy and I barely had any work, so I took my laptop to school every day and wrote long letters home. Eventually, I turned some of those letters into short stories to entertain myself. Pretty soon, I was spending four or five hours a day at school writing. When the head English teacher would come get me for class, I would feel very resentful. I stayed at that job for two years so that I could continue writing while making enough money to travel around Southeast Asia. I like to refer to those two years as my Japanese English Teaching Program Writing Fellowship.

## HS: DID YOU EVER STUDY WRITING FORMALLY?

hs: I took a few classes through a local writers workshop when I moved to New York and I went to a couple of summer workshops, but I don't have a degree in writing. My undergraduate work was in anthropology and folklore and I have a masters in philosophy of education. I've thought about getting an MFA just to add to my collection of completely useless degrees, but so far I haven't pursued that dream.

## HS: IS *ELIOT'S BANANA* YOUR FIRST PUBLISHED WORK?

hs: In 1999, my story "Sushi" appeared in the anthology *Virgin Fiction 2* from Rob Weisbach Books as one of twenty winners in a national contest for new young writers. That was enough of a goose to keep me going through the next three years of short story rejections until I wrote and sold *Eliot's Banana*.

## HS: WHAT WAS THE INSPIRATION FOR *ELIOT'S BANANA?*

hs: I'm not exactly sure. I'm one of those writers who has to read what I write to know what I think. Actually, I never intended for *Eliot's Banana* to be a novel. It started out as three short pieces, one about two kids playing games to cope with impending death, one about a man who hands a woman a banana, and one about a cat who thinks he's a woman's soul mate. At some point, I stuck them all together and they seemed to work. But I must admit, I was surprised when I realized that I had enough pages to constitute a novel.

**HS: WHAT'S THE DEAL WITH THE CAT, ANYWAY? DO YOU ACTUALLY BELIEVE IN REINCARNATION?**

hs: I feel strongly that in my most recent past life I was an insurance salesman from Toledo who died young of heart disease.

**HS: ARE YOU A LUDDITE?**

hs: Well, I wrote this novel longhand in pencil. Does that count?

**HS: IS THE BOOK AT ALL AUTOBIOGRAPHICAL?**

hs: I'm not an autobiographical writer. In fact, I never even write in first person. Always third person. For me, writing is a way to escape and think about completely different kinds of people and circumstances. The closest I get to including my life in my work is setting. I often use places that I know very well. For example, the closet and storage bench where Junie and Jacob play is straight out of my parents' house. My younger brother and I had all kinds of games in those spaces, but nothing that happens to Junie in the book has ever happened to me. I lead a fairly mundane life.

**HS: SO BASICALLY, YOU'RE REALLY BORING.**

hs: Well, maybe if you asked more interesting questions, this interview wouldn't be so tedious.

**HS: WHAT DO YOUR PARENTS THINK OF YOUR DEPRAVED WRITING?**

hs: First of all, my writing is not depraved. And secondly, my parents are incredibly supportive. They would hang on the refrigerator if they had a big enough magnet. In fact, my dad proofread an early draft of the book and loved it. My mom thinks Doyle Hane's sexual devices are hilarious.

HS: SO YOUR PARENTS ARE EQUALLY DEPRAVED?

hs: You've really crossed a line now. My parents are fine upstanding citizens who shouldn't be dragged into this interview. I think you owe me and them an apology.

HS: FAT CHANCE, SISTER.

hs: I'm not your sister.

HS: THANK GOD.

hs: This interview is over!

HS: NOT BEFORE I TRIP YOU! (CLUNK, BANG)

hs: Ouch! Take that you weirdo. (smack, pow)

FADE TO BLACK AND BLUE

# Like what you just read?

**IRISH GIRLS ABOUT TOWN**
**Maeve Binchy, Marian Keyes, Cathy Kelly, et al.**
Get ready to paint the town green. . . .

**THE MAN I SHOULD HAVE MARRIED**
**Pamela Redmond Satran**
Love him. Leave him. Lure him back.

**GETTING OVER JACK WAGNER**
**Elise Juska**
Love is nothing like an '80s song.

**THE SONG READER**
**Lisa Tucker**
Can the lyrics to a song reveal the secrets of the heart?

**THE HEAT SEEKERS**
**Zane**
Real love can be measured by degrees. . . .

**I DO (BUT I DON'T)**
**Cara Lockwood**
She has everyone's love life under control . . . except her own.
(Available June 2003)

*Great storytelling just got a new address.*
**Published by Pocket Books**

# Then don't miss these other great books from Downtown Press!

### HOW TO PEE STANDING UP
**Anna Skinner**
Survival Tips for Hip Chicks.
(Available June 2003)

### WHY GIRLS ARE WEIRD
**Pamela Ribon**
Sometimes life is stranger than you are.
(Available July 2003)

### LARGER THAN LIFE
**Adele Parks**
She's got the perfect man. But real love is predictably unpredictable. . . .
(Available August 2003)

### ELIOT'S BANANA
**Heather Swain**
She's tempted by the fruit of another . . . literally.
(Available September 2003)

### BITE
**C.J. Tosh**
Life is short. Bite off more than you can chew.
(Hardcover available September 2003)

Look for them wherever books are sold
or visit us online at **www.downtownpress.com**.

*Great storytelling just got a new address.*
**Published by Pocket Books**